TICKET ON
A CRIPPLED CRAB

a novel by Robert Kettering

ISBN: 978-1629670478

Library of Congress Control Number: 2015945679

Second Printing

This book is for **Jeffrey Lawrence Kettering**
5 September 1990 - 27 January 2015

Dear Jeff, my wonderful good boy,
again our paths have divided,
yet you remain in my heart as always,
and I look to the day our paths join once more,
happily forever, in all time, all hope, all everything.

Love,
Daddy

"My Jeff-Jeff is a super good boy; he's a never-never naughty monkey."
"How old do you think I am?"
* * *

and with thanks to my old pal Talus Taylor
18 September 1929 (possibly) - 15 February 2015
"The last to die is really the youngest."
"Is that Schopenhauer or Mae West?"
* * *

Perhaps in the end even goofy Mike understood
that time is one thing and the rest is laughable...............

CONTENTS

CHAPTER 1

RUSSIAN FAMILY
Where Mike spews poison

It's hard to get people interested in your problems…

That's what I'm thinking as I tiptoe through the godmother's apartment. My wife's godmother. It's a millionaire layout, so traveling from one end to the other takes half a minute. I snag a few knickknacks on the way. Mostly glass figurines. Second Empire whatnots. Then I'm out the kitchen door and up the back steps to the seventh floor. The top floor. We have five maid's rooms up here and one I fixed pretty nice. Too bad there's no maid. "The Crow's Nest," I call it. My wife calls it "Mike's Office" and has even painted a sign for the door. Still I'm depressed. I came to Paris to turn a collection of aphorisms into fame and fortune and wound up converting it into a novel on the advice of a friend of mine. Nobody cares for it that way either. I'm a bit down in the dumps as a result. A walking goofball, blackball and screwball. "Eightball," my father would say, which was one good reason for relocating to

France. From the frying-pan into the fire, that's how I see it. From very bad to much worse. Ten, a thousand times worse.

I'll explain everything. I hate my in-laws. We're on the outs. So I sneak up here to improve the improbable, which isn't to say I'm good at it. Ninety-nine publishers, editors and all their babysitters have said my book stinks. That can hurt an author's feelings, you know. Three and a half years, ninety-nine total revisions. Hand typed. Each one is completely screwy.

"Sloppy syntax," they tell me. "Your storyline is crooked."

Well, I keep changing my style. Nothing suits them. So I double back and remodel from zero. Hundreds of conversions and painstaking revamps. New York is not impressed. Boston either. You can't blame them really, except their high standards are getting me down lately. All the wasted time and energy, a king's ransom in office supplies, not to mention charts and graphs. Ten-pound markups. I stack them in columns with ashtrays on top, then read and rewrite and hammer the keys. Last week I became so discouraged I splattered myself around the city from dawn till dusk and vice versa. Returned early this morning with nothing to show for it but blurred vision and a herd of crabs. I'm ashamed of myself. So is my wife and her mother too, and her aunt and brother. Goddamn Russians! How many times do I have to say it? I hate them, I despise them, I don't like their looks. I'll stab them in their sleep.

The truth is I'm itching. My pants are infested and the setup here is a far cry from what I expected after reading *Hemingway's Paris*. Not with those Slavic bushwhackers downstairs. And my aphorisms forever rebounding off the Avenue of the Americas. I haven't exactly "arrived". Oh, I blame myself, don't worry. No quarrel with the experts. If it was up to me, I'd do the same as Scribblers. Give it to the poor or somebody. I'd keep the stamps.

Who knows? I get all wound up and end in the clouds, when really I ought to describe my wife's folks. That's what my friend Homer says. Start a new book, he says, based on solid facts. True life adventure.

"Stick to the bloodsuckers."

He doesn't have to live with these creeps.

We take care of old people and sap them dry. A sweet racket, even if coming right out with it may be just another way of spoiling the suspense. A minor problem. Blab everything on page one and ask *Babble of the Month Club* to pay through the nose. Except it wouldn't be that easy, this being a long tale. And my sentences are deformed. In case you haven't noticed, I show little talent for orderly progression. One yarn I wrote you have to read with mirrors. Another minor problem. Cool reception at Randy House, they sent it back glued shut.

"Because you don't plan ahead," says Homer. "Didn't I tell you to draw up an outline? Cut the crap and just lay out a good story."

"Well, it's like this..."

I pick up where I left off and have him nodding in no time. Never mind. I see what he means. It's these Russians you should hear about. My wife's godmother happens to be the present target. Rich, old and addled, that's how we like them. The idea is to fade in while Godmommy fades out and steal everything that's not tied down. We're learning to untie what is. Learning the ropes, so to speak.

Funny when you find yourself in a spot like this, looking back over your whole life like a sailor in the crow's nest, over a vanishing wake, and nothing pleasing to look at. Just a lot of foam and fish heads, a corpse or two bobbing

around, until there's not even that and the darkness closes in
and takes everything but the ass-end of horizons. Finally it
takes those too. I don't think I can stand much more.

"Oh, you can stand plenty more," says Homer. "I'm
betting in the end you even get a publishable book out of it."

A stitch too late may still save eight.

That's one of my aphorisms. I think them up while
gazing out the window, through the pigeon shit, dissolving
in the sun, if I could, and if there were a sun under these
greasy skies. The cocked rooftops of Paris. My city of many
shiny hats, slanting eyes, very young and slutty, yet awfully
old and melancholy too.

"The Keats of the attic," he calls me, which is sort of why
I came all the way over here with my typewriter and
mechanical pencils. I went to quite some trouble, a bit of
expense.

Look if you don't believe me, you ought to see my
manuscripts in every corner, my pyramids and smokestacks.
I mail them by air, they zoom home on the same plane. The
floor is sagging. Another year of sequels and this entire
building may cave in. Yet I wouldn't mind all that much.
Being called a dope. The old sadness may return, C.O.D., yet
I admit I enjoy the brooding artist end of it. Up here by the
rafters. Composing. Decomposing. Double-spaced. I close
my eyes and see success like a new dawn burning brighter
and brighter.

A king's castle is his home.

Another gem. Stringing them together into sizzling
action is the hard part. So in a way maybe it's lucky my
wife's aunt shows up like a dozen policemen.

Bang! Bang! Bang!

She has garbage on the brain and wants me to come
down and empty it.

"I know you in there."

She doesn't. I just have to let her spit and pop for a minute. This has happened before. Only my eyeballs move. The knob rattles like saber and steam shoots through the cracks, but without any key, she can piss up a tree.

"You not get away with this, Mr. Wiseguy."

A mild explosion before she stomps off for good, which is fine. I count my blessings and blow a kiss at the door. On her initial charge, she clobbered it hard enough to make the chimney quiver. My typewriter started going by itself.

She's a strong lady, that's my point. I got the clue once hearing her sneeze. Hmmm, I thought, a buzzbomb. Auntie sneezes funny, so on the first opportunity I stole to peek in her handkerchief and found nothing but fishhooks. Anti-pickpocket devices, she claims, but it makes you wonder. There's also the close-spaced peepers I want to fill you in on. I'll get this off my chest. Scarcely a trace of red. I'm talking about her eyes. Barely a hint of depth, except by way of those weird *faux pas* like the doomsday sneeze. Or the other night when we're all of us in the living room by the fireplace, the evening rose fading again to purple, to lavender, to fucking India ink. She bumps along in the godmother's rocking-chair, rambling on about a load of crap and tall stories. Lies. Always the same old whoppers. Our job is to sit like dummies. She married a duke, she says. That makes her a duchess. We have to listen to this. Hapsburg lips and high political standing. Something about the youthful dye in his mustache has her cackling to the point I want to rip her tongue out by the roots.

When all at once she hits an odd note. Her head clicks to the side and the eyes go misty and twirly. There's a roar and a moan, an agonizing gasp. Is she choking? No one knows. We all shrug our shoulders.

"Ahhhhhh!"

Her second wind. The flames leap and we get more roars and moans, a blood-curdling shriek, then she's off her rocker, the words pouring out like a fire hose, pure and unrehearsed, a torrent of sighs and simpers, black visions, yellow hordes, rape, destruction and one thing and another. In ten seconds flat she has us totally in her power, spellbound, with sex-starved Huns in every corner.

"Where, Auntie?"

"There!"

She points east and west. Thundering hooves and dirty tricks. We don't get it exactly, but she'll explain. For one thing, we're practically morons. Don't we hear the cries, the torture? It's not modern times. Hell no! A rainy day, she says, similar to this one, the clouds hidden behind fog, long ago and far away in the steppe country, where she's a little girl again, crying to beat the band because savage armies are everywhere. The good old days. She draws haunting landscapes. Muddy foregrounds. Few trees, but plenty of dark clouds and iron men. Flat noses on them. Want to know something? She's lucky she still has her noggin. That was the hardest thing to hang on to with those crazy marauders. They held a head-chopping contests and simply wouldn't behave. Day after day, as far as the eye could see, you were tripping over coconuts, bowling balls and muskmelons. The U.N. was amazed, the Police Department useless. It departed. The sheriff quit, turned in his badge and hung from a branch.

"Was it bad?"

"Worse!"

We have no idea. The sun black with arrows and business at a standstill. Zero enjoyment. You couldn't go to the store, they'd slice you up for the fun of it. They ruined the crops and broke the streetlamps. Cold steel willy-nilly. Cottages to the torch and abbreviated foreplay. Dresses up, my lady.

"Gosh!"

All our hairs were on end as the windows blew open, filling the air, as Genghis Khan rode by on her mother.

Of course she denied the whole works upon snapping out of it. The fire crackled and popped as though nothing had happened. Stash, my brother-in-law, yawned and got back to scratching himself, while his mom surprised me that night by nodding right off with a bubble on her lips. My wife also retired earlier than usual, leaving Auntie and me to hammer out the dents and nail down a few facts.

"Was that during a war?"

"Go to bed."

That's how she talks to me. I wish she'd step in front of a bus or something. I tried getting her to wash out the fuse-box, but she has no faith in my judgment. I'm an idiot, she says, which makes me terribly angry inside. So much so, I might've pushed her under the Metro if I didn't picture it only multiplying her like a chopped up worm. They never die, I told myself, but just ooze away and come back together another day like the moon and bad pennies.

Maybe she wasn't always so ugly. That's how my wife puts it. And actually Auntie herself has many publicity shots and theater programs to back this up. Class-A evidence from her days as a toe-dancer. She'll show you those at the drop of a hat. In one she's decked out like a butterfly, in another like a water lily. Cute, I admit. Budding ballerina of the Moscow stage. Her beauty is what dazzled the Duke.

Not anymore. Take my word for it. You'd have to see the puss on her. A horrible experience. Plus cast-iron extremities like gnarled roots. Fingers like carrots. I mentioned that one afternoon.

"Forgive me for saying so, Auntie, but has anyone ever told you you have fingers like carrots?"

My blunder for the day. I thought I'd never find my cap.

But that's only a sample and a pretty irrelevant one. It's my soul that worries me. I see no way out of her clutches. Like a big steel trap, that's my mental image. Bald trap with carrot fingers.

She's bald, by the way. I forgot to tell you. Smooth as an apple, with a banana nose and enormous yellow freckles the size of 12-gauge confetti. Heavy-duty springs in her legs, they give her a real bouncy hike. I could go on and on. I'm not a great admirer. I wouldn't mind sawing her in half. She could fall out a window, I figure, or I'll set fire to her wig. Just wait and see. I'll catch her off guard and let her have it with a nice big can of gasoline.

"Simmer down," says Homer. "Authors have to learn to control their material."

Which reminds me, I'm supposed to meet him at 5:00, meaning I better shake a leg. A notebook goes in a plastic bag on top of an armload of knickknacks, a few manuscript pages, then I'm down the back steps like a shadow, gliding very softly past the garbage on the third floor, trying damn hard not to make the faintest squeak. Although you can never be too careful. Auntie has ears like a beagle and the only reason I'm fairly fearless is the baby is throwing a five-alarm fit in there. The poor kid. Something like an all-clear signal. Which makes me look paternally shiftless, but never mind. We live in a very ritzy area, Passy, so my legs whirl like spokes as I make for the Metro, glancing neither left nor right at all the fancy clothes and dead eyes.

CHAPTER 2

HOMER AND A
COUPLE FRENCH GIRLS
Where the plot is sabotaged by the sex motif

At least a few things are clear. I'm headed for Montparnasse, over the river and through the trees to Homer's favorite café. The Select. That's him on the terrace, big as life. He spots me in the distance and sticks a paw in the air. He even smiles.

"Don't you ever shave? When's the last time you washed that shirt?"

Worried I'll scare the girls away. I know how Homer's mind works. "Cranks" would be a better word, except this isn't the time to go into it. I launch quickly in on my troubles instead and find I'm out of luck on that score too. Consulting Homer at a café is pure whimsy on my part due to the many legs in the vicinity, not to mention asses and tits.

"For Christ's sake, pay attention. That's a nuthouse over there, understand? She wants to kiss all the time."

"Who does?"

"Auntie, who do you think? Godmommy has go, she says. Can you beat that? I'm supposed to bump off old ladies now."

"Hmmm."

"What do you mean, hmmm?"

"It'd make an interesting end to your story."

"Are you going to help me or not?"

He slides his beer my way and signals the waiter to bring two more. "Did you finish the outline?"

I down the beer and rub my nose. "Not yet. I'm still thinking."

"Better think fast. The godmother can't last forever."

"Probably I'll go back to the States and get a job, write part-time like before."

He gives me a frosty look. "Nobody's buying a book called Chicken Shit."

"My aphorisms need refining better."

The frost turns to mud. "Look, you came to Paris to play the boy genius and live the good life. You failed because you had no story to tell. Now one has dropped in your lap and you have to do something about it."

"I'll make tracks."

He shakes his head. "You have an intolerable situation, a formidable villain and lots of money at stake. Plan a way out of the situation, a way to outsmart the aunt and win the godmother's fortune, that'll be your story."

"Auntie does all the planning."

"Throw in with her. You say that's what she wants, why not give it a try?"

"You told me she's only bullshitting."

"Sure, but you could take her up on it and see what happens."

"Help her kill the old lady?"

"It won't come to that."

"Ha! I don't think you're allowing for insanity."

"Whose, yours or hers?"

"Don't try to be funny."

He laughs. "Well, even if I'm wrong and she really wants the godmother dead, you know what William Faulkner said about old ladies. The Ode to a Grecian Urn is worth any number of them."

"Murder's against the law in France."

"A hero needs courage."

"Then how about you doing it? I mean, you're braver than anybody. I could do the writing part, but you handle the planning and action."

He waves a hand of dismissal. "Go over there," he motions, "ask those two if they'd care to join us."

"Why don't you?"

Another wave of the hand as he examines these two dolls three tables over, his lips pursing, fingers caressing the side of his glass. He's going to catch their eye if he has to stare till midnight.

"Which do you prefer?"

"Wait a second." I have a more important question. I clear my throat. "Could you let me have a hundred francs? I mean, you must've got plenty for the fox coat, right? And you never paid me for the jade chess set either. Well, here's more junk you could unload pretty easy." I plop my shopping bag in his lap. "But I need cash up front."

"Don't put it there."

I pull out a golden snuffbox and stick it under his nose. "Look."

He brushes it away. "Oh, Mike, I think they're smoking Virginia Slims."

"So what?"

"Maybe they're Americans."

"The cigarettes?"

"The girls."

"They're French, Homer."

"You think so?"

"With those goofy mannerisms?" I have his full attention now. "When did you ever see hairdos like that in the States? And the way they flutter their lashes and peck at their drinks, it's unmistakable."

"Hmmm..." He's weighing the evidence. He sighs. "Sad, isn't it? It's getting so I can't tell the difference."

Too many, that's his problem. It's not sad at all. Homer knocks off two or three a day like these two, during the tourist season especially, and at Christmastime, when everybody is balled up in the spirit of things. Nuns, window-shoppers, juniors abroad...

Oh, my! The strangest thing. I just thought for a second I could hear my wife calling. "Mike! Miiiike!" rings in my ears and at the bottom of my heart because the baby is in a dither and the godmother needs wiping. More than that, of course. Her family. They simply won't stop nagging her with all the washing and ironing and "why did you go marrying such a good-for-nothing prick?"

Homer steadies the table. "Quit wiggling."

Okay, so I go get the girls to come sit with us. Why not? Homer slips me fifty francs. That's when I notice his hand, hot as a pistol.

"The redhead," I mention, just for the record. "I'll take the redhead."

Which gets me another frosty look. "Better wait and see."

No need for that. I right away ignore the redhead and don't bother looking at her, not even at her adorable nose, her juicy mouth or luxuriously bulging stockings. Her rosy complexion? Why torture myself? Homer likes to win and somebody has to lose, so I zero in on the girlfriend instead, the blonde with the buck teeth. She's not bad. Not very good either. Long and lanky. This is the price of friendship.

Let me explain for the last time. Homer is a hog. He has hot hands. If he were a woman you'd say "hot pants." But he's not a woman, so there you have it. I forgot what I was going to say. No emotional mix-ups, no snarls of the heart. Ick and phooey. Speed-typing is my line, with a room at the top where I might reminisce more serenely throughout ten years of solitary. Beer, smoke, or just a run-of-the-mill sunset. Dreams, you could say. I play with cold fire. "Unnecessariness" would be another way of putting it. Not these tender thighs. No, they leave me cold and practically speechless. Ill-at-ease. Sex, to put it more simply still, is just not my style.

Homer nudges me pretty hard. "Change the subject."

Okay, so I put my foot in it. No problem. The girls take it in stride. They actually appreciate my candor and laugh it off. Honesty goes a long way. Of course they also steer away like from poison. Artist-dope, that's the image I project. Too wishy-washy, in plain words, I'm too scatterbrained and weak to interest any but the screwiest of screwballs, the dyed-in-the-wool sentimentalists and wallflowers. Dumbbells. Drips. Birdbrains. Idiots. But in case anyone's interested, I did get the redhead after all, then Homer got both. Confusing, isn't it?

We batted the breeze. Me in particular. The worst offender because once I get started I have trouble holding back. Words are my cross. Let's face it, I'm a chatterbox. The girls giggle and lap up their drinks, colored water and cigarettes, Virginia Slims, laced with plenty of tangled yarn from me. Not Homer. An antithesis. He buttons up to the point of rudeness.

"Hey, man, what's the plan, you pissed off or what?"

Why else doesn't he aim for center stage? That's the idea, isn't it? We're supposed to win their hearts. I mention this to get the newcomers to giggle some more, which is what they go in for. Heeheehee! Their specialty is birdcalls. I join the fun to make them feel welcome. We flutter and preen. Even though I can see they're slightly terrified of this Homer with his smoldering eyes. The whispers and sly pointing are what tip me off.

"Hey, man, you turning into a werewolf?"

Heeheehee!

We blush and fidget, me less than them, our words flying up and melting in the air, over the passing crowd, the passing wind, the sky changing colors. Really beautiful. Until the neon takes over, the nightly carnival of jugglers and gymnasts. Two fire-eaters across the way, a drum concert on our side. Then a wino with a banjo drops by and another character sells kewpie dolls from table to table. Our gigglers want one apiece. When you press their tummies, they stick out their tongues.

Heeheehee!

It's not long before I've lost the thread of my own prattle.

The girls yawn and glance around, they fiddle with my knickknacks, and even Homer interrupts with an abrupt grunt about how overcrowded the terrace has become.

"Let's go," he says, hooking Red by the wrist.

"Where to?" I wonder.

"The cemetery," he growls, and jabs me in the ribs.

"The cemetery," I agree, right on cue. "How about a nice walk by the cemetery?"

Heeheehee!

Anyway, no objections.

CHAPTER 3

SHADOWS OF THE MOON
Where homage is paid to an old wall

We stroll off under the trees, the last sunbeams rosy against the giant façades. Romantic, in a way. The bone yard is only two blocks away, and as the streetlamps flicker on, we chat softly and more intimately. One of them is a physical therapist, it turns out, the other a student of handwriting. All this is fine. We've paired off nicely and I'm thinking that later, after the bucktoothed one and I become better acquainted...When oop! Homer jumps straight in the air and lands directly on top of her. My girl, but what can you say?

"W-w-well," Red sputters.

"That's a harvest moon," I tell her, which isn't quite to the point.

The thing is, we're both on the rebound, so I'm thinking I should hold her hand. She'd rather I didn't. Still too shocked by this deranged two-timer. Come to think of it, how about me? Obviously Homer is a polygamist. I should dooooo something. Yeah? What, I'd like to know. Is her pal begging for intervention? Quite the reverse. She undoes her own buttons and plants her best foot forward. Posing. That way Homer can examine her curves better. We all do that. Red pokes me. Hell, I'm not a cop. Besides, Homer wants to concentrate.

"Shut up!"

See, we're supposed to be quiet. Buck doesn't mind onlookers. She winks and smiles, she flashes the ivories. Wow! Homer thinks that's perfect. A wiggle of the ears, then he smashes her against the cemetery wall. Red gasps and me too. I give her a fast squeeze and waltz her down a ways. No preliminaries. I bend her over a parked car, lift her dress, she slaps me, then I peel off the bra and drop the panties and stockings down around her ankles. About ten seconds wasted.

Isn't Paris grand? The city of love. There's music in the air as somewhere a window opens and a sweet piano plays, like the birth of raindrops, sad and tender as anything.

Still, she doesn't much care for this location. I have to tell her about her little pink nose and dazzling eyes, her luscious curves. Which isn't the same as lying. She's a swell dish and I have her bent way back, murmuring a blue streak in each ear. She's beautiful, she's adorable...

"Je t'adore."

Flaming hair. I'm not exaggerating. Redheads are just the thing for this season of dry trees and amber light. And with the frost on our curls and her in my arms, glancing backwards through the gingerbread of branches, it's easy to become entranced by the undulating shadows of the corner café, the Green Raspail, or glancing the other way, down the street of trees, by the empty market stalls and blazing lights. It's dark where we are. Only a handful of stars and *Belle Epoque* lamps, the moon rising over the night clouds and chimney smoke, high over the neighborhood and past the Eiffel Tower, past its topmost light even, in the distance, where the beacon flashes above the cemetery wall for Red and me and all the dead people who lay beneath all the tombstones.

There's quite a nip in the air. I won't tell you what we're doing. The branches bend and sway. The leaves whisper. Cars whiz by and I see a man walking his dog, the windows very warm and tranquil across the street. We're good friends now. All this takes three minutes, maybe five. I get to wondering how Homer is doing. It's pretty chilly, in fact, and my mind starts to wander. I'm thinking I could really go for a cup of cocoa.

When all at once I have to rub my eyes because straight out of nowhere an elderly couple hobble over and climb into the car whose hood we're using. Just like that and without a word. Which doesn't add up. French people are normally such complainers. So maybe I really am seeing things. I'd like to go somewhere to mull it over, except Red comes totally uncorked at this exact same instant. I'll never understand women. Knowing we're being observed she nearly tosses me into the branches. We bounce here and there and ruin the aerial. This two-codger audience really put the wind in her sails. We mar the chrome and dent both fenders. Where the hell is Homer? This kid has flipped. She wants to flatten the hood and crush the springs, blow out all the tires.

The Whiteheads say nothing. Our intruders in the dusk seem not the least upset about heel marks or city ordinances. Supremely relaxed behind their windshield. We clean it for them. We buff the trim and tear some loose. No problem. We're simply expected to enjoy ourselves. I'm hopelessly tangled in the wipers, yet no one hollers or says boo. So what's their angle? Do the eyes blink? No French horns or flashing lights, and no cranking engines either, not until we finish up, which was okay by me because I hate laying around afterwards anyway.

"Better shove off, honey."

No, she'd rather shake her behind at these accommodating weirdoes. She thumbs her nose and grabs my pecker. Very flirtatious. When she gallops back to exhibit her tits, I don't chase after her. Too unladylike. Besides, my balls hurt. I head for the corner café.

"Yoohoo!"

I couldn't quite make it. She flies past and breaks a heel off her shoe. Tits to the wind. That's just how she was, immodest. She whips around and blocks my way. Hands on hips and tapping toe.

"You look pretty, honey."

She thanks me, but would like to know what the big idea is. Am I trying to ditch her?

"No, honey."

"Lezz Keeess?"

Sure thing, except my heart's not in it. To tell the truth, she's slipped in my estimation and isn't so refined as I used to think. I don't go into that, of course, but ad-lib about moonbeams and the power of scarlet tresses. My writer's gift for gab. I lay it on pretty thick. It's the same with actors. Us authors are a shifty lot, light as the wind. And sincere. Why, I could shift gears with the best of them. Hem, Scott, Jones. One fine day I'll probably shift right off my rocker completely.

This touches her, this last pitch of the haunted blabbermouth. Half poet, half goat. The way I swept her off her feet, for example, and onto the hood.

"Ain't dis lucky?"

I hadn't thought of it that way, but she insists. I seem to fit in with her plans.

"You got place to live?"

This broad digs bullshit.

"How's that for stars and comets?" I want to get her interested in the sky. "Up there, see?"

No, she'd rather do something about the wonderful feeling she has. I brace her against a tree. I nibble. After all the big talk, I'm sort of obliged. I flip some manuscript pages.

"Here's a good part."

"Later," she sighs.

The chin-gas can wait. I've brought out the woman in her. But what's this with my pecker? So unresponsive to her heavy breathing. What's my excuse, hmmm? The moon, the stars...

"Am I not pretty?"

Well, I better confess about my balls. They must've clanged together during our auto show.

"Dat's okay."

Mademoiselle La Sweet Nutcracker. The smug smile indicates she's proud of herself.

We smooched more under the lamps, the leaves twisting green and gold in the light. Romantic like before, until she stuck her underwear in her purse and borrowed my handkerchief. Open wide! A dab here, a dab there. Christ Almighty! I considered making another break for it, but the café is right there, crowded and cheerful.

"How's about a drink?"

"And after? Heehee!"

I got a stroke on the zipper.

CHAPTER 4

HOMER DOUBLES DOWN
Where literature gets the business

So it's back where we started except for new surroundings. The same old beer and blather. Homer, it turned out, took the bucktoothed one to where he parks his jalopy. No motor, but it has a big back seat. He led Red there later, after I tipped him off how naked she was under the dress.

"Say that again."

He heard me the first time.

We'd gone to the toilet together, and he asks me, "How'd it go?"

"Same as always. In and out, up and down, left and right between the legs."

That's all I needed to say. His nose started to twitch.

But that's enough of that. Even Homer agrees. "Too grimy," he says. "All this gratuitous sex, it'll never make it past the Marketing Department."

"But you told me to lay it on. Sex and violence, you said. Publishers say the same."

"Not like this."

"Hot dames, you said. Dripping knives."

"Try to remember, the vast majority of book-buyers are high-minded women, cultured and refined, and even the men are touchy types, quick to take offense. You have to clean it up."

On the other hand, I'd shown the redhead my manuscript, part of it, which is why I think she fell for me to begin with. It appeals to some people. Of course that's before Homer got his dirty paws all over her. She returned disheveled and sort of sexy-sad. She likes to do it, sure, but thought she and I had something more, something fine.

Homer explained while we took another leak. "She's upset I dragged her to the car like that. Said I spoiled everything. Of course she said that after letting me bang her. Nice stuff. Meet me tomorrow and we'll get'm again. This time you can have Pianomouth."

Homer's terrible. He had them both bawling at one point, and everything stayed tearful and touchy until we all promised to meet the following day at a café in the Seventh Arrondissement. The red number gave me a big squeeze under the table. She still liked me best. I stood and proposed a toast to tomorrow, then sat down and ran a finger up her crack. She thought I was some swell sport.

Homer outdid himself as usual. I'll omit the details, even if this is what gets on editors' nerves worse than anything. I learned that much from my pen pals in New York and Hollywood.

"You can't lead them on," I confided to the girls, spreading a few letters on the table. "Probably that's one of the more serious flaws in my aphorisms book."

All flaws and no dice.

"Viceking Press," I point out. "Here's Penquill. The standard rejection reaction. They really flew off the handle after my tenth submission."

"How about MacMillions?" Homer wants to know.

Another dud, Sir. You're forever leading up to NOTHING.

"Let's see the long one."

I cringed and tried changing the subject, but finally handed it over, explaining to the girls that my ambition is to distill the babble of the human discourse into pithy sentences.

"Trouble is, book people prefer bold descriptions these days, and picture postcards. My reticent tales drive them up a wall. Ideally, every hair must be counted and cataloged according to length, breadth and Hoyle. I petitioned Random Samples for the same feedback. Big kicks in the pants unless your pages squirt juice. They demand explicit experience of chronicled crimes and no half measures."

Homer started laughing.

"Don't read aloud."

He did anyway.

I regret to report our readership won't buy it, this fairy piss of yours. In fact they buy hardly anything. They shoplift instead, empty the libraries and never return.

"Actually I think that guy secretly admires my stuff."

"Really?"

I squirmed. "Well, most editors don't answer at all, but that one even enclosed a picture of his staff washing the company car. I put up a fight, of course, told him that even if my stuff isn't the wonderful kind he's on the lookout for, plenty of outrageous crap manages to crack the best-seller list."

My dear young pretender, stop right there. Already I know what you're thinking. I exaggerate? Not true. If anything I understate, I play it down, the monumental difficulties. All to please them, out there, the man in the street and his faithful hussy. Those twerps and twerpettes. I tell you they're driving me crazy with their ten thousand fads and fetishes. Bending with every breeze. They need a good jolt nowadays. Endless excitement. They're bored and listless. The truth is, you're better off lashing their rear ends with a wet rope. Which reminds me, i.e. your book. Beyond repair, Son. Plumb pitiful. Incredibly feeble, long and dull. A regular slow boat to Pluto. Mind you, I'm used to it in spades. Five hundred manuscripts per week, completely unsolicited. Suppository writing. Every schoolteacher does it and half their students. Not to mention the celebrities, spiritual guides and demonic trendsetters. Mostly your moth-eaten clerk or your overwrought dame at the change of life. WHAT I ADVICE TO THE PRESIDENT or MEMOIRS OF A DIZZY OLD BROAD. All in the daily mail. They swap addresses and sucker lists. Two deliveries in the afternoon. Our mailman is a writer, by the way. Poems about Yellow and Jell-O. Just to give you an inkling, so as to deduce more or less what you're up against with your so-called ADAGES OF THE AGES. Pardon the coffee stains. HOMEWARD BOUND. I'm stamping it this instant. Post haste. Surface craft. Keep an eye on the mailbox. And don't do anything foolish, understand? Take my advice, if you must continue with this madness, be brief, be concise, but complete your sentences. Weave the secrets of life around easy-to-read diagrams. Document to the hilt. In other words, quit pestering us with balderdash. Know what I mean? I hope so.

> *Sincerely yours,*
> *Editor, Friend and*
> *Chief Kingpin of the Office.*

"Well," says Homer, "I guess the book trade has its criteria of quality to maintain. Have you thought of writing songs?"

"Songs?"

"We'll talk about it tomorrow. I want to catch up with the girls. Did you notice Blondie palmed that opal ring?"

"How about money, Homer? I'm taking big risks, you know. Auntie's sure to miss that Happy Buddha, for instance."

"Here's twenty."

"What if I told you I have an idea how to grab everything, the works?"

"Good. It should make a funny chapter."

"I'm talking dough, not chapters. A real haul. Not just shit like this."

I'm bouncing my golden snuffbox on the table, but he's already halfway to the door.

"Put it in the outline, Mike."

Okay, so I'm stranded after all. No problem. I'll update my notebook at a hangout called the Rosebud. That's only a stone's throw from another joint, the all-night Saint-Malo. Why don't we look in there too? You'll get a feel for the city. Wine, cognac, plenty of beer. We shuffle the sawdust until they sweep us away. Here's the river by starlight. I'll show you around, the classic sights. The Louvre, the tower, twenty or thirty monuments. If we had more time I'd take you to the catacombs or for some onion soup. As it is, we're only getting mixed up. Dawn finds me clear over on the Right Bank in search of a cigarette. No action, so let's re-cross the bridge. I stand there a minute. Don't worry, I won't jump. Just waiting for tomorrow, scouring the Seventh Arrondissement for this rendezvous café. Three hours early, I take a window table to study the breakfast crowd. Up with the sun, hurry to work. My job is strategy, planning ahead like Homer says.

"Start with a catchy title."

"A Farewell to Aunts?"

"Start again."

"How about I plug in more aphorisms?"

"Absolutely not."

Too bad. I just thought of a hot one.

The pursuit of perfection leads to the grotesque.

I can't say I'm the best outliner, but maybe this is a good juncture to fill you in further on the setup with my in-laws. The thread may be picked up a couple years back when a lovable American dunce, that's me, heads for Paris on the trail of Truth and Beauty and winds up marrying into a family of émigré Russians who make their living by stealing from senile old people. My wife is one of the characters. She has a goofy brother, a screwy mother and one diabolical aunt who enjoys hugging and kissing. The godmother, of course, she's a character, and my wife had a baby not long ago. There's also a dog and a cat. My wife has a father too, but he's rarely around much.

Confusing, no? Let's drop the whole subject and run down Homer instead. My good pal. He's been everywhere, done everything. An Englishman, kind of. He punched cattle in Arizona, fought in Columbia and Peru, divorced somebody in Barbados, spent a year in India, maybe two or three, then Thailand, Afghanistan and Asia generally. Approximately five years here in Paris. He says only six months, but said the same thing when we first met, which was almost three years ago.

I should have warned you that going into Homer's life could prove more confusing even than my comrades in Passy. Maybe you know the type. Six-one, two hundred pounds. A man of wide experience and certified vitality. Ask any of his turtledoves. He's stronger than me by far, even though I'm much younger. Twenty-five. Homer's about forty.

Outside, two sanitation workers are polishing the cobblestones with twig-brooms. Gold teeth and silver streams down each gutter. Ever wonder what the pay is? Ten cents per furlong, plus nuggets and used rubbers, torn win-tickets and also-rans, road apples and speckled oysters. With plenty to learn from what people discard. Enough to piece things together at any rate. From their want-ads and lottery systems, brainstorms and pipe-dreams. Each morning, swept cleanly down the drain. Yesterday's hopes and some from the day before. These southerners help it all along with their majestic broom-strokes. Curbstone oarsmen on the river of no return.

"Agga-magga zute!"

One of them spotted something, but it escaped in the rapids, thus plunging me into a blue funk until Homer breezes in and pays for the drinks. That cheered me up. Our cutie-pies were a little late, but brought an inquisitive friend along, a skinny Moroccan doll with a dirty mind. She seemed sweet, but wasn't above anything. Same as the other two. Innocent girls are the most rotten, I've found, even though I can't say I've managed any pithy sentences on the subject due to a paradox I feel right at the nub of the issue. Something about goodness not wanting to be good. We hit it off in spite of this, and she even listened for a while about the strange magic of aphorisms. Not later. It was just heeheehee at a hole-in-the-wall room Homer keeps for such purposes at number 83, sixth floor, overlooking the hospital grounds with its limpers and hobblers and men in white coats. The department store, Au Bon Marché, is on the far side toward the river. Not a bad view, except we got worn to frazzles chasing up and down, back and forth, from the café to the attic, trading off and drinking in the sun. It ended rather badly too, on account of guzzling so much. My fault, I admit. I struck the sour note totally on my own and without provocation right in the midst of all the hoopla. Told them I have crabs. That was pretty stupid. I broke the news and couldn't wriggle out of it. The Moroccan burst immediately into tears and the red number poured a beer in my lap. No more let-me-be-your-muse. I'm a "bloody bounder" she said, which tickled Homer. Big joke, no crabs. He never catches anything of the sort. Lucky star. Of course he always washes like a doctor afterwards. Carries brown soap in his pockets. Zip! Straight to the can and rub-a-dub-dub.

"Listen, man, before you start bragging, could you let me have another twenty?"

"What happened to the snuffbox?"

"I sold it to a fella."

"Well, you just keep that up and you'll be fine. Try nicking a little something every day."

"Hell no! You have to come up with better suggestions than that. Auntie trapped me in the pantry yesterday, understand? I had a butcher knife in my hand. When she turned her back, my whole body got nervous."

"DTs," he says.

Not much sympathy from Homer, or even false sympathy, probably because he doesn't appreciate the vast differences in our natures, being able to strut off the way he does, any direction will do, while I'm always a physical wreck on these occasions. My wife thought I'd been in a fight the way I entered the apartment, wringing wet and super somber.

"Eeek!" she says, and whips together a bowl of soup, steak and onions, with a mess of potatoes on the side.

"Delicious, honey."

We do eat well. If only the godmother could hang on a while, I think I might manage some happiness here. I'm against returning to the States just yet. Not before I'm rich and famous and successful. Universally admired, you know what I mean. Of course I'll have to smarten up my book first, make it really nice.

"Readers," says Homer, "should feel an overpowering itch to turn every page."

"Why you don't put more powder on?" says the wife. Her name is Vivette. "You scratching same like Blacky."

Blacky is the dog. He has crabs too. In fact, to forestall an explosion I've been blaming everything on him from the start. Vivette was mighty suspicious, especially with the hours I keep. It's only lucky Blacky was handy or she might've scratched out my eyes.

"Away!" she says, shoving me against the stove. "You filthy infested!"

"Now, now, gorgeous, is that all's worrying you? No problem, sweetheart. I'll be rid of these things in one, two days, and we can get back to normal."

"Normal?"

That makes her laugh, then she cries, then laughs again, and vice versa, laughing, crying, until she's completely hysterical and I feel like throwing a bucket of water on her.

"Amusing," says Homer, "but not amusing enough. And too defused. You have to focus, get things moving on an irresistible line straight to the end."

"What end?"

"Ah, there you have me. Ask yourself how you expect to get anywhere."

CHAPTER 5

TWO GERMANS THIS TIME
Where Mike mollifies Vivette and offers Homer a golden opportunity

Up in the crow's nest again, soggy turn in the weather. There's a puddle on my desk and the bed is half soaked, my typewriter swimming in rust. I forgot to close the damn window. So I juggle this notebook on my knees while touching up a final outline for Homer. Actually I have two, both pretty sketchy.

"Dramatized reality" is what he wants, but how am I supposed to know reality before it happens?

"Plan it. Do it. Then describe what you did."

The road to success.

Downstairs, the Russians are all weeping and warbling because the godmother experienced a breathing crisis during the night. When the doctor showed up, I made myself scarce. That quack sees straight through me. Although I don't know why I should be feeling guilty when actually no one did anything. Just my goofy brother-in-law fed her some walnuts. That may sound trivial, but at her time of life it only takes a couple nuts to tip her over the edge. Just a smidgen of gas and her heart starts going like a jackhammer. Which must be nerve-wracking too, like living on the slippery edge of a cliff. One false move and whammy. End of the line, sister. Hand over your tickets please and no backtalk either.

If she does kick off, that'll be the end of my writer's paradise here. Pack up the wife and kid and stick my tail between my legs. How I hate the thought! All my hopes and plans riding on a walnut. It's ridiculous.

That's how it'll be though if I don't get my ass in gear, finish my book and land a publisher. Except who can finish under these insane asylum circumstances? It's like trying to find the Lost Chord in a horn factory. And it really could have been beautiful too, probably. But it's like I can't even remember, like I have amnesia of the heart like the godmother.

Let me tell you about the old girl. She's cute, but her clock has stopped. She thinks she's six years old, just recently arrived at the seashore. Either that or she's fixing to depart at a moment's notice. Perpetually prepared, she always has her sand bucket handy and her little tin shovel. You couldn't pry those loose with a team of mules. And shouting in her ears does no good whatever. She only pees in her pants or tips something over and tries to drink out of Blacky's bowl. He hates that. Then she'll flip out completely when Auntie plays Professor Quiz.

"Where?" and "How much?" is what we want to know.

"Ask Daddy," she says, meaning me.

Or sometimes I'm the charming prince or her dead son Jacques. Once I was her husband, but wrote that off as clowning because of the twinkle in her eye, plus wiggle in her walk, in place of her customary hobble-oops-boom.

"Whaaaaaa!"

Shriveled up bag of bones, yet she's rather adorable just the same, like those dolls they used to make with cracks all over and hair falling out.

Lucky for us her nephew didn't see her in her bathing suit. He's quite a crafty prick and this would've played neatly into his hands seeing as he stands to inherit her entire fortune. That's according to him, not us. He shoves notes under the door. "Let me in!" We shove them right back. Nobody is falling for shit like that. He can shove his notes up his ass.

My wife just paid a visit with a sandwich and a carton of milk. One of those considerate gestures she pulls to ensure I'm not up here drunk or entertaining the kid from the bakery she once caught me teaching English. She rolls in on tiptoes and immediately starts dusting.

"Tisktisk," she goes. "This room be disaster, is filthy."

"Okay, honey, what's eating you?"

She has a list, nothing but complaints and grievances concerning the nut-farmers in apartment 3B. This one said that, that one said this.

"I cannot stand another one minute them!"

Which is a thick slice of baloney when you consider she's been putting up with those weasels her entire life.

"Oh, my Mikie, they stop not to calling me such dirty names!"

Another list as she struts fore and aft over my landslides and waterfalls, her eyes rolling, arms in a tizzy. She has a few names for them too, by golly. She slips, slides and nearly does the splits.

"Ahhhhhh!"

Too much literature on the floor, it sticks to her toes and heels.

"Beasts! Toadstools! Scummy bubbles!"

Those are some of the names she calls them.

"Now, now," I tell her, the most sensible one, peace and quiet is what I'm gunning for. "Here, let's sit on the bed. Come on, this part is dry. Now take deep breaths."

"I cannot stay them with."

"I know, I know..."

"Yet I gotta return. The baby ain't safe."

Right, I'll see her later.

"What?"

She turns red, white and blue. My perfunctory attitude really burns her up. I'm a stinking pig, she says. A has-been before my time. Plus a flop among flops and a lousy pornographer in the bargain. My books are all wet! She stamps her feet for emphasis. Have I no heart, no feelings? Yes? No? She demands instant answers.

Well, I should never have gotten married.

"Ahhhhhh!"

Time to jump out the window, except it's more of a porthole. She couldn't fit through if she wanted. Still, I better skip to the rescue and stroke her hair. This calms her. But what kind of husband am I? What kind of father?

"I know, I know. It's just that you should trust me more. I'm not going to let you die over here, sweetheart. I have plans."

"What plants?"

"Not plants, you numbskull. Plans. A way out of this mess. Homer's agreed to help. Then we can live anywhere you want."

"America?"

"Sure."

"Really?"

"Why not?"

She's up on her feet again, emptying ashtrays and blowing snow off my mountains.

"You mean it? You really mean it?"

"Sure I mean it. You think I like it here better than you? I only need to wrap a few things up. All these manuscripts, for instance, could use organizing into better coherence. That shouldn't take long. Homer says I'm on the right track."

I point at this notebook, but hand her a page from one of my blockbusters to lend credence to my boast. "Ooooo!" she says, and "Ahhhh!" because she's always been crazy for my book, with or without footprints, due to all dynamic sentences and explosive paragraphs. They can't go unnoticed forever, can they? Hell no! A mere question of one week, two weeks, before we're rolling in clover, my typewriter placed under glass and my brain saved for science. She was only pulling my leg a minute ago. She was angry, yes, but not anymore. These nifty passages pulled her out of it. She indicates a bouncy bit of dialogue, for instance, and several neat turns of phrase. They make her dizzy. And my word order is galvanic. So what if publishers haven't begun yet to see things her way? New Yorkers are notoriously slow on the uptake. Ha! She snaps her fingers. A bunch of stuffed shirts. But the English, well, the English have breeding. London ought to be on the horn any day. That's the light in her tunnel. She sees herself running up the stairs waving a telegram. And who am I to discourage people who own only one pair of shoes and her prettiest dress is torn, the family tree loaded with baboons? If it weren't for my bright prospects, desperation might easily take a turn for the worse. Especially when she's out in her rags rubbing shoulders with all the thoroughbreds forever milling about the snob shops around here. Being the wife of a future-great novelist blurs the contrast and puts a spring in her step, something like holding a pre-ordained lottery ticket. Not a bad excuse either for why I don't come home exactly on time. She understands, kind of, even with this three-ring circus in my pants. An artist must live.

Meanwhile, I cross my fingers while easing her out the door, hoping she goes right on buying everything I sell. Even if she is only one person, the burden seems much lighter somehow and I can get on with more pressing matters such as rolling a cigarette.

Auntie's been skimping on my allowance. Not even enough to buy Gauloises. So I crumple the butts and roll my own. They're so strong, half the time I'm chirping like a baby bird. Tiny smoke rings, that's what life's become. If Homer doesn't come through pretty soon, I'm really sunk. He'll drop by today if he's bored. That's how he put it to me.

"See you tomorrow if I have nothing to do."

I only hope he has the sense to scoot directly up here and not be lollygagging with them in the apartment. He gets on their nerves. Auntie especially can't stand his face anymore.

"This man," she says, "this Homer friend for you, he be awful bad influence."

"I'll say! But isn't it funny how you saw through him and I'm just starting to?" That puts a smile on her lips. "The things he says about people. You, for instance."

The smile vanishes. "What says?"

Well, I don't guess she'll murder him on sight, but it's best to keep them as far apart as possible or the atmosphere becomes too electrical and we could be in for a hell of a bang. If they ever seriously lock horns, I picture not much left but a smoldering wig and a pile of brown soap.

Oho, I hear him on the stairs now. Boom! Boom! Boom! He takes them two at a time and hits the door like Auntie.

"Open up! I know you're in there."

The same line as her too, but for Homer I throw the latch. Whooosh! Straight to the window to wave at two *au pair* girls in the courtyard. He picked them up on the way over.

"Germans," he says, "the spoils of war," which has to do with a theory of his regarding defeated nations and the psychology of the feminine mind. Japs he puts in the same category. "Easy as pie, Mike. They'll always feel cheated if they don't get violated by us victorious Americans."

"But you're English, old bean."

Same difference. Another theory. He has dozens on every subject. I have to cut him short. "I finished my outline."

"Great. Get dressed."

"Don't you want to see it?"

"Later. Where are your shoes?"

"Under the bed."

He's after them in a flash. "Wash your face," he says. "And your hair, shit, comb it."

"Actually I have two."

"Shoes?"

"Outlines. I'm blending them together."

"Sounds messy."

"The first one is a kind of heist-type story. Then I got to thinking about obstacles and conflicts and all what you told me about dramatized reality. That's when it hit me, a kind of masterstroke, something that could set us up for life."

"Yeah?"

"Yeah."

He's on his hands and knees, holding one of my shoes, looking up while I stare down, the two of us only eyeing each other because I've decided to aim for dramatic effect and not elaborate right away. I light a cigarette.

"Well, let's hear it."

"Well, the thing is..." I blow out the match. "Just as I'm going over the first idea, the heist-type story, it dawns on me that Auntie is a villain, she's my main obstacle."

"That didn't dawn on you before?"

"Sure it did, yes, but then I got to thinking, what if she dies somehow, you know, mysteriously...See what I mean?"

"Button your shirt."

"First tell me what you think. Come on, it's only three pages."

He skips back and growls, but finally snatches the outline from my hand and devotes two seconds to each page.

"Who's Adrian Porter?"

"My hero."

"You have him acting like James Bond."

"That's how I see him, like you."

"Me?"

"The competent type."

He smiles. "Why don't you shave off that greasy beard? You'd look more competent."

"But you see how it could work, don't you? Lots of stuff hasn't been sold yet. Stocks and bonds and stuff like that. The artwork moves slow, the way Auntie Jews her prices, but with you on the job, I figure we could speed all that up."

He yanks a blanket off the bed and flings it in my face. "Here, we can use this."

"Wait a second. How about the safe-deposit boxes? Auntie still hasn't located all of them exactly. Two in Zurich. You have to ask yourself what's in them. The godmother was from one of the richest families in Russia. That means something, doesn't it? Are you listening? Her father owned coal mines in Poland, forests here in France. Who knows what all? Those boxes wouldn't be for seashells, would they? Damnit, Homer, you said yourself there must be other boxes, the same like the one you helped Auntie steal."

"I didn't steal anything."

"I know, but you saw what was in it. Gold. Diamonds. Lots of valuable stuff. Some of the artwork you'll admit is priceless. Matisse and what's his name, Modigladooni? The way I see it, Vivette and I make a quick haul and skedaddle. Two, maybe three weeks is all we need. Kick Mama and Stash out on their asses. No problem. Piece off the nephew. It's Auntie the obstacle. A great big fat one. She has to go."

"Go where?"

"The dark side of the moon."

"You mean kill her?"

"Of course. I see no other way. That's where you come in. For a hefty cut, naturally, same like always. Thirty percent, what do you say?"

"Zip your pants."

"First tell me what you think. I have to know right away."

He jerks me by the elbow and shuts the door with his foot. I nearly break my neck on the stairs.

"Damnit, Homer, why can't you answer?"

"The outline's fine."

"Really? You really think so?"

"Say hello to the girls."

CHAPTER 6

MRS. WILCOX
Where good-neighborliness trumps bad behavior

Well, he was right about them anyway. Easy as pie. The most dazzling moment came before we even reached the street, running into Mrs. Wilcox in the courtyard. While I may not have mentioned it before, I'm a bit smitten with Mrs. Wilcox and she caught me completely off guard. I could've killed Homer, except I couldn't move. I stood perfectly still, wishing I could melt, but I froze. My emotions sort of crystallized on account of the idiotic way I'd been acting with Homer and those stupid *au pairs*, a dirty blanket flung around my neck and no shoes. I forgot. Homer was carrying them for me, holes and all, while she, Mrs. Wilcox, stood with her dogs, her two wolfhounds, looking oh so beautiful in her million-dollar clothes, kind of watching. Damn! I was never so embarrassed. Not even fully clothed. I must've looked like Huckleberry Finn.

I'll often run into Mrs. Wilcox while out walking Blacky. This is a thrill for both of us, probably Blacky more than me because even if I'm slightly obsessed, Blacky is head-over-heels in love with her dogs. They're both females like her, very sleek and lovely beyond words, yet just as untouchable as two angel wings. Which is a problem for Blacky. He can't bring himself to sniff their rear ends. Nor will he investigate their stuff. He's not good enough, he must figure, and he's right. Of course accidents can happen, never deliberately, but sometimes while we're out bopping along, minding our own business, we'll stumble across a couple piles that he can't help but catch a whiff of. He carries on then like a madman.

"Hey," says Homer, "that's a good-looking cunt. Ask her to join us."

I rushed him to the street, fast. The girls too. Very vulgar types. They wouldn't stop snickering.

"Shut up!"

"What's the matter?" says Homer. "You're puffing like a steam engine."

"I could knock your block off."

"What for?"

"She's a lady, that's what for."

"Lady? You say that because she's wearing designer clothes."

"My neighbor, damnit! She lives up there."

"Don't tell me you're in love with that rich bitch."

"Ha!"

You can never admit such emotions to a bozo like Homer, even though she's a lady all right, a real one, seeing as she married a lord. Lucky Lord Wilcox. He's an Englishman like Homer, only classy. Lord Malcolm Wilcox, Fourth Earl or something of Bass-Charington or something. I checked with the concierge and found he's totally on the square, a money magnet, with a whole floor of offices by the

Tuileries. And with chauffeurs and butlers and pin-striped suits. The works! Plus he's handsome as the devil and a perfect gentleman on top of everything. You don't have to look twice. It's the way he carries himself, never staggering down the lane like Homer. No collisions with the lampposts. You won't catch him shoeless either, or with my million o'clock shadow. A complexion like ice cream. So I'm guessing he must shave every twenty minutes. Yet he's not unmanly and more than one startled shopper has dropped her eggs at his feet. The erect posture is what gets them. And the majestic stride as he glides along the storefronts and under the trees. When he disappears into our building or his Rolls, the effect is almost unreal and would put a lump in your throat, like reading a page from the Legend of Arthur.

His wife deserves no less, believe me. Some people don't just inspire destiny, they put it through the wringer. In Mrs. Wilcox's case it's on account of her whole body, the face in particular, the unflinching beauty of it, like the consequence of some strange and unexplainable series of dreams-come-true. Gold hair. Silver skin. Eyeballs the color of greenbacks. As though a miracle must've started snowballing way back somewhere, in some place like ancient Greece, at a time when the gods still had kids. This would suggest a stroke of luck on our part to have her with us today in Passy and not buried with the rest of them in the mists of time.

The woods, the Bois de Boulogne, is only a short hop around the corner, where Blacky and I have waited for her on many an evening, along about twilight, as regular as clockwork, at sunset. We talk to each other on these occasions, Blacky and I, making wagers, sort of, as to whether we'll have to wait half an hour, a whole hour or two. This makes us look psychologically dangerous, but we're so gone on our lady and dogs we don't give a damn.

Time zips by like a rocket and soon we're frozen stiff. We grit our teeth and don't care to breathe. The only movement is from our big eyes scanning the horizon. While Blacky has only one eye from playing with the cat, he's usually the first to sense the impending arrival on account of his remarkable talent for smell. A nose like radar. I watch it twitch, very gently at first, like the hatching of an egg, before they're actually in sight. That's my cue to grab his collar. When the tail flies up, it's too late. His ears flop back and a high-pitched whine springs plaintively to his lips as even I may notice a faint stirring at the very tops of the trees. The air shatters and drifts down like snow. There's an explosion to the west, the clouds do zigzags and a bird comes tumbling at our feet like a wet rag, Blacky bawling like a baby now, his nose sailing around like a conductor's baton. Huge tears fill his eyes and the blind one turns red as the sun. It seems to spin. He might squirt a little too. He can't help it. Already his brain is on fire. I clamp a thumb over his good eye and try holding his nose, but there they are, far side of the boulevard, the traffic stopping on a dime as they cross over. Not even a squeak. The only sound is like music, sweet and dreamy.

They generally take a good long walk then, with Blacky and I in our glory but at a safe distance, dodging along from tree to tree, kicking and biting each other in our playful excitement. I'm a fast runner and Blacky can almost catch pigeons. We streak down the bridle path like zebras. Blacky is also a good jumper. We have lots of fun. The only trouble is some crazy ideas I get, especially when we're staked out in the underbrush and I'm admiring her ass. I hate calling it an "ass". It's more of a valentine. I love it and have trouble holding my eyes in from the sway in her walk. I get woozy. Blacky gets woozier. He wants to mount a Hawthorne bush, and it's at about this point the scary part comes, the crazy ideas. I hate myself for saying so, but sometimes while admiring it, her rear end, I get a tremendous urge to dash over and squeeze with both hands. With all my might! A terrible sensation, even though I never actually do anything but shiver with self-control. I break out in a cold sweat and walk backwards, slamming myself against a tree. The earth shakes, the sky cracks and a squirrel's nest hits me on the head as a dull echo jumps back and forth through the forest, Blacky howling like a banshee now. He knows exactly how I feel. Except we have to bite our tongues because even Mrs. Wilcox may cast an eye toward the thickets. Straight at us! A good thing there's nothing to see. Only one broken tree. Blacky and I are hiding behind it. She arches an eyebrow and my cap flies off. That's all. Blacky may forget himself and start honking again. I give him a good clout.

And a magical moment may elapse during which I imagine she can see us. I blink my eyes tightly closed and blush so deeply all the snow melts within a ten-yard radius. The wind whistles, the bows groan and the faintest whisper of singing creeps through the weeds as I pretend there's a smile crossing her lips. Nothing else. The walk is finished. One of the wolfhounds stoops gently to the ground and makes a bouquet of perfume. End of story. They turn on their heels and I get to watch them go, all by myself because Blacky is floating on fumes. They disappear toward a pink cloud, it's the only one left. A few stars have appeared. The sun took a nosedive, so there's no point hanging around. I square my shoulders and hunt for my cap, booting Blacky in the pants to set him on course. He's practically in a coma all the way home, yipping, yelping and showering me with kisses. A regular slob. His head is completely clogged with vapors, yet he won't stop sniffing. Those walks really take it out of him. I lay him by the fire and cover him with his rug. He's such a sap, I have to laugh. I pat his head and he licks my ears.

CHAPTER 7

ON MEETING VIVETTE
Where historical boners litter the path to victory

Two days went by without much happening. The old lady pulled through okay and everything is back to semi-normal. In the morning I wrote my parents.

Dear Mom and Dad, out of money again...

At least the sky hasn't fallen. No police, no summonses. No cigarettes either, since Auntie still holds tight on the allowance front. I guess she figures I'll have to cave in pretty soon and do what she wants, then we can run off together like a couple teenagers. What an absurd woman!

Homer laughs. "She's jerking your chain, testing the water on your brain. If the godmother's death were really necessary, what could be better than letting her drift away, more or less naturally, like they did with the others? In her condition you could actually poison her with table salt."

"Then why's Auntie keep hounding me? One minute I'm a worthless good-for-nothing, the next I'm the idol of her dreams, the one person she can trust."

"On Madison Avenue they have a saying, run up the flag and see who salutes."

"What's that supposed to mean?"

"She's framing you for a fall. Why else have you register at the Prefecture? At least officially, you are now in charge. When the godmother dies, you're going to have to move very fast or find yourself in a room without doorknobs."

"I'll kill her."

"Who?"

"The aunt of course."

"Mysteriously?"

"Sure mysteriously. I can peel a banana, can't I? Scatter BBs on the stairs. I'll smash her to pieces."

"Well, at least that way you won't need an accomplice."

"Ha! I knew you weren't listening." I shove my outline at him. "See, while I'm at the other end of the city establishing an air-tight alibi, you're here in Passy rubbing her out."

"Adrian Porter is."

"That's you, damnit! Weren't you paying any attention at all?"

"I don't like the name."

"Pick a new one. I don't give a shit about names."

"How about Pablo?"

"Pablo Porter? It doesn't sound right."

"I mean our friend Pablo."

"Pablo the painter?"

"He'd be perfect."

"But Pablo's crazy."

"That's why he's perfect. Try to remember you're writing a comedy."

I sputtered and choked, but couldn't get him to relent except to sympathize a little about my nicotine problem.

"Those ebony cats," he says, "I'll give you a carton of Lucky's for the pair of them."

That was Tuesday, no word from him since. Nor from his naughty Germans. Those were super sluts. After escorting them to the woods, we spread them on the grass like liverwurst. You know the type, black stockings and heavy on the lipstick. I could see Homer in the bushes with the other one. Elsa or Ilsa. She had a funny face on her. Beautiful legs though. Glasses an inch thick, that's what I remember. Mine had goose bumps on her belly.

Framing me for a fall isn't going to work, and she can hint around until she's blue in the face. I'm not as stupid as she thinks.

Which reminds me, I think I said we haven't been bothered by the police, but it was them who brought Stash home last night on a flood of tears after working him over in a doorway somewhere. You should've seen the shiners they hung on him. It did my heart good. One eye was purple, the other a kind of solar eclipse.

"Fascist pigs!" he called them. "Bureaucrats! Provocateurs! Blue swine!"

The sergeant wanted to haul him downstairs for Round Two, so we had to lay on the charm in heaping gobs. Mama especially is a master of the soft-soap technique. Auntie shelled out fifty francs apiece, but it was Mama who saved the day with her crosses and love-taps.

"The city's finest!"

That gave Stash fits. We held his arms and legs, then the baby burst out crying and Blacky roared in with a flea up his ass. They wanted to check his license.

"May God be with you! May God be with you!"

Mama blessed them up one side and down the other until no one knew what to make of it. In the end, they had to accept a small piece of cake. No coffee, thank you. They shook our hands and even saluted on the way out.

Then Stash was in for a hail of heavy whacks. Auntie and Mama joined forces because he shouldn't bring the fuzz home, understand? How dumb can you get? The last thing we need is a reputation at the station house. Suppose the good officers had spotted our mental case, hmmm? With her sprinkling can, no less. Her eyes all goo-goo. What questions might be asked? Bim and bam, they chased him out of all his hiding places.

"I do nothing!" he says. "Nothing! Nothing!"

In a way, that's true. With Stash it's more like second nature. You plug him in and right away he shoplifts a television set - walked straight out the store and they picked him up loping down the avenue bold as brass.

Vivette is the only sane one of the bunch. How she ever made it this far without blowing her stack is beyond me. The miracle of conditioning, I suppose. After hanging by your thumbs for twenty years you can get to thinking that's life.

"Maybe," I've told her, "Maybe, just maybe, you have it backwards. Maybe life isn't so horrible."

You'll notice I don't like to overdo it. Even before our marriage I suspected she was on to something, the way our plans kept turning sour all the time, not quite up to snuff. But I thought this could be a passing phase, an April shower. I told her as much, even suggesting we while away the hours looking for silver linings.

"When my book gets published..."

"Ha! Ha! Ha!"

She knew far better than I. We were smack in the middle of the most vicious circle you ever saw. It took me a bit longer to catch on. That nothing changes. If anything, we only sink deeper and deeper, until it's like pearl-diving in a cesspool. Nothing but clinkers. Our best bet these days is for a fresh revulsion to turn up, one not so slimy as before.

You know what bothers me? I spotted everything practically from the start. That's what's eating me. I'm not sure how to explain. Before meeting them, whole months slid by when I couldn't stop laughing. The earth was an apple in those days and me the worm, the sun more or less an orange. Three years ago, this was, at a time when I was freer and easier than I am today. An intellectual tornado, cosmic lover and whizbang of the four winds. Unemployed, of course, I was just fucking around. Yet by yielding to Paris and her bohemian ways I did seem to be formulating some new, for me, approaches to the perils of preposterousness. Nothing put me off, not the imitation artists, the tongue-tied raconteurs or the out-n-out deadbeats. The worst villains had my sympathy, the stupidest idiots my ear. Whole cafés were cheered by my smile and easy-going manner. People didn't scare me one bit, which, to quote Homer, is because I wasn't thinking too good.

I was hard to recognize too. I wore clean shirts in those days and had an invisible beard. Also a pocket full of hundred-dollar bills. The thing to keep in mind is that world-beaters of my caliber never travel long distances solely to get laid. Ambition filled my heart just as paper filled my knapsack, enough to last a lifetime. No shortage of pencils or pens to wear out, a pound of paperclips, plus many heartwarming vignettes from my extravagant teens, the Senior Prom, etc., all wedged in neatly between five changes of underwear and two thousand aphorisms. Ready for action, in other words, my noodle cram-packed with horse feathers.

This last part hasn't changed much. The money is long gone, yet I've managed to retain my fond notions of writing and of Paris. Still my City of High Hope. I look on it now in the same spirit of romance. The jumbled rooftops, the mist on the river. It's a sickness with some people.

Meanwhile, I discovered that we actually more bars here than street corners. This helped out plenty when my sentences snarled and I got to noticing how my brain isn't so hot after all. It was on one night during this period that Vivette entered the scene. Actually it was two nights. I couldn't distinguish properly because everything at that time flickered by in the twinkling of an eye. I'd been making the rounds for three days, three nights, straight, around the clock, always one jump ahead of myself. No sleep and no food either. Come to think of it, I needed nothing but beer in those days. Beer and the city. The sun would come and go, and so did the moon. Flowers opening and closing like in fast-action movies. People to work, home from work. Metros. Taxicabs. Back and forth with the world, turning and whirling.

My friends were in stitches, but not very durable. Only one managed to hang on through those three particular days, all the way up to that one fateful night when I ran into Vivette. She said we'd met before, Vivette did, which was my line, I thought, but my friend Austin, who's from Boston, agreed we did meet her before, three nights ago, in fact, in that very same dive. This was our second time around. Vivette said she liked us better the first time. Of course she'd been home three days running and had a chance to think things over. It wasn't fair and I told her so, explaining that for my part I wasn't quite sure she even existed and didn't much care in the second place whether she preferred us in the first place because I was one sad laddy in any case, my heart being in the Highlands. I proved this by downing a double scotch and rolling my Rs. The Robert Burns routine.

And believe it or not she fell for this head first. I was right down her alley.

"I too be poet."

"What boat?"

"No boat. Poet."

Auditory interference. We were up against an eight-piece band, and to make matters worse, Vivette's thick accent had me wondering if she's more Scottish than Burns.

No, she's French, she said, but her parents are mushrooms.

"Russians! Russians!"

Henri's White Night Inferno is the madhouse where we were. You come off the Boulevard du Montparnasse, duck down a dark passageway and into a strobe-lighted echo-chamber full of hooting and hollering and ear-splitting music. Henri himself is perpetually hysterical.

"A dancer, man! She's a real dancer!"

Yes, but different. All the other jitterbugs were imitating harried beekeepers. Except me too, of course, I'm more the funnel-type imitator. We both had style, that's the first thing I noticed about her.

"Hey, honey, you have style."

"No childs. Ain't married me."

More acoustical distortions. I finally had to grab her arm and shout in her ears, clutching my wallet with the other hand because Henri caters to a lowdown mob of pimps, punks and pickpockets. I saved her from all that. I bought her a Coke and invited her to my place for a wrestling match.

Sex doesn't intrigue her, she said, as we strolled off through the bright autumn night. We discussed literature instead, as well as life in general. Dancing, it seems, is only something she does to free her spirit.

But how does she feed herself? Does she have a job?

"Not zactly." Then she came right out with it. "My family be crazy."

Interesting but irrelevant. I'd been blabbing too much as usual, so as we neared my building, I decided to kiss and feel around more so she doesn't get the wrong idea. Not until we were mounting the stairs did I notice the powerful legs on her.

"Hey, honey, I can see you're really built for dancing."

She thanked me and blushed. "I dance only because I *have* to dance."

That was okay by me. We'd made it to the top floor, only an inch below the shingles. I always seem to be stationed near the stars. I warned her to watch her head, then showed her around. One chair, one table, one tiny bed.

"Let's sit on the bed."

"You understand, no?"

She was starting again about her folks. They're all nuts. Okay, so I sympathized. She needed to get away from them, I could see that. But how with no money? Damn, I forgot. Flat broke. She'd already told me. They liked to keep her that way.

"In bandages?"

"Bondages."

"Oh."

I was dozing off now. If she had any dough, do I imagine she'd be caught dead at a clip-joint like Henri's?

"No, honey."

The thing is, chicks at the Inferno could drink free of charge, and Henri himself often popped for French fries and would offer to drive her home. Or she could stretch out in back on his Tunisian divan.

"That's nice."

Besides powerful legs, Vivette has remarkably frizzy hair, medium brown, and an unusual back - long, wide and strong as an ox. That's about all I got to see though, except for medium-size breasts, because she wouldn't let me take her pants off. We only necked and cuddled until I passed out in her arms. The sky had just begun to brighten around the edges. I noticed the back, etc., during semi-conscious peeks while she sat at my table composing poems about what a good-looker I am.

When I awoke, she was gone. That's when I read the poetry. Like music to my ears! Illiterate and weird, yet it had a thoughtful quality too, unlike anything you'd expect from a chance pickup. Another thing, this sweet kid had fixed breakfast for me, toast and jam, which came as a big surprise because I never stock that stuff. So she must've brought it with her. I noticed my electric heater too, tipped upside-down to brew coffee. What a clever girl! Actually the pot was smoking, the water having boiled away. Still, this was breakfast in bed. I felt rather clever myself and wondered if I'd maybe screwed her after all. Obviously she'd gone to some trouble here, even dragging my chair around so the door wouldn't swing open for my neighbors to see me sprawled out snoring. Really, very considerate.

I stuck the pot out the window and hunted for clues. I couldn't bring her face to mind, but could still see that frizzy head of hair and her muscular back. The breasts weren't exceptional, but those legs!

"Damnit, where's my cap?"

I found an earring behind my pillow. Lucky me! I'd return it with a wink and a kiss for her hand, making mention of the aristocratic taper. Although, confidentially, she has mitts like a bricklayer. Shapely but large. Meathooks run in her family, otherwise she's much finer than those other skunks.

My money petered out around this same time, so I did some lying and began to receive a little from home. "To go to school" is the line I took. Of course everything continued to dribble down the drain at the Select. No matter. I ate like a bird and had to pay next to nothing for that cubbyhole I called "my studio." I quit shaving and bought no clothes. I picked some up, I'm not sure how. People give you things when you least expect. Especially if you travel in drunken circles. And I was always either loaded or hung over, hitting the bottle for three or four days, then I'd fold up and sleep twenty hours at a stretch, only to start over again like a marathon freak.

Vivette helped me stop that. Almost from the start I quit the breakneck pace and wasn't sliding downhill anymore, at least not so fast. I took to coming home nearly every night and even dabbled a bit at my masterpiece of confusion. Short sentences and long walks in the park. Vivette, for her part, slunk around meek as a mouse, cooking and cleaning and retrieving loose change from the floor, then squealing with delight if I happened to tear off a full page.

"Better be careful," was Homer's advice.

"No problem. She can't have babies."

"That's what they all say."

My room wasn't much bigger than a four-door Ford, so of course she packed three suitcases and moved right in. The second week I knocked her up. To show how dizzy she had me, I even got a bit gone on the idea of pregnancy. Waking up in the middle of the night just to give her a kiss, I'd scurry to the corner at the crack of dawn to buy hot rolls for breakfast, so she might arise on high spirits. My friends started calling me "Daddy". Even lowlife who owed me money. Everybody could see I was flying by the seat of my pants, ready to marry this girl anytime, anywhere, almost.

Later, when her family swooped in with all their black visions of abortion, I got fighting mad. Flush it down the toilet? What a suggestion! I puffed way up and burst into tears along with Vivette. I told them point blank I wouldn't tolerate such outrageous unspeakableness. I hit the ceiling and bounced on the floor. My beard turned into a torch. "Hell no and get out of here" is the position I took. Which did the trick. They must've seen murder in my eye because they backed off fast. Which should've been the end of it. I should've tucked Vivette and her belly under my arm and headed for the hills like a wild man, never to mess with those killers again.

But I'm an easy-going guy. I think I hinted at this before. A regular *comme-çi comme-ça* type, always searching for the good in people. What a fatal mistake! Let's face it, I was an awful greenhorn, loaded to the gills with whole lakes and rivers of humanitarian hogwash. I put up with the damnedest crap. Why? IQ problems to a large extent, but also a kind of cosmic confidence. I'd cast caution to the wind and let life take me where it would, the prospect of change being always so fascinating, isn't it? Such a luxury of youth to lean back and wallow in possibilities.

Meanwhile, everybody else leaned forward. Were my shoelaces tied together? Why else didn't I skip for the border? Actually no one felt this more than me. Marriage? I simply couldn't come to grips with the idea. So I wore a mask and put up a big front, like playing stop-the-clock chess at Death's Door, pretending everything was working out perfect. At the same time, it seemed a good idea to keep an eye peeled for any fortuitous shifts in extenuating circumstances, such as maybe she's not really pregnant.

Homer snorted. "Don't be ridiculous."

"Anyway, I like kids."

I sucked in my belly and puffed out my chest. Real officer material. My voice even deepened. I knew exactly what's what. Queen's knight to black rook nine. I pawned my electric razor and bought her a lovely bunch of roses. We almost set the date.

"Soon."

"How soon?"

Needless to say her family was on pins and needles from start to finish. Having raised Vivette from the year zero, they naturally had her doped out to a T. But what about this Mike character? An American, he says, but is that how they make them over there, actually willing to marry this swollen and penniless waif? I didn't add up. So they placed us under surveillance, at least one look-in per day, my mother's letters being the first objects of interest. The return address. Stash saw me remove a bank draft from one and his face lit up like a skyrocket. I noticed that much. Then he must've tipped off his mom because I saw her sneak the empty envelope into her prayer book. Cute, I thought. At the time, cancer might've amused me. If she were to try that trick today, I'd break a bottle over her head.

And my parents started to receive strange notes and idiotic questionnaires, in pidgin English and slip-slop French, demanding absurd articles and serial numbers. My father especially grew extremely alarmed. Had I finally begun to operate on the wrong side of the law? He'd been predicting such a calamity for many years. But what did I have against American jails?

"For God's sake, return immediately. America is your home."

I got a plane ticket out of him and a wacky set of letters, a kind of cross between *Mein Kampf* and *The Great Gildersleeve*.

"Boy," I told Homer, "why can't you jokers leave us alone? I know what I'm doing, don't I? Or do you think I'm stupid?"

He had the answer to that one, but not the heart to tell me. He beat around the bush.

"Take a vacation," he says. "If you love this girl, she'll wait. You have to put your thoughts in order, mull things over for a long time."

"How can I do that with a kid on the way? Vivette would be pissed off."

"You know, Mike, if you want to be a writer you're going to have to be selfish. Not that you're not already very selfish. But you have to allow yourself time to master your craft. I'd say you need at least ten years."

"Ten years!"

"Probably twenty."

Holy Christ, what a wet blanket! Although he did go on to explain that I'm not the first aspiring author to have trouble pleasing editors. Even great masters of the past hit snags with their first books and routinely balled them completely up. Take Victor Hugo as a case in point, dashing off approximately fifty duds before eventually hitting pay dirt with three or four gems likely to stay in print longer than the greenback dollar. And how about the Divine Joyce? Skin and bones, yet he kept at it like a bulldog for years on end, stumbling around Paris with ink in his eyes. That made me feel better. Joyce got practically nowhere until after he died.

"But in twenty years I'll be old!"

He could lower his estimate, I figured, even though I admit to feeling some misgivings myself, that cheerless rushing sound at the back of my dreams, as though someone were flushing the chain on my destiny. The answer was to write like ten maniacs. What choice did I have? I'd been putting it off, that's all. Postponing the day. While all the while I knew, as I said, in some prudent part of me, Homer was not only correct on the subject of marriage, indeed I was flirting with a nightmare, but my prospects in the literary sweepstakes weren't much brighter.

"The truth," I'd admonish my keyboard. "You must write the unwritable."

Wealth, I hoped, would come as a by-product, like a rash, as I strove to hack through the jungle of everyday happenstance to that wonderous valley of artistic excellence, from whence I would rise like a volcano to the very summit of linguistic gas.

Meanwhile, ideas were no problem. They popped out like pimples into mile-long plots, complete with earthquakes, typhoons and damsels in hot water. These latter playthings I naturally kept quite scantily clothed and like putty in my hands, growing beauty-marks, dimples and even wings, unfolding like a storm over my lyrical seas, very dainty and pure, yet perfectly capable of more sweat and raw passion than all the whorehouses in France.

This was the correct approach. I knew people preferred the bright side to a lot of punctuated bellyaches. Trouble is, I miscalculated. Shooting for the moon, I hit a flock of cuckoo birds instead. It took a while to sink in. I kept fishing for fresh angles. A pinch of beguilement perhaps? Finally a pint of brandy, this being such a thirsty business, this world of the sublime, up here in the clouds, at the very heart of imagination, where hope, luck and happiness reign. Right in the middle of nowhere.

Even now, as I look back on those days, on all the heartache and eyestrain concocting an impeccable snowflake, it's like someone else did it. I'll go through page after page, chapter after chapter, and agree wholeheartedly. "Yes, yes," I say, I'm very pleased, until the time comes to shut the covers and ask myself, "What was that all about?" I mean, it can give you the shivers. A great weakness grabs hold and soon I'm a billion miles away, reading between the lines and clockwise, searching for a word, a phrase. Anything, damnit! Am I going blind? Occasionally I'll scream, but it's always there in the end, the emptiness, staring me in the face like a great hole in my canvas.

Funny this hasn't stopped me from mailing it around. The rejections and rude brush-offs, they gnaw at my soul, yet haven't put a damper on the visions of the jackpot, the turn of events. You can never tell. Publishers are only human. Vivette thinks so too. At least she did in the old days. We use to go around convincing each other.

CHAPTER 8

HI, AUNTIE!
Where love's young bluebirds
seek family blessings

We lasted several months in that cozy space-capsule of mine, and each night screwed ourselves silly, first laying around chewing the fat about life and death, then rolling over for an encore when the ideas got flying too thick and fast. This took terrific endurance and rarely ended before sunup, when we'd sort of simultaneous conk out in each other's arms like exhausted athletes, huge black and blue marks from head to toe.

We were learning a good deal about each other in the meantime. She learned, for example, I could talk a blue streak but had practically no real action in me. I was just a big bag of hot air. She learned that pretty quick. And if there were to be any wedding around there, she'd have to be the one to do the necessary paperwork and such. I was all show and no go.

"Yes, yes," I'd say, and "Sure, sure," then would sail off into the most touching windstorms, spelling out exactly how much I loved her. I meant what I said too, every word. It's just that when the time came to produce a definite move, one foot in front of the other, I was hard to locate. She could talk herself hoarse, cry and whimper, I was always one jump ahead, sneaking out the door, or she might catch me at the corner tap or making a fool of myself at the Select. My policy was firm, keep yapping about something else. It hardly seemed relevant how enormous her little tummy was getting.

"I'll marry you, certainly."

I only needed time for psychological adjustment. Marriage isn't like a waltz in the hay, you know. It's legal and social and the whole French Republic sticks its nose in. It's more like joining a religious cult really. There are many, many, many odd codes and unnatural protocols.

Her family wasn't too snotty yet. True, I didn't have to deal with her aunt until later. Meanwhile, the other two treated me like a prince. Stash told all his comrades what a progressive guy I am, and Mama dished out pretty much the same bill of goods. In fact, when it comes to emotional effusions, Mama can be much worse than Stash. She bit me on the nose once showing me off to her chums from church.

"Mine future son-in-law, Mike the Yank!"

They could pinch my cheeks if they wanted. She'd demonstrate how, then muss my hair and cross herself.

I got my favorite dishes too. Every damn day the two of them would breeze in on us with bulging shopping bags full of great packets of grub. Buckets of borscht even. I hardly had time to swallow before they'd dash out for more. Whole hams and chickens. You could hear them on the stairs, crushed under the weight and cursing my name, then broad grins when I opened the door.

"Duck and dumplings and that ain't nothing!"

Everything was cooked to a turn in six different gravies. Marinated plums and sour-cream popovers. Russian specialties. Ural surprises. My guts started to blow up almost as fast as Vivette's. The seat of my pants tore out one day. Quick as a wink Mama found me a pair of Stash's.

"That makes of you into brother."

Vivette cut six inches off the cuffs to make them fit better. We received a radio at the same time, so I might retain my mother tongue with the BBC. These were wonderful folks, only slightly fanatical where my comfort was concerned. That's because I kept my muscles too tense and wasn't relaxing enough to suit them. I should just unhook my belt and let myself go.

"Puts feets up. Have other slice of cheese. When you getting married?"

Auntie is the dynamo who finally got the ball rolling. The executive type. Like I said, we didn't meet at the beginning. She'd been away quite a spell in Greece, concocting a rotten deal whereby Vivette was to marry a well-to-do Armenian down there. This was ninety percent in the bag, so she naturally felt put out about me getting to Vivette in the interim. She raised the roof, took one look at me and said "shitfuck". What an ungrateful pig Vivette had been! Abortion was the only remedy, the only way for this balloon-belly to square herself. The same suggestion the other two had. And of course this was my cue to charge forward again, not too steadily, but I rose to the occasion and spoke my piece. Which didn't impress anybody. My declarations of love went over decidedly flat that night.

"Quiet!" says Auntie, ignoring me while lambasting the others. "Listen," she says, "this Mr. Xyzian may forgive from generosity of heart. He be old, see? Or why he must know anything? Men are such dogs!"

I raised my voice, but so did she. I just couldn't get it through her thick skull I was willing to take the plunge myself. I'm not the type, she pointed out, and quite frankly I had to agree with her a little bit.

"This ragamuffin?"

Well, my clothes had seen better days and I'm no giant like Stash. Only five-eleven. But that ain't short, is it? Especially by French standards. And I'm good-looking by any standards. Everybody says so. Tall plus handsome. My genes are excellent.

"Ha!"

She dismissed me with a wild sneer and a magnificent sweep of the hand. I was striking her funny. Even so, I stuck to my guns and showed the whole gang what I'm made of. It gives me a swift pain to remember. I was mighty chivalrous in the old days, and that particular evening is what you might call a culmination, the turning point of my tender years about which I have not stopped turning.

We awoke in the middle of the afternoon, as I recall, although you'd never have guessed by looking outside. Rain and great sheets of rolling mist. My bed was like sleeping in a rubber bathtub, the walls cold and sweaty, and about a foot from the ceiling hovered a bluish gray cloud, right in the middle of which dangled our only source of light, forty Watts of naked bulb. Vivette sprang to her feet like a schoolgirl to click it on, so that it went faintly yellow in the cloud, like a sunset in a fogbank.

"Why the acrobatics?"

As if I didn't know.

"Oh Mikie, my Mikie, I be so scared!"

"What for?"

She was taking me to meet her aunt, of course, the family big-shot. I knew this and also knew it wasn't such a hot idea. My strategy was to continue playing dumb clear to the finish. Inside I had to be at least twice as keyed up as Vivette. This was partly due to our discussions of the evening before about what I should and shouldn't say, on account of Auntie is so "temper mental".

"She awful angry, my Mikie, for trouble we put her in Greq and now this." She indicates her bay window. "You not understand for years losing husband from her and dancing, till she grow old, very hard woman. Only thing what matter now can be us, her small family and money."

Bitter bitch, that's the image I was forming. I wasn't wrong. After learning something of the steep decline and how nothing compared well with the idyllic past, I could see definite grounds for crabbiness. I also wondered if there's not a good chance she's nuts. Apparently her husband the Duke had been rubbed out by political gangsters. There was a child too, lost in the shuffle along with a brilliant ballet career and everything else that mattered. An entire way of life pulled out from under her.

Most of this I gathered from Vivette during the wee hours of the morning, in whispers and sobs, of how Auntie and Mama had escaped through seven armies to set up their senior-care business here in France, raising Vivette and Stash on hand-me-down rags and four hundred different schools, careening with their saintly mother from village to village, sickbed to sickbed, their hosts always on the way out, the smell of death everywhere, buckets of slime and shifty-eyed quacks with their potions and pills, needles a foot long. Then Auntie at midnight. That part never changed. They'd grab what they could even from the very poor ones. The wedding-ring maybe. Always something you'd never expect tucked away with Grandpa's watch. That's how Vivette remembers it. The eerie prayer sessions and inquisitive cops. Auntie's knock, followed by muffled voices and a few gold coins.

Godmommy is their best job ever. First because she's filthy rich and second because she really is Vivette's godmother, thus lending a delightful aura of legitimacy to the whole stinking business.

During those first months when we were left more or less alone, Vivette used to visit her godmother every once in a while. Mama put her up to it. I saw no reason to object, especially since she always returned richer with a five-hundred-franc note or a charm bracelet and things. The bracelet was gold, incidentally, which I foolishly presented to a sloe-eyed floozy in Montparnasse for helping me with my French.

Vivette's French is no good, by the way. I speak better. Even though she was born here, she still goes at it sideways and with a Slavic brogue, same as the others. With Russian she does fine. Super fluent. That evening at Auntie's I got a full dose in both ears. The truth is, they're all of them too fluent and extra juicy. Five minutes in the same room takes the crease out of your pants.

To impress the old girl, I wore the corduroy suit Stash gave me. Size quadruple-X. That made me feel like the Incredible Shrinking Man. Vivette laid it out on the bed to "freshen it up", and had me submit to a haircut, just around the edges, a trim.

"First impressions be so important!"

Okay, so I scrubbed my face like a choirboy and combed all the lint out of my beard. I was sorry now I'd grown it.

One look in the mirror told me I didn't have the kind of puss an old dame would trust. Anyway, that's how it struck me. I wanted to shave, but Vivette said not to talk foolish. I should just act natural and get a move on. There was a train to catch.

She boiled coffee on the contraption we were using as a combination cooker-heater, and while sipping the stuff, I sat at my table with a pen and notebook watching her polish my shoes with a piece of crayon. We didn't have any regular polish and this broke my heart a little bit. The childish cut of her brow and tender eyes, sparkling now. I couldn't help loving her. Women glow in pregnancy, everybody knows that. Their skin turns to moonlight.

"Just work on the scuff marks, the rest doesn't matter."

"Oh Mikie, my Mikie, if things go bad tonight you take me to the States like you promise me, yes?"

"Hmmm...Wow!"

The coffee was mighty strong, but I mainly didn't answer because she'd never understand anyway. In America I'm just another jerk, while over here I'm an artist.

"Mikie?"

"Quiet. I'm trying to work."

I wrote the word "the", then gazing out the window I wrote the word "rain". To hell with America! Even though I sympathized deeply about the lack of material comfort and a good diaper service. I genuinely desired her happiness too. It's just that she should forget the States, leastways until word gets out about what great books I write. Until then, I figure I'll never be an out-n-out flop as long as I stay put. After all, managing to survive here as an artist is quite an accomplishment for a young fellow, just in itself. It takes a rather clever bloke, in my opinion.

"Mikie?"

"Quiet!"

"Must go."

"Sure. But I was thinking, honey, why today? I mean, why can't we go tomorrow?"

Nice try, but no sale. Even bucking the bitter-cold wind, she dragged me down the street with such headlong determination I was sweating bullets by the time we reached the Metro. No letup on her pep-talk either. Auntie's back in town! I wound up whipped into a frenzy and full of big nervous farts. Bashful me. At the last minute I'd put on a tie in honor of the occasion. She was using it to pull me along better, like a mule, because I didn't care for these family get-togethers. I still don't! Given the choice, I'd have taken a sightseeing tour of Montparnasse or maybe hid out in one of those picturesque bistros where I could soak up the sexy atmosphere of groaning architecture and gusting skirts.

We couldn't decide when the sun went down. The streetlamps were on since three o'clock, and in the glow from the small shop windows, the whole city appeared terribly forlorn, yet absolutely gorgeous. The slick cobblestones, glistening under deep gray skies. That's how I'll always remember this town, like a wet dreamy song as we splashed merrily through puddles and over waterlogged leaves, my heart pounding, my cap drooping, drenched and cockeyed, like the rooftops themselves, yet with the whole works simply dripping with beauty and whatnot.

The crowd on the Metro had us nose-to-nose all the way to the station. No one offered us a seat either, since Vivette didn't appear very pregnant exactly in her bulky coat. Just husky. To top it off, some creep must've lifted the box of bonbons we'd bought for Auntie. Thirty francs! Vivette couldn't get over it. We didn't notice until reaching the station platform, whereupon she opened the sluice gates.

Another evil omen, for Christ's sake! I'll be damned if she didn't faint on me. I saw her eyes roll and wondered what's got into this kid. I hate these scenes. Then down she went. A passing hero helped me lay her out on a bench. She's not light. While he ran for water, I fanned her with my cap, pretending I'm a stranger here myself. I'm only helping this lady and don't know her from Adam.

"Where am I?" she says.

We were at the Gare du Nord and I knew a pretty good movie nearby. The answer was no. The train ride would perk her up. I should just be gentle and take her arm so she doesn't land under the wheels. We climbed down an hour later at a grubby little station way out in the sticks, about fifty kilometers from Paris. That's where Auntie keeps her hangout. A low-rent district of rundown shacks and vacant lots, a few vegetable gardens. If it hadn't been for the downpour, we'd have been able to make out the garbage dump in the distance.

"Is that east or west?"

She was pointing at a curtain of footlong raindrops and a bucket of black spray.

"Climatic conditions are much denser out here, aren't they? Looks like we'll have to take our bearings from the whistle of the goddamn wind."

"Who been?"

"I said this is shaping up even worse than I expected. Let's wait for it to let up, okay? We can have a drink."

That's when the objections began, but I didn't hang around. I beat it across the road to the hick café they have there. Vivette trailed in a minute later.

"Want coffee, honey? You don't mind standing at the bar, do you? I'll just finish this beer and I'm going to have one more."

She smiled bravely. She knew this could go on for hours. I ordered a coffee and another beer, then hit on the idea of cognac. The little rascal next to me was of the opinion that calvados is equally appropriate during such a gale and cheaper. Okay, so I bought him one too. He thanked me and I thanked him. But how about a cigarette? Sure. And why don't I sample his wine? Beer is for Germans, he says, and Polacks. Well, he had a point there, so I switched to the red stuff.

"And another for my friend."

We were discussing nuclear proliferation and harness racing, when Vivette started tugging my sleeve. Is she having another dizzy spell? No, it's just that there's a two-mile hike ahead of us and she doesn't much care for this dump in the first place because the patrons are ill-mannered hayseeds who belch and bellow too much. They're steaming up the windows. Especially those boisterous suction-pumps at the far end. One was plucking a duck and all were full of helium. The worst though was the idiot by the door eating mustard with a spoon. An honest-to-God syphilitic nose on him! His trick of catching dribbles on his tongue really turned Vivette's stomach.

"Just don't look at him."

Problem solved, except the proprietor himself would never make the glamour pages with his poisonous leer minus thirty-two teeth. The cast in his eye didn't help, but his lewd remarks are what finally set Vivette off after he spotted her belly. He wanted to talk about fucking. My pal introduced us.

"Mikie, I go."

"Come on, honey, it's still coming down out there."

With a little luck, it might rain all week. She knew what I was thinking behind my big sheepish eyes. I'm not sure why, but I felt at home among these halfwits and their beautifully colored bottles. What better place to meditate? On the past, for one thing. All those interlocking debacles that had become my life. And now the future, out there, in front of the darkness. I couldn't see ten feet, of course, beyond the windows and blurring rain except the reflection of us comedians.

Anything for a laugh, my friend tells me. On Saturday mornings they give each other haircuts and never fail to ball up the job entirely, mostly on purpose. The lattice effect is what they gun for. We take a minute to admire the patchwork, the uneven tufts. Later, he says, the fun really starts. They juice up on wine and wild stories and play cards to all hours. Ten-handed rummy. It's a crazy life. Night after night he's missed the Eight O'Clock News. Some go in for checkers or dominos or writing backwards on the windows. Others head for Paris to have their pockets picked. Not for long. Paris stinks. They always return to their comfy café, their intimate haven. It's like a private club for these gentlemen. Otherwise you have to travel five kilometers to a low-class dive and drink with a lot of bums. Everybody prefers it here better.

Vivette is the exception.

"Jesus, honey, why can't you relax? I want to finish my wine."

She was on the verge of tears the way they kept refilling my glass. And before I could polish off the last one, she slapped my cap off the bar and sailed out the door.

"And call me not honey!"

I had to hotfoot it to catch up, her coattails barely visible on the far side of the tracks.

"Hey, slow down!"

"I hate those people! Hate that filthy place! All my life I want away from such filthiness!"

"Sure, me too."

"You lie!"

"No, Vivette. Shit, be reasonable. I only wanted to get us in out of the rain."

"You mean it?"

"Sure I mean it. We have to think of the baby, don't we?"

"I love you, Mikie."

"Me too. Now let's go back?"

"No."

"I have to pick up my change."

"No! No! No!" She was stamping her feet and bawling. "We leave now, boohoo, this instant. You forget your damnit change."

"Okay! Fine!" I was flying off the handle myself. "Have it your own way. You always have to be the damn boss."

"Oh, Mikie."

"Oh Mikie, my ass! That's what I get, isn't it? Perfectly reasonable, I suppose. Four francs down the drain. What the hell do you care? Just feed me lots of Mikies and turn on the faucets. Sure and certainly! Since I'm the one with mental problems, am I right? That's what you're thinking, isn't it? Why not say so? Your considered opinion. Who cares if my parents had to work hard for that money? Piss on it, I agree. Better yet, we'll leave it at cafés, wipe our rear ends with their savings. What could be more fitting? More ethical? I ask you. Please answer. And while you're at it, maybe you'll explain what I'm doing knee-deep in a cow pasture. Am I a fencepost, would you say? Am I a tree with an owl in it? I'm waiting for enlightenment, dear doctor. Are these bats in my branches?"

"Please, Mikie."

"Oh please my bouncing balls! You're always getting me to jump through hoops. Why ain't I home writing my book, can you answer me that? Because I'm standing here in the goddamn rain, that's why."

"If only you know how important this be to me."

"Oh, important, important. A date with your aunt, what's so important? Tramping through ninety-two tornadoes. The old hen! Why don't she meet us in town, huh? Do I look like I need an excursion to the country? Oh, but excuse me. I plum forgot. This be important. Naturally! Whatever *you* want is important. Not what *I* want. Hell no! Perish the thought and lead the way. Don't worry your head about me, master. But let's step on it, okay? If you please. Holy Christ, is that asking too much? I want to get this over with."

I should've kept my mouth shut. She had us going at a gallop in no time, puffing and panting like fugitives from a chain gang. Downhill mostly, but my knees weren't bending properly, and with the treacherous crosswinds and rugged terrain my equilibrium was off center. We didn't miss many puddles either. Her shoes would disappear and it was my job to retrieve them, my own footwear being fastened on better. Ankle-high boots is what I had. Good but not perfect. They wound up squealing and slurping up the soup as fast as hers. In the end we sounded like a flock of geese coming down the hill. Twice I landed on all fours, gagging on foam. I'd wobble to my feet only to catch a breathtaking squall square in the pipes. Another gust up the ass. Ten rapid blasts on each side. It wasn't long before my ears were ringing. I'll be damned if she didn't give me a big encouraging grin.

"Only little further ways."

"Go to hell, you damn fool! We'll drown out here. Why do I ever listen to you?"

"Oh, Mikie, you must this once be strong for me. Auntie expecting us for eight o'clock sharp."

"Well, she can see it's a hurricane, can't she? We'll be lucky if we don't fly away with the birds. Shit, I don't see what she has to do with this in the first place. If I'm acceptable to your mom, why's your aunt stick her nose in? You're practically of age to begin with. And what's this about a marriage in Greece, to some gaffer you never even met? Doesn't she know that went out with the Pony Express? She's not crazy, is she? Damnit, Vivette, I think she has a lot of nerve, and I don't care if she is, like you say, head of your family and all that malarkey. If it was up to me I'd tell her where to get off."

"Please don't say it to her."

"Hell no! That's not for me to say, that's for you to say. I'm just a stooge on this journey."

"She awful angry."

"I don't see why."

"Sure you do."

"Yeah, well..." She had me there, with that paunch in front of her. I was getting scareder by the minute. "I only hope she doesn't have the wrong idea. Your mom must've explained I'm willing to do the right thing and all."

"Oh, she don't listen to Mama. Mama listen to her."

Good, the top boss in charge. Head loony! I was seriously considering ditching Vivette then and there, feeling I'd otherwise be reaching the point of no return. I dragged my heels, but that's about all. Inertia carried me forward like an irresistible nightmare, downhill like I said, with my better judgment sort of clinging to the bushes. At one point I did manage to wriggle free, but then offered her my arm almost instantly, having suddenly been stabbed by that twinge I always get before changing my mind from doing something rotten to doing something stupid instead.

We'd been following a mud path through a strip of weeds between the railroad tracks and garbage dump. The tracks to the right, a mountain of tin cans to the left. It was so dark, we couldn't see our own feet and kept tangling our legs like a couple flamingos. Then the tracks veered off, leaving a row of shacks in their place, and the path opened out onto a gravel road. Auntie's shack is about a mile down, all by itself, separated from the other lean-tos by more weeds, a few trees and a lot more darkness. Stash had his jalopy parked in front, and I could see a thin stream of smoke spinning out the chimney. Otherwise no sign of life. It looked deserted and dilapidated and sort of caved in. Extremely uninviting. In fact, haunted. Heavy shutters covered the windows with boards were nailed across and rags stuffed in the cracks. Not a speck of light. No sound either, except the crashing rain and Vivette yakking on about how I should sober up quick and mind my Ps and Qs.

"Would you shut up!"

That's all you need when you're on edge is to have a neurasthenic broad needling you.

"Keep your fingers out of my face!"

I thought I heard something, very faintly at first, like a clarinet being tuned. Then all at once the air filled with whistles, like a thousand train wrecks, as someone pounded out a number on Auntie's organ.

"Stash," says Vivette.

The way he played gave me a terrific chill and made us zigzag more in our approach. A high iron fence finally slowed us to a halt, the music growing louder and louder and more and more delirious.

"At least it's not the Wedding March."

"Why you must everything make worse than really?"

"Because that sounds like the Phantom of the Opera in there."

She gave me a peck on the whiskers and laid her head on my chest, catching a good ear-load of heartbeats. A noble soul. She was as nervous as me, of course, and I felt ashamed of myself for being so mean, so cowardly. At the same time I couldn't help wondering what I was doing with her in the first place. Could this really be the purpose behind all the twists and turns of my life, the years of education and dental appointments, not to mention the four tons of vitamins my mother pumped into me, to end up on a swampy road with this blubbering blimp? Why wasn't I somewhere else? I looked up at the sky and got a facefull of raindrops.

"Mikie?"

"Clam up!"

"We go in now."

"Sure...but...but..." Hell, I didn't know how to break it to her. "Listen, honey, let's make it another day, okay? We'll take a rain check. Really, I don't feel well tonight."

There was a heartbreaking whimper and a fluttering kind of frown-smile, then her whole face fell apart at the seams.

"I do what you say."

That was easy, except she went on wilting and I knew I was sunk. I'd have to go through with it. Shit, I knew that anyhow. Things had gone too far.

"Oh, all right. But button your lip, would you?"

CHAPTER 9

THE AUNT'S SHACK
Where east meets west in an ironclad bargain

I took a gulp of air and snuck over and rattled the gate a little. It was double-hooked, triple-latched, wired, roped off and generally hogtied. To be on the safe side, Auntie had about ten feet of rusty chain wrapped around with half a dozen padlocks.

"Won't it open?"

"Hell no it won't open!"

Nothing appeared to have been touched in years. The shack is on about an acre of fenced-in junk, one pile covering another, the whole yard a hideous mountain range of bald tires, twisted steel and incidental crap. I didn't like the looks of it.

"No one's home," I said, which was a ridiculous deduction considering Stash kept tickling the ivories loud enough to make the shingles flap. And no sooner did I open my mouth than Blacky bounded out from under one of the mountains, his fangs in a froth and howling mad. That's the first time I met him and right away he tried to kill me.

"Arf! Arf! Arf!"

He was skinny as a rail in those days and mighty vivacious. I skipped back fast, not yet knowing what a sissy he is.

"Hold me," says Vivette.

"Oh, balls!"

The rain fell harder and to make matters worse the wind joined Blacky in the howling game. Whooosh! Ahooooo! We had a duet. My socks rolled to my toes as I silently cursed Vivette good and proper, wishing I'd never clapped eyes on this crybaby or her belly or anything like the aunt's musical house. Everything was rolled up in one for me.

By the way, you know how she inherited that shanty of hers? I didn't find out until later. The whole works came from the former owner and original builder who popped off unexpectedly after drafting his will. "Poisoned," the neighbors said, but really he fell off the roof and nobody could prove otherwise. The only question is, what was he doing up there in his pajamas when everybody knew he had a limp in both legs? Clear-cut decrepitude is how the cops had to write it off. Apparently it's not uncommon for lamebrains of advanced years to get funny ideas about walking on air. This one they found by the rain barrel, his nightcap bashed in, his feet snarled in a clothesline. They still talk about it around there. The Case of the Russian Clothesline. Auntie hung him out to dry, that's the local consensus.

"Look," says Vivette.

"What?"

"Listen."

She was pointing at the door, but there was nothing to see. I couldn't say she was wrong about noise though, very definitely. The rattling of keys and turning of locks. More locks! Plus a really strange commotion similar to orange crates being crushed, as though someone were trying to tear that door to pieces.

"Shshsh."

"Don't tell me to shut up."

She cupped her hands to her mouth and shouted, "Auntie!"

No answer, but the crunching stopped. So did Blacky. No more King of the Mountain. Stash gave it rest too. No more dancing fingers. Only the slow creaking sound of rusty hinges. And pitch blackness. Although the door must've opened because Blacky darted inside. Only for a second. He darted right back out again, yipping, yelping and traveling in circles before tripping himself up on a pile of oily rags by an upturned wheel-barrel.

"Who dat?" came Auntie's gravelly voice.

She speaks with a marked accent and imposing volume, like French through an imported foghorn. Peeking over Vivette's shoulder, I could make out only a dull flash, as though she were shining a dirty mirror at us.

"Auntie, put that down."

"Is you, Vivette?"

"Course is me."

"Who dat man?"

"Michael."

"Aha!" and again "Aha!" as she bounced to the gate like a big round ball, a meat-cleaver in her hand.

Gulp!

"Hi!" I said, but she maybe didn't hear me.

Thump!

The cleaver got buried in a stump, then out with the keys, mumbling, grumbling and making terrible faces. I guess the lighting wasn't ideal for working on locks. I could see Blacky though, creeping on his belly, inch by inch, until the gate swung open and he made his move. Zip and clunk. Two seconds of excitement before she caught him with the heavy end of her key-ring. A jailer's model. It had him walking slantways and flatfooted back to the rags.

"Humph!" she says, looking me over.

"Hi!"

"His name Michael."

"Hi!" Repeat performance, this time I get my Adam's apple to jiggle while rummaging for a more intelligent remark. "Blugga! Blugga!" I do expressive hand-motions.

She hooked a thumb at the door. "Inside!"

Ladies first. She shoved Vivette on ahead and jerked her chin at me. "You. Come."

"Me? Quee?" Meaning damnit, why can't I just curl up with Blacky?

I wasn't prepared for this guardian of the ash cans, nor for Vivette's depressive reactions. Bawling again. Although I'll admit it fit in perfectly with the rain. Let her cry her fool head off! I had my own problems, after all, and could practically see myself at the Select, pie-eyed but handsome, among all the jolly faces that would soon be old. As I would myself, now that I thought of it. Us boom babies had to grow up some day, didn't we? Our livers would demand it. As would our hardened hearts and shriveled dicks. Our destiny of sagging breasts and then what? Shit, I could see it wouldn't be long I'd be pushing up daisies. This really made me panic, as though I'd been trapped in a dream where I can't find the gangplank. Missing the boat, goddamnit! I'm actually headed the wrong way. Away from the fun and laughter and the clink of friendly drinks, the friendlier drunks, not to mention the warm women of Montparnasse and the chance to partake of some passing enchantment. The gay hijinks. Sparkling chitchat. So vital and alive. Yet fading too, like a memory, moving off with the immortal present while leaving me behind, the assholes, to vanish ever deeper into the background until I'm offstage entirely, buried under a horrible kind of void of false recollection, dull and empty and hardly worth mentioning to the worms even, since they too need to move along in the great scheme of things, turning up their noses at what once aspired to a definite brightness in the future.

"Michael, come."

"Oui! Here I come."

There I go. So well-behaved. I rarely listen to myself. I follow like a woolly lamb, stumbling over the threshold, then I wipe my feet for about five minutes. Mama had to come fetch me.

"Oh, mine Michaeleetskoo! You coats, you shoes, you feets be soak it. Not to feel so good?"

"No-no, good-good."

I only wanted to clean my shoes better.

She placed a finger on my chest and made a bunch of tiny crosses, then gave me a good pull.

"Dis be mine sister."

"Hi!"

I couldn't see her, but nodded seven or eight times in three or four directions.

"Be formidable womans," Mama added. "Is nice you meet friendly."

"Yes! Yes!" I was all for that. "Good morning. Good evening. Howdy."

"Hee! Ho! Ha!"

That was Stash, he just thought of something funny. They were all there. Stash is the bruiser by the organ untangling his fingers. I felt so ill at ease, I was actually glad to see him, except I couldn't very well on account of the dimness of the lighting system. Oh, here he is holding my arm, he's taking over the introductions.

"Already you meet Mama."

"Sure! Hi!"

"And my sister previous."

"Yes, of course." I was with him so far.

"Now Auntie come back."

"Good. Please-to-please-to."

"Here you meet Poopa."

"Poopa?"

"Papa," says Vivette.

Same difference. Who's Papa? And *where* is he? Stash had me aimed at some deeper shadows between a big brass bed and an old icebox, but I could see no Poopa, Papa or anybody. The only light in that dungeon came from half a dozen candles and a mound of coal in a Ben Franklin stove. I'd never heard of any Papa either. He came as a surprise. Whenever I asked Vivette if she had a father, her answers always came out so gloomy and evasive I figured he must've died a sad death or worse. Maybe he's the Unknown Soldier? I didn't really think so. To tell the truth, knowing Vivette, I rather suspected suicide and chose not to press the issue. I've always been a great one for diplomacy.

Here we go again. "Hi!"

No answer.

Boy, I'm thinking, another one, invisible this time. Even when I edged closer, I couldn't get a beat on this shadow man. So why not march boldly forward? I'll stretch out my hand and turn on the old personality.

"Away!" he shouts, and I jumped three feet. "Keep that mackerel away of me, understand? Keep'm away."

"Oh, Papa!" says Vivette, taking my hand and making me sit with her on the bed.

"Sorry," I mumble, I'm not sure why.

Auntie goes "Humph!" and ricochets a chunk of wood off the stove. It lands in a pile of cinders on the floor. A dirt floor, by the way. Dirt covered in dust.

I'm noticing other things while relaxing on the bed, my eyes adjusting somewhat to the dreariness. I already mentioned the candles. Three on the organ, another three on a table by the boarded up window. Two extra rooms, I found out later. A kitchen in back. No toilet. Auntie does it in a bucket. There it is by the door, a wooden affair with a rope handle. The door can't actually be described owing to blind spots. The walls too seem perfectly capable of drinking every drop of candlelight.

Caa-hoo! Caa-hoo!

That's the stove. It shimmies and shakes whenever the wind cuts loose, then every once in a while we get a big black cloud puffing down the chimney.

"Aren't your eyes burning, honey?"

"Shshsh."

Vivette thinks I talk too much, unlike her old man, our Papa of the shadows. Quiet as a mouse these days and still missing from action. I can see Mama though, seated next to Stash on the organ bench, smiling for all she's worth. Stash too. The goo-goo twins. I avoid looking at Auntie and count pots and pans instead, eight or ten of them, strategically placed to catch the seepage.

Caa-hoo! Caa-hoo!

We pretend that's nothing. Everything is nothing. No "how you kids been doing?" or "would you like a hot toddy?" Probably because they gabbed plenty before our arrival, tearing us to pieces. I'm not sure why. Or am I?

"Well," I say, I'm the first to crack. But that's all I say. Vivette shoots me frown after frown after frown. I fiddle with my cap. "Go to the movies" is what I'm thinking. I have this voice inside.

"What whispering?" says Auntie.

Sensitive ears. She's seated across from us, a little to the right, staring into space, lost in thought, cracking her knuckles and sucking her teeth, otherwise peace and quiet is what she values. Which gives me a chance to steal a gander at the puss on her. You don't run across many like that. Framed in black, a seething mass of tortured viciousness. Skin on the yellow side. Eyes like slits. Oriental? Could be. Except the way her jaws are revolving she may be chewing tobacco, which might indicate she's from Kentucky.

She hauls off and spits. Smack! She hits the floor by the bucket, startling me so much I'm tempted to dash over and clean it up out of sheer good manners. I nudge Vivette. What's the deal, honey?

"Shshsh."

We're supposed to sit motionless. Imitate Papa. Reticent to the vanishing point. Even when I bend forward, I might just as well bend backwards. I'm squandering my retinas on this tar-baby.

"Akkkkkk!"

Auntie again, she's clearing in her throat and rising to her feet. This must be it. I'm ready for her. The candles leap and I'm practically all set. At least I won't say "Hi" anymore. Probably I'll kick her in the bean if she gives me any sass. First I better smile. I feel I should.

"Humph!"

A favorite expression, but what's it supposed to mean? And the contemptuous look I get. More and more I have the feeling I'm being insulted around here.

How about Papa? Al Jolson over there. I turn sharply his way and receive the same vacancy. What kind of attitude is that? Plus the welcome he handed me. I'm a mackerel, he says. I'll give him a mackerel! Goddamn bogeyman, I'd like to see him start something. I'd like to see him period. Cards on the table. After all, it's his daughter I've supposedly ruined, not the aunt's. Out with it, I say. Confront me with the facts. I'd like to get things at least partly in the open.

I could also use some elbow room. Vivette's a terrible squasher. Mama hops over, so now we're three on the bed with me in the middle, a visiting sandwich. The only freewheeler is Auntie, pacing the floor once, twice, twenty times. Stem to stern. When Stash monkeys with the keyboard, she clips him on her way by. Noise is out. Only clump-clump from her feet and swish-swish from her skirts. A ballerina, Vivette says, but how do you explain the tonnage? Very impressive shoulders. I'd like to see some twinkle-toes spin her over his head. I can't help admiring her build in general, the rearview in particular, undulating under the drapery. Wow! A regular Hottentot swagger.

Caa-hoo! Caa-hoo!

That stove will be the death of me. Not only smoke, it can really put out the heat. I wet my lips and dry my palms.

Now my tie is crooked.

"Thank you."

Vivette's a big help with ties. I loosen it and sneeze. Why can't we open a window? I guess it'd take a crowbar. I count slugs while we wait. I just noticed, ten or twelve of them, like fat caterpillars cruising the floor. Black ones, brown ones and most are iridescent. They pass each other like ships in the night, the floor being their sea, defying eternity and meeting it halfway between Auntie's footfalls.

Sometimes I wonder how she has her shack decorated today. The dirt floors could be covered in Persian rugs and the soot-caked walls by fine paintings. She might've even gotten rid of her handy bucket. I notice Godmommy's Christofle tea service has been missing for over a month. That really burns me up. I think I mentioned I'm getting nothing out of this but writer's cramp. Not a pot to piss in! Which looks bad for my manhood.

Hey, speaking of manhood, I just caught a glimpse of Papa when he bent forward to poke the fire. White shoes and a pink jacket. Also four glowing peepers. Let's think about that. White and pink are okay, but four eyes is too many. Because I'm not allowing for cats. Mystery solved. When he bends forward a second time, I see he has Puss-Puss cradled in his arms and they both have eyes. Excellent! I put two and two together. Now maybe someone will tell me the tune he's humming. Russian? Gypsy? A mournful son-of-a-gun. The only other disturbance is from Auntie's great clodhoppers still clumping from corner to corner, smashing hell out of the poor slugs.

"Want cookie?" she says, suddenly wheeling on me.

I look to Vivette for guidance.

"I speaking you."

She's speaking to me all right and I'm taking too long to answer. The thing is, I'm not sure we're talking about real cookies or doing metaphorical aspersions on Vivette.

"I'm not sure."

"Not sure? Ha! Ha! Ha!"

I'm cracking her up. The others too. Heehee from Mama, hoho from Stash, and even Papa is either laughing or strangling the cat. I could use an interpreter, but Vivette seems to think she hasn't cried enough. When I slip an arm around her waist, she buries her face in her hands. What's that make me look like?

"Want cookie or no?"

"Sure," I say. What the hell. "A cookie would be fine."

"I get'm," chirps Mama, happy as a lark. She heads in six different directions. "Where they are?"

"Sit."

Auntie will handle this. She has cookies in her pockets. Now where are her pockets? Oop! Up go the skirts and here comes my cookie. She wears man's trousers underneath.

"Is good?"

Hmmm, a mouthful of dust. I'm growing angry inside. Not outside. I smack my lips and beam at her ingratiatingly, a real dust fiend.

"More?"

"Oh, no thank you very much."

That's telling her. My voice slides smoothly into falsetto. Isn't this nice? Cookies in our pockets. I cross my legs and rock back and forth, my hands locked to one knee like a Ziegfeld girl.

"Unusual weather we're having."

Cahoo! Cahoo!

"Vodka?"

How do you like that, she carries vodka in her pockets too. She shows me. Three tiny bottles of maybe two ounces each. I'm encouraged to take my pick. The red one looks interesting.

"Is good?"

Like fire, but not bad. Actually it hits the spot. I'm examining the label, turning it this way and that, when she jams her face at me.

"Were you born?"

"Yes, ma'am." This aunt is nuts. "What?...Oh." Silly me. She wants to know *where* I was born. "In the United States...Yes, ma'am...of America...I beg your pardon?"

I don't believe it, she wants to see my passport. I have it right here. No I don't. I thought I did, but Vivette's been keeping it safe for me. Hand it over! A little damp. I apologize. It's also a trifle frayed and a bit sticky where I taped the binding.

"More light."

Move over some candles, we're going to play Customs Agent. She snaps her fingers for Stash to get his head out of the way.

"That photo," I explain, "was taken some time ago."

"Is nice photo," says Mama.

"I didn't have a beard."

"You Jewish?"

"No, ma'am."

"Much traveled," says Auntie.

Well, I did skip around plenty before bogging down at the Select. Twelve countries per month.

She runs her fingers over the seals and endorsements, counter-endorsements. Too many visas to suit her, too many frazzles. When she angles it for better focus, a lottery ticket falls out, an Italian one. She gives me a look, I'm a rolling stone.

"Ever be to Roooossia?"

"No, ma'am. You'll notice I stuck mainly to the tourist routes. The Black Forest and places. Westminster Abbey."

I'm not a hobo, in other words.

"You writer, my sister say."

"Yes, ma'am."

"Ever you pooooblish?"

Damn, I hate that question. "No, ma'am, unpublished."

"Speak up!"

"Unpublished. I'm just getting started."

That deserved another look. "Four-flusher" is what she's thinking. And in all honesty I have to go along with her on that. Already I stopped telling people I'm a writer. Gibberologist, I say, or else I lie and claim to have been published in absentia. That baffles them, but not as much as it does me.

Finally she hands back my passport, but won't let go. It's the strangest thing. We're each holding one end, my passport in the middle, and she brings her face really close, smiling at the same time, which is pretty strange in itself.

"Mmmmmm," she purrs, kind of sexy. "Such beautiful boy."

Our noses touch and I see a fine set of teeth, trimmed in stainless steel, only one is missing, and while all this goes on I can't help wondering what happened to the meat-cleaver, worried that weird antics may be the benign tip merely, like an iceberg, of some really dark and dangerous mental catastrophe yet to be revealed. After all, vodka is one thing, but what kind of hostess serves cookies from her pockets?

"So beautiful, beautiful," she purrs, caressing my whiskers. "But think you afraid me of, no?"

That makes me blush. "No, ma'am."

"Yes, I think so, yes."

Damnit, what am I supposed to say? "How did you like Greece?"

"Leave him lone!" shouts Vivette, flying between us. She grabs my passport and flings it in my face. Her own face is white, the lips trembling. "Apple-snap!" she says.

"No!" says Auntie. "Ripple-snip spinach soup!"

Stash burps and I feel guilty.

"Tejlozwalpierychiablagnzol!" says Vivette.

"Zacaiwkablawlaprozac!" says Auntie.

"Oh, la-la!" says Mama, shooting me a pained look like she can't believe her ears. "You hear what they say it?"

I hear okay, but don't know what to make of it. One way or another all hell has broken loose. Claws spring open and buttons pop. Teeth and nails flash like daggers. A Russian riot, in other words, even though I'm dubious about content. Plaster drifts from the ceiling as dust rises from the floor, all of it meeting in the middle with the contestants. They thrash, twirl and polish the air with their hands. You never met such dedicated conversationalists. I stand up twice and they shove me down ten times. Which seems unfair. I don't see why I should be the only one. Even Papa is allowed to chime in with an occasional squawk and squeal.

Hey, come to think of it, I can see him plainly now. George Washington, that's my first impression, except he's more distinguished than George and not so pudgy. Kind of willowy, in fact, if you know what I mean. White hair like George's, he keeps it knotted in back and Marcelled in front. But there's something odd about him too. I can't put my finger on it until I spot the lipstick. That's feminine, I'm thinking, and so is the eye-shadow and face-powder. His voice sounds deep enough, but the more I take in, the more horrified I am by cosmetics. Hell, he's painted up worse than a Hollywood Indian! This finally hits me between the eyes and leaves a bad case of the heebie-jeebies. He notices and winks. Damn! I pull up my collar and put on a tough mug. Nobody will guess how scared I am. These aren't just colorful kooks anymore. I'm afraid I got mixed up in something really sinister this time, more or less like the Moor Murders, where my literary ambitions will have to settle for a splash in the morning papers, my dismembered body located throughout several sections of the countryside.

If Vivette ever finishes insulting people, I intend having a word with her. I figure the time has come to go. But she's still nose-to-nose with the aunt, still slinging the mud. A stiff breeze gets going. Three candles are out. Papa relights one and becomes absorbed in wax. He plays with the stuff. The others are free to glide and slobber all they want. Stash bangs his knee on the stove and knocks Mama in my lap. She's up and after him in a flash. They swim through the air and bump heads.

"No worry," says Mama. "Ever tink be hunky-dunky."

Really? I can't get over her optimism. But Stash seems to agree. He runs over and shakes my hand. So maybe Mama's right. I stand and mumble. Vivette shoves me down. Mama smacks her for that and there's a fresh surge of saliva.

Oho, I'm getting it from Auntie herself now. Directly overhead, she's talking like Donald Duck. At least I think she's talking. She could be irrigating the fields. I don't think I should just sit here without an umbrella. I stand. Vivette lets me. I want to interject harmonious tones, a few saws and wherefores, plus my plans for the future and good intentions.

"Shut!" screams Auntie, "up!"

Boom! I'm rolling on the bed again. I think somebody tripped me. Vivette picks up the ball, then Mama. Auntie cuts them both short with every name in the book and some from legend. The truth is, she goes too far, sparing nothing, not even the unborn. Vivette's mid-section. This is a low blow. I gather as much by paying strict attention to hand signals and Vivette's quivering chin. The poor girl is appalled, her lips sealed. Never in her wildest dreams did she imagine her aunt could be so vile. Her belly is sacred, after all. She hides it with her hands. She protects her wee charge.

"Tatarijekap!" she says.

"Schibblebip!" says Auntie.

You can't faze the old girl with maternalism. If anything, it puts zip in her invectives and adds zing in her innuendoes. I guess the time isn't ripe for reconciliation. One unforgivable follows another until we're even deeper in the shits.

Vivette's sniffles have really cheered Auntie up.

"Blaggaplook," she says. "Ha! Ha! Ha!"

A radiant smile.

She tilts her head at me and crosses her eyes. "Boo!" she says, real screwy.

Tooting like a horn, she stomps back and forth, her stomach way out. She points you know where. Poor Vivette, her aunt is an impressionist. She ridicules her condition and apes her waddle, strutting across the floor like a squad of marines. Which has a bad effect on my honeylamb's composure. Her posture droops. I don't think she's going to make it. I'm weighing my options while she sways in the wind. Get her home, I decide, when a bloodcurdling shriek shoots straight out the top of her dome.

"Okay," I tell the others, snapping to attention like a five-star general. "That will do. Let's make some room here."

I'm worried about Vivette's complexion. She's pasty in the face and threatening to topple. I prop her up.

"May we open a window, Madame?"

"Sit down, stupid."

"Please, Madame."

"Klapznakschiet," she calls me.

A fine how-do-you-do.

"Let's get out of here," I tell Vivette. "Come on, if we step on it we can still catch the midnight show at the Odéon. What do you say?"

"Grrrrrrr."

Not much of an answer, besides which she shakes me loose and pulls away, shoving her thumbs in her mouth and tearing at the nails. And before I can ask what she's up to, she spits them smack in Auntie's face.

"Ovchegivoff!" she snarls, which must mean something like "here are some nails for your coffin".

An awful thing to say. We all suck wind. Auntie especially. She staggers against the wall like somebody hit her with a hammer. Paralyzed and speechless. But for how long? It's my opinion we're likely to look back on this dull interlude as the calm before the grand calamity. The way her eyes bug out, I'm sure she must be near the boiling point.

"Mine God! Mine God!" says Mama, wringing her hands and kind of chanting. "Why people can't nice be to one another?"

That's what I'm thinking too. I rise to my feet, all set for another stab at harmony, then Vivette and I can beat it. But Stash slams the organ at the same time and I nearly keep on rising clear through the roof.

Auntie hates that as much as I do. "Aggerjagger," she calls him, and attacks like a windmill. Bing, pow and lots of stimulating slaps, only stopping after a minute, after he's mostly under the bed. She turns and glowers at the rest of us, her head ducked low like she's ready to charge. No, she's examining the floor. Slugs on parade. One must displease her because up goes her foot, practically over her head, then down, bang and splat, she flattens him like a rotten pickle, with such force the juice makes it ten feet in one squirt to sizzle against the Franklin stove.

Sickening but climactic. I figure the party should break up now. Except nobody moves. We only eye each other while the slug juice sizzles. A couple loud pops followed by smoke. Mama stops chanting and our breathing becomes more regular as time passes. You can almost hear the dust settling.

"Heeheehee," says Papa, spoiling our magic spell.

Why is that? He won't say. He pats his hair.

"Sorry," he says.

Oh, that's okay. He shouldn't apologize. Just let us in on what's so hilarious.

"De cat! De cat!" he says.

Yeah, so what? The cat is trying to scrape slug juice off the stove, is that anything to crack up over?

"Yuk! Yuk! Yuk!"

He stands, points and sits back down.

"Ho! Ho! Ho!"

We don't see the humor. We see the cat okay, but what's the big joke?

Mama shrugs. "Cat be hungry, afraid he burns feets."

"No! No!" says Papa. Mama is all wet. "De schmell! De schmell!"

He's nuts, but it's catching. In ten seconds flat he has us all in stitches. One of those infectious convulsions. No rhyme or reason, we simply feel like splitting our sides open. Me too, even though I don't really get it. Something about the cat and the smell of the disemboweled slug.

"Yeehaha!"

"Holy smoke!"

"Papa's right!"

"De schmell! De schmell!"

Five minutes pass without coming up for air. Again I'm worried about Vivette, wincing between guffaws. She may be losing water. Yet I can't help bubbling over myself. Tears stream down my face and off the tip of my nose.

"Enough," says Auntie.

"Cat got your tongue?"

"Weeheehee!"

We rock back and forth like a chorus of penguins, grinning at each other like chimpanzees. Auntie has an attack of the horse-whinnies, topped off with a high-C heehaw.

"Done," she says. "Everything be settled."

"What's settled?"

CHAPTER 10

THE ENGAGEMENT PARTY
Where Mike wins the day whether
he likes it or not

I think I missed something. There's a general round of applause followed by hugging and kissing. I don't know why. All at once, everybody acts extremely relieved and inordinately jolly. Vivette collapses next to me, suddenly serene. I guess because we're supposed to put our differences behind us, forgive and forget. We should also dance. They're choosing partners. Stash plunks down at the keyboard and Auntie breaks out the booze. Soon I'm walking in circles with a dizzy look on my face. Mama congratulates me and Papa both, but she should lay off the bear-hugs. Papa wriggles free and scurries to the kitchen. He returns with a saltshaker and a fistful of breadcrumbs. This is a new gag. The salt goes on my head and the crumbs on my tongue for good luck. An old Russian custom. Only one thing bothers him, this business with the music. It puts a bounce in his ass. He'd like to be the first to dance with me. I better check with Vivette, except she's crying. No, she's laughing. Anyway, in Russia boys dance together on the flimsiest pretext. Papa assures me himself. No cheek-to-cheek stuff until later. My beard made a big hit with that guy. What the hell, I let him nibble at the fringes. We do the Bunny Hug, then the Murmansk Shuffle. Vivette prefers the one-woman Mambo. Off and on, she blubbers like there's no tomorrow. Boohoo and haha, she's on alternating current.

"Come you," says Auntie, beckoning from the bedroom.

I'm supposed to follow. If only I could see her. She takes my hand and leads the way. Still I fall down. She helps me up and shows me the sights, her bedroom by candlelight. Too bad there's no bed. The bed is in the living room. Here, we can sit on these boxes.

"Kiss?"

Just a friendly embrace and buzz-buzz-buzz, she's bending my ear about the old country and its topsy-turvy history, plus the eightball family she's saddled with. Her burden of difficulties and responsibilities, her rotten luck. I take it she feels Mama, for one, is hopelessly soft in the head due to an unhealthy devotion to the saints. And what about Stash? All set for a straitjacket. That leaves Vivette and the old man. Well, let's leave Vivette out of it for the time being. But I must've noticed this Papa character. Off the beam obviously. His frilly clothes and languid manner, that probably shocked me a good deal. Well, to tell her the truth I did seem to pick up on certain deviations from the norm, a picturesque quality, the way he swivels at the hips, for example, like a two-bit hussy. On the other hand, maybe his shoes don't fit. Or am I talking out of turn straight down the middle? Not at all. She appreciates my delicate sense of decorum and good citizenship, but wishes I'd stop making excuses for the old fairy.

"Be fine lines from depravity-insanity."

I could see what she means.

"More kiss?"

Common courtesy. Besides, I had no desire to spoil this meeting of the minds, flattered as I was at being taken into her confidence this way. Into her arms, in fact. My primary concern, I was maybe agreeing too much, especially when we got on the subject of Vivette and her flagrant indiscretions, her wanton lustfulness. That's some nerve I have, since it could be pointed out that I too had a hand, so to speak, in recent reproductive mishaps.

"Ack, love be always same for the young peoples!"

Another kiss, then she wants me on my feet for a tour of her bedroom-storeroom. I'm reminded of a pawn shop. I see a bicycle wired to the ceiling, broken furniture here and there, with maybe fifty crates and boxes stacked against the walls, mostly overflowing with rags.

"Dis be mine husband."

That made me jump, but it's only a photograph. She brings it down from a shelf and shows me.

"From first days of marriage."

"Yes, very handsome."

The Duke of Splish-Splash. I don't catch the name, but gather he was a lion among men and a true devotee of the dance. Those were wonderful days. He use to wait for her each night with candy and flowers. A stage-door Johnny. He wined her and dined her until she agreed to marry him, then they hopped on this sleigh in the picture. I see the two of them seated behind a big shaggy horse, snow in the foreground, a large mansion in the background.

"Lost world," she says, a tear snaking across her cheek.

Both were bundled to the ears, so it's difficult to judge age, but I'd say Auntie was much younger than the Duke. If that's her in the picture. Nowadays she looks more like the horse.

"Gone," she says. "All gone."

She blows her nose and tosses the picture aside. No use raking up the past. She uncorks another of her miniature vodkas, and shows me, boy, a whole drawer full of them, plus a display of the rarer brands by an icon cabinet. Is it a hobby? No hobby. All these bottles were collected by the skydiver who used to live here.

"What's in the cabinet?"

"Ahhhhh!"

I had to ask.

"My baby," she says. "My little boy."

Sure enough, inside the cabinet is another photo, her kid this time, cracked and faded and yellowing with age, propped up beside a pair of high-button booties and a toy dog made of crumbling rubber, the whole works arranged like a shrine with candles and biblical illustrations.

"Sad."

"Yes."

"He's dead, I presume."

She nods and gently closes the cabinet.

"Cognac?"

A welcome change of pace. I'm free to choose from others, mostly vodkas and brandies, but also rums and gins and a wide array of whiskies. A fascinating exhibit, except later I had trouble reading the labels.

"Get out!" she says, which sent me toward the ceiling again.

But again a false alarm. It's only Papa she's yelling at when he pokes his head around the corner, a shit-eating grin on his face.

"Better we return."

They were calling to us from the living room.

I danced a few rounds with Mama and Stash, until Papa cut in. Auntie took over later, after I showed I could do the Murooska. She prefers to lead and really she should. Training will tell. She's actually lighter on her feet than Vivette, which is really saying something when you consider Vivette's youth and natural vigor and the extra weight the old bag has to spot her. We hardly ever touched the floor. We touched the walls okay. And the stove.

"Yeeeow!"

My pants were steaming, but she saved the day with a quick twirl and neat dip, sending her tongue down my throat for a toe-curling kiss.

"Yippee!"

Mama conducted a séance toward midnight, trotting out the cards and right away predicting a bright future for Vivette and me, with gold-ended rainbows and a carload of kids.

"Hallelujah amen!"

Auntie monopolized most of my time during the wee hours, cornering me in various shadows to discuss serious business. In her own way, you know, she's a very affectionate woman. Crazy for smooching, that's her weakness. She only ran her hands down my pants once, after catching me outside taking a leak. All in good fun, I thought, even though I can't say I trusted my own opinion. I was plenty scared of that woman, even then, the way she latched on and took control, instructing me about the birds and the bees, I guess that was the idea, while Blacky spied on us from the junk heaps, pretending he can't really think, which is pretty much what I was pretending myself.

The party ended a little after four. Auntie was feeling me up on the dance floor, when Vivette rounded things off with a tremendous crying jag, a terrific flood of tears, which Papa took it in his head to copy. Time to hit the road. Mama came up with a Saint Christopher medal, which I foolishly pinned to my cap, thus pissing Vivette off. Auntie defused the situation by hanging it on the most prominent bulge as a parting joke. We all roared with laughter until I couldn't help spitting up a little. Vivette too. She hiccupped, burped, then all at once she was outside tossing up the works.

"Well, so long everybody."

"Sleep tight, you one fine boy."

Auntie stuffed a hundred francs down my shirt before doing her routine for us with the locks and keys.

"Till we meet again."

Hankies in the wind, mist in the eyes.

"Ha-ha-ip!"

"Aren't you finished, honey? Come on, what you need is an aspirin and good night's sleep. Me too."

Out of sympathy, I puked some more myself. Papa ran after us with my tie and a bag of tangerines, then slunk off the opposite way. I wished him happy trails. You could see his white shoes disappearing down the road like the Invisible Man. The others kept on waving, their final salutations. I wasn't in the mood and only looked back a couple times as we climbed the hill. The rain had let up and the path wasn't so slippery. Still, Vivette kept me busy with pit stops and teardrops. Such a sad girl! We had to wait over an hour for the Paris train, which didn't help her disposition any. The station smelled like dry piss.

"Oh, Mikie, my Mikie, you must run away fast before they eat you, them cannibals. To see how weak you be. Is only reason..."

"How do you mean cannibals?"

Vivette talks crazy. I was used to it, of course. All the same, there's no denying I felt some pensiveness myself, deep down, as she drifted to sleep on my shoulder, crying and mumbling, in half-French, half-Russian.

"America, America, America, my Mikie, Mikie..."

Not until that afternoon did I learn we'd just had our engagement party, the date firmly set for April twenty-first, about three weeks away. No more ifs, buts or howevers. Auntie would see to that and everything else.

There's a group photo that I think gives a good inkling of the pickle I was in. The whole gang of us on the steps of City Hall. The Wedding Day. Auntie is in the middle with me on one side and the expanding Vivette on the other. Homer is toward the rear, our Best Man, side-saddle on the railing with his nose in a newspaper. *Racing Times*. What a picture! At least a thousand details I'll never get out of my mind.

"Hey," says Homer. "I never noticed that, Auntie's smoking a cigar?"

Yes, and Papa borrowed Vivette's veil. When it comes to offbeat characters, I guess I could've done worse. A writer has to consider these things.

My book progressed nicely until the kid was born. That happened toward the middle of May. Then we ran into trouble making ends meet. The weeks passed and the months. Finally I decided to try our luck in England. We had to come right back. No money laying around over there either. Auntie let us stay at her shack while she and Mama tended to an old lady by Park Monceau. Another Russian throwback. That was their last job before the godmother. Mama had already begun to ease herself in at Passy, and pestered us to do likewise on account of the deep affection the godmother had for Vivette. She wasn't so batty yet. Still, I didn't care for the setup. We dropped by a couple times and Vivette agreed. We preferred being on our own. It took fifteen hundred francs to change my mind. Auntie promised five thousand per month thereafter, which naturally boiled right down to room and board and dirty dishes.

At first I was bashful in the midst of so much wealth. Later I got ideas. What if she dies? I could see the knickknacks alone were enough put my kid through college several times. And there was a will, supposedly, leaving everything to Vivette in the final analysis. Pretty good, I thought. Soon I'd be lord of the manor! The godmother was obviously no match for another winter. Built like a coat-hanger in those days and she still is.

Then her nephew chased me down the street one day and I realized our true interests were upside-down. If she dies, we're cooked, Vivette and me, on account of registering as her guardians. Homer says we'll be the laughingstock of Devil's Island.

Sometimes I envy the godmother, for even if she's nutty as a pecan and in many ways deader than ten doornails, nobody can say she's losing any sleep over it. The trick, I suppose, is to get yourself stuck between tic and toc, then paddle like hell for ramparts.

The phone rings at all hours. If it's not her nephew threatening judicial annihilation, it's old friends bugging us for info. Why can't they visit?

"Out of kestion," says Auntie.

She whistles me over.

"Doctor's orders," I tell them.

Meanwhile, I chew my fingers from stem to stern. The godmother digs another fortified bunker and sticks a long cat turd on top.

CHAPTER 11

BEER AND BANGLES
Where Homer exposes the hard core of ambition

We're at the other end of the city today, Homer and me. Actually he's upstairs with one of his regulars, his third of the afternoon, while I lounge around this tenth-rate café, drinking, writing and watching the world slide by. I get about five hundred words per gallon.

Church is the opiate of the steeple and a bird in the hand is worth two if by sea.

This whole routine started around noon with Number One. Now we're on Number Three and the sun should set any minute. Wine-red sky. The Metro climbs above ground across the street, so I'm guessing we're by Porte de la Villette where the wholesale butchers are located, meaning I can switch from beer to warm blood if my waiter keeps playing hard to get.

The first one was their first time, so Homer dallied over an hour. My purpose is unclear. I study the office-workers passing with their last-minute shopping. Maniacs in high gear. The boss will set them straight in the morning with a little kiss this and please suck that, which may sound like sour grapes. I guess I wouldn't mind trading places. Only fifteen francs are left from the eighty Homer paid me for an antique watch and a dusty old tapestry.

There's a big dog by the door with a blue tongue on him like Auntie's. Otherwise it's an okay place, Depression-era décor, the tail-end of sunlight from here to the tracks.

I intend giving him a kick on my way out. The dog, I mean, not Homer. The waiter too if he keeps ignoring me in terms of refills.

"Down in a minute," says Homer.

He has to help her move something. A ton of bullshit. I pretend to be writing letters so people don't think I'm just guzzling.

Oop, here he is again, far side of the window, buttoning his fly and pointing at his watch. Five fingers means five minutes. No problem. Some things take precedence over others and I understand time can lose lots of relevance when there's a pit wrapped around your pendulum.

More beer!

A quick sketch while we wait. Our man of action. The spitting image of Errol Flynn, turning in the sun and smiling, waving, the envy of all bookworms.

Later, after he finally does wind things up, we're neither of us too surprised to find I'm stewed to the eyebrows.

"Sorry, Mike, couldn't tear myself away."

"I know that and don't care. I'm at the end of my rope."

"What's at the other end?"

"Auntie."

He laughs. "Come on, we'll go to Montparnasse."

Good idea. The Café Select, where nobody knows each other. That way maybe I can lose myself better in beer bubbles, a drop of whisky on the side if somebody's buying. Irish whisky with soda-water for my effervescent soul.

"Soul bubbles."

"Something eating you?"

"Beer, beer, beer and I'm still at the end of my rope."

He guides me across the terrace, under the hum of green neon, through the swinging doors to the end of the bar, plunking me down on the last stool.

"Two beers, please."

"Is she on the level, that's the question."

"Are we still talking about the aunt?"

"Her and me being partners. You think she means it?"

"Of course not."

"Then what should I do?"

"Try drying your eyes."

Another good idea, and maybe I should switch to *panaché*, a sugar-water drink they mixed with beer over here. I tried those yesterday in hopes of staying sober.

"It didn't work."

"What didn't?"

"I had forty-five."

"Forty-five what?"

"Bubbles, bangles and beads, and elephants to ride on."

"What're you babbling about?"

"Tweeds, tea leaves and the tyranny of high fashion."

He points at my glass. "How many of those have you had?"

"Well, if you want to get specific, I was only reminded of my sports-coat when that layer-cake slunk in dressed like a fortune cookie. Have you noticed how I keep changing the subject? But that's not the same as babbling."

"Better taper off."

He's right. It's just that I wanted introduce my sports-coat because it sets me apart. I bought it in London and am the most conservatively clad in the entire Select.

"Excluding the proprietor."

"Knock it off, Mike. You'll get us tossed out."

"He admires you, did you know that?"

"Who does?"

"Monsieur Select. Edwardian greaseball. Always a flower in the lapel. See, he's saluting us with champagne."

I return the compliment, minus champagne. I throw some beer in the air.

"Salute!"

He steps over. "Good evening, my friends."

"Hi! Can you say chrysanthemum-mums?"

"Chrysamasa-sums?"

Homer bumps me against the wall. "Never mind him. Who's that young lady?"

Tough question. The Select is a magnate for young ladies and many aren't old. Homer means that one, however, and is very precise with his index finger.

"No," says the proprietor. "That's my son."

"Gosh, Homer, what an eye you've got."

"Not him. Her."

"The one with bells on her toes?"

"Shut up. I seem to remember..."

"Sure, the kid with four-pound earrings. If that's the question, the answer's easy. You got her last summer or winter, around June or December."

"Oh," says the proprietor. "You mean the dark one perhaps?"

"Right. Dark orange hair and vermillion dandruff."

"Stop babbling, Mike."

"She's an actress."

"You don't say?"

"Sure he does. But now I'm confused. Lost her in the crowd. With all these talent scouts and sugar daddies, she ought to wear phosphorus. She practically blends in with the walls."

"Why don't you shut up? And get yourself something to eat. Your face is brick red."

"Faking a suntan. You too, as long as we're being personal. I didn't want to mention it before, but I notice even you've been striking poses. Unconsciously, let's say. Everybody would like to break into the movies. I have this profile."

"How'd you like me to flatten it for you?"

"Ha!" I can see he doesn't understand. "Cockatoos and painted rainbows. The perils of authenticity, you could say, or would a titless Taylor suit your purposes? Me, I'm more the watered-down Burton type. We make up for it with our costumes and mud-flaps, rhinestone upholstery, each different in the same way. Tinfoil underwear and rear end reflectors. Zipper smiles. Their outfits are gaudy, Homer, that's my whole point. How do you like my sports-coat? You'll admit they go in for the more blinding hues. And the jibber-jabber, my God, we're practically secret agents by comparison. So drown out the fucking church bells! Otherwise modesty gets us where? Back to America, you'll say. Emulate the pilgrims and eat square meals. Early to bed, early to rise. Is that your prescription, Doctor Knowledge? I need guidance."

He's not listening. He swivels on his perch, goggle-eyed by the "in" look and "now" expressions.

"Regulation non-conformity," I tell him, "even from the old fossils. First you bathe your isles of Langerhans in Egyptian formulas, then shine up like a new garbage can.

Plastic birthmarks, ovaries and rubber balls. All spun of the dreams that stuff is made of."

Oho, now I've done it. Shifting in the saddle, he jabs a finger at my heart. "What makes you think you're any better?"

Artsy-fartsy babbler, above-it-all skeptic, that's how he sees me. Melville with no harpoon, I'm Mark without Twain. Just another drip in the bucket of Montparnasse dropouts. Champion of the barstool and master bubble-eater, with no reason to expect anything but a complete, dead, total loss. Same as the others. And here I'd been counting on an award ceremony or two. It won't be long, I've always figured, even though I knew it would never happen. So why all the optimism? At the same time I've given up. How's that for double-talk?

Mad! Stupid! Insane!

There, now I broke my pencil. Switch to the ballpoint quick as a wink. The dauntless scrivener on the outskirts of the night. Faithful recorder of the bum lead and the false clue.

"Big mistake."

"What is?"

"Losing sight of the high cost of printing."

He taps my notebook. "Write, don't talk."

Yes, us babblers have to fill up space. A return to our heroes of the east seems in order, or I might dish out more smut on Homer and his dollies from the Follies. Really put him on the spot. After all, I know what I know and nine-ninety-five is pretty steep for beer and bangles. The incomparable gash-hound versus the world-renown Parisian female. Battle of the Titans, that's what keeps the pages turning. If only they weren't such clowns for contempt, grist for Homer's humor. Mine too, now that I think of it. We prefer the homespun variety such as is scarce at this hour and on this particular corner. The only trouble, I have to watch my step on account of Homer won't tolerate people adopting his private point of view. The first glimmer of agreement and he's liable to attack with a broken bottle. That's because his scorn is paternal and perverse. He loves and despises them simultaneously. A complicated subject and a good area to avoid. No abysses until the Witching Hour. By then I expect to have this tipsiness out of my system, this Scott Fitzgerald gimmick of the consummate prodigal with music in his fingertips, his blue eyes fading...

"His candle flickers."

"Dry up."

Grumpy old Homer would like to spoil this entire lyrical section before I have a chance to describe the Select. A spot of grease in the night. Boxed in, he has me on the last stool, my back against the wall, directly below the barometer where I'm told Ernest Hemingway used to like it during the Roaring '20s when men were men and beer was a nickel a quart.

"I wonder why he bumped himself off."

"Who?"

"Troubled spirit. Me, I could sit here forever and wouldn't get troubled. Cafés retain their memory, don't you think? The smell of sawdust still. A clear view of every mirror. The pendulum clock, the rubber-tree plants..." I'm pointing, but he's not with me. "He lived around the corner, did you know that?"

"Thanks for the beer."

"Por nada."

The fool doesn't realize he's paying. On the other hand, I see a twenty-franc bill on the bar that could very easily be mine. In fact, now it is mine.

"Your turn," I tell him. "Whether it was or wasn't, now it is. That's what makes economics a difficult science, old sport. The flow of capital and wobbulating ownerships, obligations, the velocity of the franc. The godmother, for instance, says everything is mine. Take the works, she says. Did I tell you? She surprised me in the dark and bequeathed everything to yours truly. With her negligee wide open, eyes like fireballs. I think I told you. Then she slipped me that watch I sold you. It's hers and she can give it away. Why not? I see you don't know why not. Are you listening? Doesn't matter, not really. But before we drift too far afield, I believe it's still your turn, and to show my heart's in the right place, I'm sticking with beer."

"That one's mine."

"No it isn't."

"Yes it is."

Stealing my beer, what a low character. Let him try it again and I'll bend the barometer over his head. Or sing him *Annie Laurie*. Sleep it off when the sun comes up. Under the shadows, my way-station in the night. Afraid I'll miss something perhaps. Some twist, some turn, some new and much darker wrinkle. Then curl into a question mark.

"Unlock the heart, that's the ticket."

"Are you still talking to yourself?"

"Loneliness, Homer. Why else do they leave their rooms? The search for significance and they don't know where it is. Me neither, so what can I say?"

"Try nothing."

"Nothing?"

What a funny suggestion. He expects me to sit out eternity in silence. I shake my head to show how sad that would be. Life, I'm thinking, do you love me?

"And are you sincere?"

"Jesus, Mike, would you give it a rest."

"But she's such an attractive heartbreaker, forever pulling the wool over our eyes. Which is more a question of perception. Perception deception. Or the other way around. The violation of darkness. A small chink in the void. I don't go for the growing-old business, do you? Or the other thing. Brrrrrr! The spirit world, I mean. Hobnobbing with the clouds. Can you picture yourself as a wisp of smoke? How about a ring around the moon? That doesn't appeal to me."

"Okay," he says, dragging me off my stool. "You need some exercise. Go ask that one if she speaks English."

Well, he's getting better with his suggestions but can do his own asking. I'll just write her a note.

Do you speak English?

"Too bad about this bar, makes such a damp desk."

"Straighten up."

"Rheumatism of the elbows."

"Get moving."

"Another thing, I'm bound to feel mighty disgusted some day for learning the alphabet. You wake up screaming, determined to stop smoking."

"Crummy deal."

"I'm glad you agree."

"Now ask her."

"I have to take a leak."

Downstairs, that's where you get good ideas.

First dream, then die.

It's a shame I can't find my notebook.

"Hey, Homer, have you seen my notebook?"

He sure has, and he's messing it all up with maps and phone numbers and invitations to breakfast.

"The shack, man, the aunt's shack. If we go there tonight, we walk away rich."

No, he'd rather narrow the field. First Brigitte, then Lana, then Sophia from Lorraine. He ruffles their feathers on their way to the can. A cheap trick, he admits that himself. Always the same questions, same answers. It lays me low. Homer operates on a percentage basis and won't mess with the tough nuts or clever coquettes.

In the midst of so much poetic license, however, I think I neglected to mention he corralled the kid with the bangles. A whimsical choice when you consider the depth of his hypochondria and how this type smokes hemp, spits blood and consorts with known creeps and dribble-dicks. A sentimental exception, I'm thinking, seeing as we knew her before she was barely off the ground as a young hopeful. Homer never actually screwed her, but got her to blow his bugle in the men's room. About a year ago, if I remember correctly. The girl herself is faking amnesia, trying to pass everything off as a joke, café humor. Homer has to pat her ass to calm her down. But let's have no more talk about the retracement of footsteps. The crapper is out.

"Isn't that what she said the first time?"

I'm noncommittal on account of my big heart. Anyone can see she's in a tight spot. No uppers or downers or real friends.

"She'll do it for moment's companionship."

"That's pretty goddamn sad, asshole."

He gives me a pat too.

"Hey," I tell her, "I bet you're an actress, you're so good-looking."

Gallant but inaccurate. The bags under her eyes are green, her gums receding, and the veins around her nose have begun to swell into starbursts. On the other hand, you have to admire the way she covers up with Happy Cream and tall talk about tryouts and booking agents, the juicy parts coming her way, only balking a bit when it comes to petting in public, shivering uncontrollably when Homer passes a hand under her blouse. He whispers in her ear.

"No."

"Come on."

"No!" in a higher key, smiling in such a way she may be trying to hide a rotten tooth.

I know how to smile that way too. We both flinch when he hooks her arm and gives me a wink, creating one of those awkward moments. Difficult to know what to say. But she goes with him anyway, blushing through the greasepaint. Outside this time. No stairway to the toilets. They glide off for the corner church where there's a children's park in back with benches under the trees.

How do you like that? I'm only mildly astonished when they return like honeymooners, transformed and transfixed, and she's a clinging vine, with fingerprints on her neck.

"Daaaaarling," she calls him, and gives me the elbow. She wants my seat, so she jerks her thumb. Beat it! Even though it was I, was it not, scarcely ten minutes ago, who found it in his heart to pity this fallen starlet. Homer was being rude, wasn't he? I'll say! But after wrestling her head down, everything is reversed and peachy. Now we have Lassie with courage. She's even dolling up her lips for more of the same. Or how about a hotel? A better idea. Just wait and see. She'll have him steamed, cleaned, then she'll press his jeans. Sound good? Great! What're we waiting for? More lipstick, see? Let's go.

"Some other time."

I could have told her this was coming. Already he's casting out fresh feelers, licking various legs with his lashes. I think I'm going to get my seat back.

"No money," he lies.

She offers to pay, but he forgot his pajamas.

"Homerrrrrrrr!"

She wouldn't mind it between the legs for a change, and even the urinal has gained some allure. This kid sure knows how to change tunes. I'm mildly disgusted and feel like telling her so, except I have kind of a yen myself.

"Hey," I tell her, "I'll go to the hotel with you."

What? Drop dead. Am I ever crude plus crazy. She thinks my manners leave everything to be desired. My body too, the genetic malfeasance. She tells me as much. My features are irksome, my presence nauseating. She absolutely recommends I poison the atmosphere somewhere else. The thing is, students of life such as she know how to pierce through the flimflam in people, straight past the pretense to their souls, and mine is rotten to the core. It gives off smells. So why not hurry before I miss the cross-town bus? Better yet, I should stretch out in front of it. Either way, the conversation is finished. Not another word. Maybe a dirty look. I have it coming. Ten dirty looks. Twenty! From every angle. With a toss of the head. She'll show these upstarts what it is be faithful. A one-man woman. I see that now. Why am I so stupid? I apologize and tip my cap. I shake her hand and spill my beer. Homer orders another.

He leans over. "She's going through that stage where they take on too many men. It warps their brains."

"Are you kidding?"

"I'll fix it for you."

"Don't."

"Then wait at the Dôme. I want to wash. Did you notice that rash on her neck? I'll be over in a minute."

CHAPTER 12

LOVE AND MONEY
Where Homer calls for action and
Auntie does him one better

I wish I didn't have to put up with such nonsense. Too many notebooks get spoiled. People might even take me for a surrealist when I claim to see five or six Homers trotting across the boulevard. One trips over the curb while the others plow through the terrace to slap me on the back.

"Why the long face? Did you really want that hippie?"

"No."

"You can have her if you want her."

"No, I was just thinking. The godmother and everything. And I'm worried about Vivette."

"Worried about Vivette," he mimics my squeaky voice. "Save your worries for yourself. She's used to that family, you know. If you took her away, that's when she might really crack. Have you thought of that?"

"What're you talking about? She cries noon and night, and I'm scared now she'll bump herself off, maybe take the kid with. I mean, you're always reading that in papers where somebody kills themself, but first they do it to their kids."

"How about you?"

"She wouldn't kill me. She loves me."

"She loves the kid too, that's not what I meant."

"Anyway, I'm the boy who has to watch her eyes puff shut like a boxer every night. You can laugh, but I'm the one who has to come up with a way out. She's getting more and more depressed."

"So is everybody."

True, the Dôme had taken on real draggy tones. The windows turned cloudy, the patrons weren't rowdy, and the ladies of the leopard-skin mode, normally so gay and attentive, were shying away from poor Homer.

"You know, Mike, I waste a lot of time on you."

"Yeah, I'm sorry. I appreciate it."

He can go fuck himself.

"I don't suppose the aunt's come across with more money."

"Well, she says I can have the dining-room furniture if I sign more papers."

"Don't sign."

"I already did. But that table must weigh four hundred pounds. How you want to get it to your place?"

He slouched low in his chair and folded his arms across his chest. "Better start the ball rolling. Have you talked to Pablo?"

"About the table?"

He drew a finger across his throat. "Murder Incorporated."

"He's not the man for the job. You are."

"Give Pablo a try. If he doesn't work out, maybe I'll lend you a hand."

"Why not now?"

"Comedies need comedians."

"Is that so? Maybe I should run right home and tell Vivette, get her to take her head out of the oven."

"Never feel sorry for women, Mike."

"Me then, am I supposed to play Abbott and Costello while Auntie swipes everything from under our noses, stuff that should rightfully go to Vivette?"

He slouched lower in his chair and closed his eyes. "Someday I'm going to tell you the one great secret of life."

"Tell me now."

No answer.

"Listen, man, I know you think everything I do is crazy. Murder and all that. And I agree. But we could rob her shack, couldn't we? I mean, there's nothing crazy about that, is there? I'm sure she hid lots of stuff out there. We just bust in and take it, what do you say?"

A gentle wheeze from his nose.

I stood and slapped twenty francs on the table, figuring that might get a rise out of him. "Okay, I'm paying for the beer...Homer?...Tomorrow I'll do what you say, I'll go see Pablo. That's what you want, isn't it?"

Busy day. I decided to leave it like that. I retrieved my twenty francs and headed up the Rue Delambre for the Passy Metro, figuring I'd visit a few haunts on the way, even though I was too drunk to see them for what they are. Still too happy even. That's what gets me, the lack of personal progress, when even fleas can be educated. Dogs learn to sit up and seals spin their balls for a price. Hookers too. Both sides of the street. They hop, skip and make smoochy noise with their lips. Thirty francs standing, I find out the hard way. Dark hallways are their nether world.

We enter furtively and exit economically after imitating Homer against number 37.

Now I'm down to five francs, like a silvery moon in my hand, which I take to the last-chance dive across from the Metro, slipping in among the riffraff, the only writer at the bar. A dignified figure. I prop my notebook against the peanut machine and get down to business.

Toulouse Lautrec stuck close to the deck with legs unsuited for sport. Rounding the bases, he tripped on his laces and came up proudly but too goddamn short.

I close the covers and scratch myself.

"Pants rabbits," someone says, trying to teach me new words.

Winos with crazy eyes, crazy angles on life. You can't tell them the first thing about lice, Lysol or garlic salves. They want the last word on home remedies and stinky applications.

Greeting me at Passy, I see Auntie herself is equally bullheaded.

"Drunk again!" she says, propelling me into the living room, where I sprawl on the floor, willing to hear her side of it, if only she'd stop zigzagging and understand how it is when the sweat starts to flow.

"Pants rabbits take a stroll."

"Is you insane?"

"No, is you be?"

I shouldn't have asked. She knocks me over with a feather, actually a pillow full of feathers, then rounds the bend with more this and that, you good-for-nothing crabwagon. It turns out I'm the stupidest of stupes, the vilest of vipers. I'm detestable, indigestible and actually one hell of a swine.

Okay, she has a right to her opinion, but why pick this time of night to hash things out? Three in the morning and she wants to test my head for sour notes. I cover up, but she thumps it with a tuning-fork, then slams the piano. They don't match up. She's quick to point this out.

"Bastard! Villain! You slippery dick!"

"You angry about something?"

"Angry? Angry?"

"That's what I said, Sugarpuss."

Insolent, I admit. It gets me trebles, sharps and heaving tits. Not the easiest thing to ignore. I try staring at the ceiling, deep into the unknown, wondering what life might have been had I married a girl named Beatrice. She'll reach a climax eventually. At least I hope so. Then maybe I can help. With acid in the bathwater, for instance. Or I'll rip her open and sew her up, minus everything. Bury her before the police arrive, then dig her up later. Bury her deeper. I'll use cyanide dirt. Carve "shucks" on her headstone.

"What?"

She thinks I said something, but I'm only relaxing on my elbows, listening to the baby. What a racket! Two rooms away, practicing for the end of the world. Stash too. That's him on the daybed, moaning like a trombone.

"Stash have a toothache?"

She points at the floor, I'm supposed to stay there.

At least Mama and Vivette had the good grace to go to pieces in their own rooms. When I flew in, they flew out. Blacky wasn't so lucky. He's over by the fireplace, imitating a frying-pan with a flexible handle. I pat the floor, but he'd rather stay put. I should omit the handshake.

"Here, boy."

No, I'm snubbed by a one-eyed dog.

Swish-swish goes his tail.

But what's that other weird noise? Aside from Auntie. The godmother, I might have guessed. Sawing wood in the sand, snug as a cootie. Every planet in its place, every atom in its orb. No grips or loose ends. No eardrums. So maybe it pays to be wacky.

Okay, now that we know where everybody is, let's hit the sack. She can yell at me in the morning.

Her eyes get big. Again she points at the floor.

"Mind if I smoke?"

"One time I needed you, you both out drunken."

"Not me," says Stash.

"Drunken pig!"

"No, my Auntie, you talk so stupid."

What? Stupid, is it? She picks him up and lays him out, in order to teach him. That way maybe he'll stay home where he belongs instead of gallivanting all over town with his left-footed pals, especially on important days like today when the nephew drops by with a raiding party of lawyers. Poor Auntie had to throw them out single-handed.

"Yeeeeek!"

She boots him this way and that and square in the ass, then misses completely and dashes her own ass on the floor. Now we're really in the doghouse.

"Tee-heehee!"

My intrepid silliness. I can't get a handle it until she grabs a letter-opener and threatens oblivion.

"Coward," she says, because that's how I'm acting. "Afraid you for defenseless womans."

This tickles her no end.

"Ho! Ho! Ho!"

It's her turn to be jolly. I'm such an alarmist, it fills her full of chuckles. She slaps her knee and her shoe falls off. Then she's up on her toes, buzzing the room like a Swan-Lake Zeppelin. Stash takes the opportunity to blow, which is wise of him. I stand, bow and hear a vase crash over my head, then a blue figurine. She wants to play catch with the knickknacks. I merely bat them aside.

"I have to pee, then I'm going to bed."

"Sit!"

"Okay, but only for a minute." What's one sleepless night to a coward? "You crazy old bitch."

"What?"

"Nothing."

"I hearded you."

She didn't. I barely heard it myself. Still, as she trades the letter-opener for a cast-iron poker, I curl into a very small target. Blacky scoots over and licks my face.

"Stop," she says, because we're too affectionate.

She stirs the chandelier to give us the idea. A few practice swings. She lops a candle in half. Probably Blacky is next if he doesn't economize better on false moves. I don't know what's got into him. Suddenly he's digging at the floor like he'd rather live downstairs. That's out of the question. And we don't need so many toothpicks. Finally she hauls off with her foot and aims for the moon. His tail gets away from him, but he catches up. I wish I could run that fast. I hear his nails clicking on the kitchen tiles almost before he got there.

Now, instead of commiserating about kicker's cramp, I tell her I don't care if her whole leg turns green and drops off. Something she can't believe I would say. So I reiterate and elaborate and don't watch my language. I'm fed up. And still pretty drunk. But it's fascinating the way her cheeks begin to tremble. The flab, it sort of vibrates. Her poker hand too. She keeps it straight in the air like the Evil Knight.

"Tally-ho, you old crow!"

She warns me, but why worry? I'll tell you why. That damn poker. It bothers me up there. Directly overhead, shivering like the stroke of noon. Her whole body does the same, swinging into a kind of rigid blur that detracts from her appearance and I tell her so, even though she has the upper hand when it comes to pokers. I wonder what's holding it up? Some quirky law of physics? The real question is, when does an aching pause become the future in retrospect? My ten thousand days squeezed into a teardrop. No pain. Just a silvery splash of white-hot memory as a gentle wispiness touches my dome and sends the sawdust blossoming into a long line of zeros, splattering the walls and ruining our curtains, streaming down the windows like rain.

"No, no," she sings out. "No cry you." Which is what I'm doing. "Darling," she calls me. "Is her."

"Godmommy?"

"Hate her, no?"

"Why should I?"

"Stealing."

"What?"

"Money."

"Whose money?"

"Mine."

"Yours?"

"Ours."

"Wait a second."

I open my eyes, half-expecting to find an angel in my arms or Mrs. Wilcox, instead of this screamadonna with her hands like emery boards, fumbling with the zipper.

"Kiss," she says. "Hold like this tight."

"First things first."

"Ahhhh!"

She understands in a flash. I'm always so broke. She tweaks my nose and pats my head. I should rest easy in my mind. She skips to her room and returns with an envelope, sealing it with a wink.

"For me?"

She nods, yes, everything is for me, then dives like an eagle with ten claws. Which isn't as bad as it sounds. At least it's dark.

"Love me?" she says.

It's not that dark, but at least I have the envelope. I crack it open and count to a thousand.

"Gee, thanks."

"More later."

"When?"

"In safe place."

Dodging the question. Nobody asked her *where* it is. Anyway, I think I already know.

"Did you bury it at your cottage?"

"So happy we."

Same kind of answer. I let it pass. Let her have her fun. Then first thing in the morning I'll make a list and drop the word. Killer wanted. Pablo most likely, as long as he doesn't fuck everything up. The main thing to avoid. Chop her up like chopsuey, but leave no dental records laying around. Mama and Stash too. Blacky I'll pack off to a triple-A dog college. Send Vivette on a world cruise. A trust-fund for the kid. Endowment policies. A new daddy.

"Here, let me help you with that."

I'm glad that's settled.

Godmommy, of course, is in for a smooth ride out. Not in one of those government glue factories, but a really reputable home for the living dead. Plenty of sea and sand. Top priority! Where the twilight of her days might slip gaily into night. With strict orders, she can go on breathing as long as she wants. No horseradish in the oatmeal. Generosity will be my hallmark. Heaps of fair play. I might even see fit to unleash my better instincts and do the grandson act. Except I'll probably be awful busy with my books and stuff. Polo, they say, is terribly grueling. Not as grueling as my books, yet who's to say I can't switch media and make a movie of my life? Somewhat fictionalized. One of those delectable success stories told by a down-n-outer. A dollar per page and throw in a river of booze. Stick him in the maid's room maybe, my ghostwriter in the sky. Give him a goose for Christmas.

"Yeehaa!"

"You blockhead, I heard that one already. So has the Man in the Moon and the lady in pink tights. Sure I'm sure. Copyrighted by the Incas. Don't you ever buy a newspaper? Why, I could shake better gags out of a chestnut tree. Certainly I'm serious. Centuries have passed and many delightful eras. You've heard of Egypt, haven't you? Surely King Rootin Tootin rings a bell. You ignorant numbskull, I believe it's even turned up among arrowheads and stuff. Stone Age devices. Damnit, it's older than the goddamn planets! Give me my dollar back."

CHAPTER 13

KILL CRAZY
Where Mike hires a hitman

After a romp in the woods with Blacky, I caught Vivette dragging her nose through these notebooks and had my hands full smoothing her feathers. I guess it's quite a shock to learn what goes on in here behind my boyish grin. I'm such a two-face prick! Needless to say I launched quickly in on the old runaround about her eyes are like the starry nights and her hair like the high seas, except it didn't go over too well. She said I could go screw myself. And to think how respectful she was in the old days, how my notebooks were sacred stuff. It won't be long she'll have me back in the States earning a living for her and Snookums.

That'll be the parting of the ways, of course. Let her hold hands with a sonic boom. I'll fly so fast she'll wonder what's keeping my hat on. Then she can empty her veins down the sink and I won't care. It'll be her own fault for the way she treats me.

"Liar!" she says. "I tell you lie why, when not to know the first precept of art is love. Yes, my Mikie. L-O-V. Is from love you must."

Laughing such things off is the best approach, even if my laugh sounds hollow. I get her rolling in the aisles while promising her the moon, skinning my knees, then sprinkle her with sweat, sweet-talk and lots of hokey expressions. Time degenerates nicely that way, love becoming a lullaby, until the pigeons coo and the sun breaks forth like the truth itself.

"Is you, Mikie?"

"Who else would I be?"

"I seem I can't touch you."

"Never mind that. Here's a hundred francs. Buy yourself something. And don't wait up. I'm messing with Pablo today."

"Pablo?"

I should never mention his name. She hates Pablo ever since he lifted her dress in broad daylight on the Boulevard des Capucines and tried to pull her panties down.

I hurried and shook a manuscript in her face. "I know he's crazy, but this is business. He's designing a cover for me."

That caused enough confusion for me to gather a few things and back out the door with great charm and grace. Life has enough complications without marrying a bloodhound. I shot directly across the boulevard to the large café by the market, my heart set on a couple beers before tackling Pablo. But the market was at full blast and the café packed, so I barely managed one before becoming embroiled in knees and elbows. Then Mrs. Wilcox slunk by the windows and my hormones overheated due to the rhythm in her walk. I was all set to tag after her, when Vivette's mom popped into view among the fruits and vegetables, prancing and shouting and badgering the local sad-sacks.

"Praise the Lord!"

Many tourists find this fascinating and delightfully Parisian. The Japanese take photos. I'm the jackrabbit in the background, bounding down the stairs to the Metro, where I'm again hemmed in. Lots of dreary faces. No use trying to explain, this sense of superiority, the deep emptiness of murder. I also didn't want to miss my stop.

After changing trains at Montparnasse for direction Porte des Lilas, Pablo's stamping grounds, I lost focus again due to a candy-eyed brunette with the kind of don't-kid-me look I adore. Luckily another creep horned in.

"I have to get married by midnight or I'll lose my inheritance."

What a jerk! He seemed to think I was counting on him to keep from jumping the tracks. As it is, my determination deteriorated all on its own. I just couldn't picture Pablo killing anybody quietly and on purpose. So when the train stopped at Saint Michel, I hopped off and hiked over to my friend Max's place, a fifth-floor walkup he shares with a woman named Margot to whom I introduced him about a year ago, although Margot says they met five years before that. Max was on a bender both times and couldn't remember or care less. Perfect for my plans, in other words. Mean as a snake. The only problem would be the profound contempt he has for other people's ideas. And nobody kills for friendship anymore.

All this occurs to me while I'm mounting the stairs. I pause halfway, recalling a remark Max made about beating the shit out of me the next time we meet. The reason escapes me, but I'm thinking I should probably phone first. On the other hand, I came all this way, so I continue on up and knock on the door. Margot answers.

"Miiiiike!"

Arms around the neck. Boy, is she ever glad to see me. Max, the brute, hasn't been home since Wednesday. She shows me a calendar with Os for the days he's missing and Xs for the days he's only blind. I don't ask what the swastikas are for.

"Look at these bruises."

Sure enough, he whips her with his belt. That's good. He can skin her alive for all I care. Nothing would make me sadder than dying for somebody else's love.

When she parts her robe to expose more X-rated contusions, everything floods back why I'm more likely to get murdered around here than Auntie.

"Out of cigarettes," I tell her, and hit the stairs like my life depended on it.

No more playing the sap. Which is what Auntie expects, a continuation of my fall-guy syndrome. It's in this way I'll fool the great lard-ass. The surprise of a lifetime!

"You, Michael?"

Yes, the dimwit she expects to flicker Godmommy for her will in truth be the diabolical Fu-Manchu of her own demise. Brilliant! Indicating I may be a genius after all. A bent one admittedly, yet of a superior order nonetheless. I mention this because it's been bothering me ever since school. I can't say I did awful hot in the classroom. But if my teachers could see me now! Not the way I look, of course, but the ideas I'm getting, these megawatt brainstorms. One old bag would probably poop in her pants. "Boogerface" we use to call her. Similar in appearance to Auntie, she made my life miserable. Dead-set on having me graduate into prison. Back then, my ambition was to trap her head in a vice under conditions where mercy wouldn't enter the picture. It still wouldn't. I'd laugh at her screams and wouldn't stop turning until her hat looks like an envelope. Kill the killers! My new motto. All I need is a triggerman. I'll be "The Brain". Nothing physical because I'm afraid I'd pass out. I picture myself laying down with the corpse, a total failure.

Come to think of it, isn't this where Auntie's own plan lacks logic? A fatal miscalculation of my aversion to blood. Quite a puzzler too, when you consider how accurately she dopes out everything else. This could be her tragic flaw, of course, her blind spot and Achilles' heel. Which leads me to wonder if she's in love with me after all.

Good God, what a thought!

I put it out of mind. Down the street. I find a trendy café that caters to students and dangerous radicals. The beer is warm, but I have an excellent mirror behind the bar for contemplating my man-of-the-moment aura. Cocking my cap, I frown for all I'm worth, except it doesn't come across the way it should. Babyface Nelson. The barman inquires if I'm planning to be sick. A wiseguy. The students too are very quick with their pitiful witticisms. I give them tit for tat on my way out, ridiculing their pimples and ideological hair.

All wrong for my purposes. Whereas a nice greasy hoodlum would be more like it. I don't know why I didn't think of this before. I stumble across a whole gang on the very next corner. Polluted eyes and half-inch foreheads. I nod approvingly as they huddle around a motorcycle, stuffing carburetors in their pockets. They don't go for the attention, but they'll get over it. A discreet wave of good-fellowship to show I'm not a cop. It loosens them up and makes them laugh. We all relax. I wink and they nudge each other. Even funnier! But I'm starting to get the drift myself.

They take me for a queer, goddamnit! I strut off fast and circle the block. Finally I'm wasting too much time. I drop back in the hole and go see Pablo.

Paolo Marcagiano is his real name. Italian, not Spanish. He emigrated with his parents from Florence to New Jersey at the age of two, reform school at ten, paint-therapy at Belleview, followed by felonious mischief and Greenwich Village horseplay, a 30-page rap-sheet, before he heads for Paris to make a name for himself as an avant-garde nut case. Nowadays he lives with a French woman in a small house not far from the Metro.

I like this Pablo even though he's meant nothing but trouble for me since the day we met. That happened at the Select one night when I was chatting up a couple Canadian dolls at the bar. I heard this menacing voice behind me.

"Why don't you shut up, stupid?"

We became friends later.

I mention this to show Pablo doesn't mind violence. Actually it's written all over his face, a mass of bumps and tiny scars, with his nose a kind of central abstraction that could be painted in two dimensions and named "Battle Bugle".

That's why I'm hesitating in the street, wondering if I should give Homer another try. I could beg the asshole.

Please! Please! Shit!

I vote myself down and head up the passage to Pablo's garden in back. Mostly weeds and two puny trees, a few sunflowers. The house is to the right. White, trimmed in green, two rooms and a kitchen. The garden is the showpiece. Sometimes you'll catch the great artist out there in the milder weather, painting pictures or rolling around drunk. Which is something else I should mention. Alcohol. It works on Pablo like nitroglycerin, inflaming the lesions on his brain and causing him to kick, spit and he will definitely piss in public. Today everything is quiet. I'm guessing he's in jail or flopping in some gutter. But no sooner do I raise my knuckles to the door than it flies open.

"He's dead," says Pablo.

I look him over, wondering if I woke him from a nightmare. He's not wearing pajamas but a paint-spattered smock, pink beret and ragged tennis shoes of mismatched colors.

"Who's dead?"

"Him," he says, pointing with a palette knife to a ball of brown fur by the sofa. "He died on me."

"Good thing. What would the neighbors say, you keeping a beaver?"

"He's not a beaver, stupid. That's a hedgehog."

"Where'd you find him?"

"Didn't find him, he was given to me as a gift. Too many fleas, that's what got him. They ate him alive."

"Funny you should say that. I just read something about hedgehogs, how they have a trick with fleas."

"Ah, tricks, tricks! I don't want to hear any shit about your tricks or practical jokes."

"But it's interesting how they do it. With a leaf. They balance it on their snout, then back into a river until all the fleas scramble aboard, then poof."

"What poof?"

"Downstream. The fleas float away with the leaf."

"I used kerosene."

"It killed everything but the fleas. Why not touch a match to him while you're at it?"

"Snotnose!" he says, and tries to push me off the porch.

"Only kidding, Pablo."

"Well, don't. I feel bad enough. Look at him so peaceful."

"Sure is."

"Shut up!"

We stood several seconds in respectful silence.

"His eyes closed like that, like he's only sleeping."

"And no fleas."

"I told you to shut up. Help me bury him."

"Aren't you going to paint his picture first?"

"What for?"

"Your duty as an artist."

"Duty?"

This caught him off guard. He ran his fingers through his hair, mumbling something about "it's too hard", then glared at me and said, "Fuck you!"

We threw the poor creature in the weeds and turned a washtub over him. Pablo sat on the tub and lit a cigarette, then bounced to his feet to shake both my hands. He'd forgot we hadn't seen each other in an awful long time.

"So how's the wife, the Polack?"

"Fine."

"And the kid?"

"Fine."

"You're in hot water."

"No, not exactly."

"Sure, I can tell. Up to your ears in manure, aren't you? I knew it the minute I laid eyes on you. What is it this time? On second thought, leave me in the dark. Change the subject. I'd rather not know. Anyway, you're barking up the wrong tree. I'm broke as usual. No dimes, no nickels, no tin. Just look at these shoes. Swiss cheese. See, the socks shine through. And it's winter yet! The other one's no better. Equally perforated. You don't believe me? Shit, you think I'd hop around on one foot just to show you a shoe with a hole in it? Ha! Ha! Ha!" He shakes his head and grins from ear to ear. "Impossible, Mike. You're bleeding turnips. Can't be done. Hang up the towel and browse around. Judge for yourself. Don't let this belly fool you. Meaningless. Absolutely misleading. I eat practically nothing. Next to zero. Oh, a smidgen of rice now and then. Yesterday's breadcrumbs. Once in a while a carrot. I can't remember my last peanut. I keep no diary, as you know. I'm a painter. But examine the cupboards if you've a mind. You'll find the same crap under the bed. Dust. Nothing but corners. Go ahead though, satisfy your curiosity. You can go through my pockets on your way back. But take my advice..." He darts a wary eye over the fence at the house next door. "This thing is worthless."

"Your watch?"

He removes it to show me, front and back, plus the flimsiness of the wristband. "Flashy but phony. A complete waste of time. Doesn't work and never did. I wear it for show, Mike, for the neighbors. Know what I mean? Sucker bait. Three for half a dollar. They peddle them to the school children. Some kind of chewing-gum substance. Made in Swishyland. It turns soft in the sun. Honest! You don't believe me? Shit, take the sonofabitch!"

"Don't be silly."

"I'm not silly!"

"Simmer down. I only wanted to talk to you a minute, a little problem I have. Maybe you can help."

"Not a penny."

"Not money. Help. I have money."

"What color is it?"

"Let me explain. This could be important for both of us, financially and other ways."

"Jesus, Mike, I think you must be deaf. Didn't I just tell you I'm broke and busted? Accept reality. I have nothing for you. Nothing! Nothing! How many times do I have to say it? You're not only bleeding turnips, you're beating dead horses. Isn't that plain enough, easy to comprehend? Or do you need an ear-trumpet?"

"Can't you listen for a minute?"

"You're a nice lad, but you're stubborn as a mule."

"Just listen for one minute."

"One minute?"

"Let me explain."

"Give me my watch back."

"Here…You remember when we talk last summer, I told you about Vivette and me, how we're living at her godmother's place in Passy?"

"With Vivette's mom."

"Yeah, and her aunt."

"There's a sister too, ain't it?"

"No, a brother."

"And a dog."

"Blacky."

"His name's Spotty, I thought."

"Let me talk, okay? I told you about the lousy setup."

"You wanted to kill your mother-in-law."

"No, the aunt."

"She's getting on your nerves."

"More than that, Pablo. She's stealing everything."

"What everything? You ain't got nothing."

"From Vivette's godmother. She's rich, see? And the aunt's stealing it all. Bonds and stuff like that. Siphoning it off to Switzerland, Homer thinks, and by rights it should go to us."

"Us?"

"Vivette and me. There's other stuff too, jewelry and things like that. I'm pretty sure she's hiding it at her shack."

"Whose shack?"

"The aunt's. It's a small house she has outside town."

"So we bust in and take it."

"Right. But first we have to kill her."

"Who, the aunt?"

"Yes. She's dangerous, Pablo. I'm afraid if we don't get her, she'll get us."

He shakes his head. "The thing to do is let her try, then it's self-defense."

"That may sound okay, but you don't know that woman. I won't feel safe until she's out of the way."

"You can make it look like an accident."

"That's a good idea. Actually I was thinking along those lines myself. Trouble is, the police sniff out shit like that. And I'd be the main suspect, see? If I had a partner though, someone fearless like you, I could be somewhere else."

"Where?"

"It doesn't matter. On top of the Eiffel Tower."

"Why up there?"

"It doesn't have to be there, of course, just so I'm far from the scene of the crime."

"What crime?"

"Jesus, don't you get it? While you're sneaking up on her with an icepick, I'm miles away."

"On the Eiffel Tower."

"I told you it doesn't have to be there. It could be the movies or a museum, anywhere, just so lots of people see me. That way I have an alibi."

"Why can't we both have alibis?"

"No reason, except it's not necessary. I mean there's no reason to connect you with her."

"I want an alibi too."

"Okay. I just thought it wouldn't be necessary. If that's how you want it, it's okay with me…What's the matter?"

"I just got a feeling you're serious."

"Sure I'm serious."

He sat on the tub again and cradled his chin in his hands, his elbows on his knees, looking up with big sad eyes. "Better move out of that dump. You don't belong there. Come live with us. We'll feed you. You can buy yourself a sleeping-bag. Write in the off hours. Most of the time it's quiet."

"Come on, Pablo, you think I came here for that? I really appreciate the thought and everything, but this is business, pure and simple. I have a job for you and I'm willing to pay."

That's when he turns purple. He's not a businessman, he says, he's an artist. Artist! Artist! Artist! Not only that, he's Italian. And not only Italian, he's from the north. "Way far up there!" He knows nothing of the Mafia. His mother was an Eskimo, his father practically Swedish. He flips his lid, his pink beret, and flings it in my face.

"A thousand dollars," I tell him. "More later. I figure ten thousand for the whole job."

"Whole job? Whole job?"

I'm not sure he heard. He reels back and tips over, landing on his ass, then bounces up so fast I think he hit on a spring. He throws his palette knife at me, an inch over my head, and starts running in circles, around and around the washtub, faster and faster. I don't think he's going to make it.

"Arrrrrrrrrr!"

Sure enough, he twists his ankle and drops to one knee, squealing in agony. Which makes me laugh. Not for long. He lunges and knocks me flat. I scramble to my feet and he does it again, this time against the birdhouse. Everything breaks and we're swimming in weeds, my one elbow in his armpit, the other in his mouth. I want to keep it there so he won't eat my ears. I told you how he is. It's a good thing about my elbow. Except it makes him furious. His eyes get really wild. I jam a thumb in one and knee him in the groin. That calms him. So I do it again to make him really limp. Enough is enough. I ask him to wait while I fetch a sprinkling-can. I give him a shower.

"You okay?"

Sure, he's coming around. He grabs my throat and we're plowing up the yard again. We wind up by the plum tree. Six times we roll over the rake. Still crazy for my ears, so I keep a good grip on his sideburns. Let him chew my collar. I'd like another shot at his balls, but my legs are too bent. No leverage. This gives me an idea though, about dog shit. I see a nice juicy clump on one of my shoes, between the heel and sole. I wonder if I should. I'll have to move fast. I slam an arm under his chin and show him what I found. I get him to gag, then paint a nice mustache. It makes him woozy. His eyes roll and I can slug him where I want. All the starch gone. I ease off a little and watch. He seems harmless enough, but you can't trust the bastard. I hop to my feet and skip back, huffing and puffing. I look him over. His eyes are shut, his knees raised to his chest, his hands cupped to his ears, smiling and mumbling, probably only dreaming. The mustache actually suits him, like Clark Gable. I trot to the house to wash my hands, and return with a soapy rag. He's still there, still smiling. I wipe off the handlebars and get him conscious. First I pin him down. I kneel on his shoulders.

"Hey, wake up."

"Ho-hum."

His lashes flutter. He yawns and glances around, combing his fingers through the grass as though nature were a never-ending joy.

"Twenty thousand," he says.

"You mean you'll do it?"

"For twenty thousand, not ten."

"Fine. Twenty thousand is nothing."

"Nothing?"

"I'd even pay more."

"I want more then."

"First you have to do it. Once I know it's done, I'll pay right away."

"What's done?"

"The aunt, you have to kill her."

"Right."

"Is it a deal?"

"I just said so, didn't I?"

"Do you promise?"

"Sure I promise. Say, what're we out here for anyway? Get the hell off me, Mike. What the hell you think you're doing?"

He seemed perfectly sane. I helped him to his feet and shook his hand, wanting to seal the deal right away. I dusted off his shoulders on our way to the house.

"Want a drink?"

CHAPTER 14

BRINDLE AWAY!
Where the love of justice spurs poetry in motion

"Oh, Pablo, you don't know how happy this makes me. To have a partner, finally!"

"Yeah. Great."

He went to the kitchen to uncork a bottle of wine while I stretched out on the living-room sofa, admiring the twelve dozen paintings he has covering all the walls. Mostly still-life studies of wrinkled fruit and dried bouquets.

"Which is your favorite?" he asks, handing me a big tumbler.

"The sardines, I guess."

He wags his head proudly. "Yeah, they're going ninety miles an hour."

We ran down our mutual friends for a while before swinging back solidly to the world of art, him lugging out a thick stack of canvases from the bedroom, flipping through them very quickly, preferring not to linger on the obvious, such as why his picture of apples is better than Cezanne's.

And actually it is a little better, or about as good. Anyway, not much worse.

"But why not the hedgehog?"

"Forget the damn hedgehog. What is it with you anyway?"

"I just thought you should paint him. I think Picasso would."

"Picasso?"

Now I've done it. Introducing the extraneous. He invites me to be the judge and he'll be the jury. His paintings are proof enough, aren't they? I should examine the "line fold" and "negative texture."

"See? See?"

"Yes. Yes."

He presents them six at a time.

"You don't like that one?"

"Sure, it's nice."

Out the window anyway. He rips it to shreds.

"But I did like it."

"Tough shit."

One grand gesture deserves another until half an hour passes and I'm able to introduce some serious business. He uncorks a second bottle while I embark on my thousand and one tales of how low and despicable the aunt and them are. Dull gossip, in his opinion.

"Put it in a can, Mike. Tell me later." He checks his watch and dashes to the radio. "I want to hear this program."

That's not going to stop me. I propose a toast to Auntie's most wonderful and timely death just as *Woman's Hour* comes on the BBC.

He fiddles with the dials. "Would you pipe down!"

"But you have to understand, I wouldn't dream of killing anybody unless I was driven to it."

Yes, yes, he understands perfectly, totally and probably better than I do myself, but wants to hear this radio show. It's his favorite.

Well, obviously it's essential that he comprehends my motives. How else can he sympathize or consider helping?

Damnit, he sympathizes from A to Z, but wants to hear about Marie-Antoinette. It's a serial the lady on the radio has been reading to him for over three weeks, up until today, just when the poor queen is facing the big chopper, the final episode, I have to barge in with a brass band in my mouth.

Okay, but as soon as it's finished he has to promise to hit the switch and put on his thinking cap, lest the morality of our action is lost or distorted by the extremely immoral nature of the very act itself.

"Of course not, shit!"

"I don't want that."

"Me neither!"

"If we were to make such a mistake, I figure one of two things would happen, both of them bad. Either we end up on Easy Street but feeling guilty about it, or we could land in the bucket."

"Right. Here's to crime."

"Mainly it's the pattern I want you to see, the way Mama has of worming her way in on these old people like the Salvation Army, for no pay, never complaining, forever moaning and praying and keeping everybody awake with her damn incantations."

"Ah, stow that crap. Let me tell you about last night. I walk in the Falstaff and see this guy buying a rose for his girl. He has a bowl of soup in front of him and she's got a plate of spaghetti..."

"But I want you to feel this deep down, Pablo, the way I do. I want you to hate them."

"Don't worry, I do. Now let me tell you..."

"But you can't say they don't deserve exactly what they get."

"Sure they do."

"The old ones, I mean. Mostly they're deaf and blind and very soft in the head. Mama and her staple-gun go practically unnoticed."

"She uses a staple-gun?"

"For her crosses and bleeding Jesuses in every room, his guts hanging out. Even Auntie gets a pass. Probably they think she's Mama in disguise, snooping around in the dead of night, making her appraisals, her evaluations, until boom."

"What boom?"

"She lowers the boom, of course, once Mama has made it possible. But that's not the same thing, is it?"

"I suppose not."

"I mean ethically."

"You want some peanuts?"

"On the other hand, maybe it's worse. Mama is on the square, see? An honest-to-goodness saint. If it weren't for her, the old ones would smell us out in a second. Her act is flawless because it's not an act. She's exactly what the doctor ordered. Angel food."

"Okay, let's talk about something else."

"But I don't want you coming to me afterwards saying you're remorseful and all that. You're the one who has to do it, remember, and you'll be doing it for my motives, not yours. I want them to be yours too."

"No problem, our motives are the same."

"Too bad I can't be part of the actual killing. That would be better, but I can't. You see that, don't you?"

"Sure I see it. Why go on and on? I said I'd do it and I will. Alone. All by myself. You won't have to lift a finger. I'll jump out a window. I mean an alley. You can go to the damn movies."

"But you don't want to be unfair."

"Hell no!"

"Because you can't say they have much choice."

"Who?"

"Like the godmother. She has nowhere to turn and no one to take care of her. Looking at it that way, Mama and Auntie are performing a useful function from society's point of view. Even the stealing part. I mean, so what? It's not like she could ever spend all she has. And no one to leave it to but a greedy nephew who's already rich. Her husband and son died years ago. So who gets her money?"

"We do."

"I mean in the abstract. Say a person lives past everybody around them, all their children are gone, no grandchildren, what happens to their dough?"

"They can leave it to charity."

"Some maybe, but most goes to the state, to France. The government takes the lion's share. What's the point of that? Think it over."

"I don't have to think it over. It's getting damn chilly, ain't it? Let's go to a café."

"For the sake of argument, say you're ninety."

"I don't want to be ninety!"

"You would if you were eighty-nine. And if you're ninety, you'd eventually want to be ninety-one. What's the sense of it?"

"None. Boy, you're really..."

"Right. None. None compared to the difference between being rich and poor. I'm talking of people young enough to enjoy it. Not these old coots. Immortality, that's their ambition. Pure egotism, see?"

"Yeah."

"They figure if Mama brews enough rejuvenating tea, she'll have them growing new teeth and playing on the swings again. Selfishness, nothing else. No regard for the next generation, people with their whole life in front of them. You're not so young, but you still want to get ahead, don't you?"

"Yeah, ahead out the door."

"Maybe you think they're grateful. That's where you're wrong. They couldn't care less if Mama drops dead in her tracks, except needing a new sucker to hammer in the ground with all their aches and pains and pass me the liver pills. So in a way you have to go along with Auntie. Just because Mama gets a kick out of it doesn't really matter."

He stood and took the glass from my hand. "Okay, you're right. Now get up. You're sitting on my sweater."

"First I want to tell you about the aunt."

"Fuck the aunt!"

"But you agree people get more or less what they deserve. It's really nobody's fault."

"Damnit, Mike, you're talking too much."

"Why should we let it bother us?"

"Come on, you want to leave the bottle or polish it off on the way?"

"Millions die every day. Here in Paris, I'd say one or two do it every minute. And things disappear."

"Good. Lets us disappear. It's getting damn chilly."

"Wealth is like that, you'll say. It's created to be passed on, hand to hand, and that's a difficult process to follow. Impossible if you're dead. But suppose you're only half dead? Or ninety-nine percent? Our civilization wasn't built on that, was it?"

"Know what, I'd like to enter your chin in a six-day bicycle race."

"Two, maybe three months is the best they can expect from Auntie. Pretty short notice, wouldn't you say? The godmother only takes longer because she's richer."

"You're on a real jabber-jag, you know it?"

"The last item is the heartbeat."

"Would you shut the fuck up! I said I'd do it and I will. Now button your lip and button your coat. I'll croak every last one of them horrible pricks."

"Just the aunt."

"Ants! Fleas! Give me a thousand."

"I only have nine hundred. Francs, not dollars."

"Hand it over."

"Five hundred. I need the rest for shopping. But it's a deal, isn't it?"

"I'm taking your money, ain't I? You just name the time and place and how high to stack the bodies."

"Just the aunt."

"Ants! Fleas!"

He tips the bottle to his lips until the corners dribble, then smashes it on the floor and drops to both knees, clutching his throat like Dr. Jekyll.

"To face to face," he says.

"What's the matter?"

"And come up swinging. Clinging! Verging on the verge of the void of the gyp without the rosy cheeks of shad rowing."

"You're kneeling on glass."

"From bad to bad to the bottom of the pickle barrel, to pick the peppered, pickled rose. Springing up!" He hops on the sofa. "In flight to night to daytime nudity, we pluck the rose and turn away. Away! Away! Crying for her boy, dying to live in Roseland with a girl named Who."

"Okay, let's find a café."

"Who killed Cock Robin?"

"You're talking a lot of horse shit, Pablo."

"Rosy did, the snot. Why not? Stupid boy with the toy of an idea. An iflea! To stop the cops. See, it's we. Kill, I will. Lots is tops."

He stabs a painting and kicks a leg off the table. The radio gets it next, the old one-two. He whips around and glowers at me. Except I'm not there.

"Where are you?"

He can't find me in the kitchen. I'm not in the bedroom. He returns with an apple on his knife. He checks under the cushions. Actually I'm on the porch. He doesn't look there.

"Where'd you go?"

The last thing I'll do is tell him. I'm halfway to the street when I hear a crash. Windows fly open and the neighbors start honking.

"The rose garden of yesterday," he sings out, "is a drugstore. And man a pickle jar. So brindle away, goddamn you. Away! Away!"

CHAPTER 15

WHO'S WHO AND WHY
Where Mike battles Auntie in the
realm of the fantastic

I take his advice and am two blocks south in less than a minute. Five hundred francs lighter, but you could say I got off easy. At least now I have a partner. One with luminous black eyes, not Homer's steely gray ones.

And how about the slapstick poetry?

Everything seemed strangely in league to ball up my plans. Even the temperature dropped. Pablo was right about the weather. Thick fog rolled in and weird critters took shape, tall ships skimming the rooftops with their sails unfurled clear to the street. Something I find extremely irritating. I enter a café to think it over. An hour later I'm still thinking, sagging a bit. They offer me a chair, but I prefer shivering and stomping with the other draft horses, steam pouring off us. The windows drip. Bubbles rise in my glass while silvery rings multiply across the bar in overlapping loops, riveting my attention. Until the barman takes it in his head to whisk a crumb from under my nose. As if anything could be that easy.

"Like ordering a cup of coffee."

"Coffee?"

"It wouldn't be that easy."

Not that I'm asking a whole lot. A modest pension, let's say, with a humble perch from whence to take in the seasons and rot a bit longer on the vine. Once all my lessons are learned. Like at school. See and go. Or the last stool at the Select.

"My first choice."

"Beer?"

"Let's just say more would be better, but millions aren't essential."

I'm invited to leave under Section Eight. Slip and slide to a warmer café, slick frost covering the ground, pigeons scooting here and there. All shot full of chilblains. Or they hang upside-down like bats. As though spring may have decided to skip Paris this year.

"Two weeks in Hawaii, please. I'm getting married at midnight."

Actually the best I can do is a candy-bar between coughing fits. Beer plus whisky. No cake. I bounce spit off the pavement while changing course for Montparnasse and the blaze of lights that flare like matches only to fizzle into a cool burn like neon ice. Lucky green looms suddenly, taking my breath away. I hadn't expected to be lucky. I barge straight through the swinging doors, past the posers and attitudists, to where it's more peaceful and subdued, only semi-packed, and more in keeping with my deep, dark, mysterious allure.

What a fascinating character!

My admirers can't contain themselves for all the hypnotic magnetism Auntie electrified my face with. It turns them on.

"Yes, isn't it phenomenal the star-quality one amasses simply hobnobbing with lunatics?"

Personally I can't stomach these rubbernecks without belching. I stick out my tongue.

"Loafers! Dicklickers! Go jerk off in a napkin!"

It's not their fault, of course. I better apologize.

"An American joke," I tell them.

No point taking a pack of autograph hounds to task for what really amounts to a legal problem. And the soupy weather? More of a meteorological problem.

Clues, fingerprints, flying saucers.

"Goddamn Pablo!"

I discover a moth in my beer, then stare at the floor for about an hour. I play with my fingers, count my thumbs. The clock chimes. What if this happens or doesn't happen or only seems to happen? Fuck! Once one thing is clear, another clouds over, flapping through the doors like a grizzly bear in drag.

It's Auntie all right, decked out for war. Furs, diamonds, the works.

"What're you doing here?"

"Where?"

"You followed me."

"Sizzzzz," she hisses like a radiator.

"Same to you, Boogerface."

"Booger-ger?"

"That's Godmommy's mink you're wearing."

"Mine," she says.

"Oh yeah? I suppose the earrings are too, and the necklace and bracelet and that jumbo sparkler."

"All mine."

I wink at the others. "My mistake."

Gales of laughter, scattered clapping.

"Don't encourage her."

One knucklehead has the nerve to inquire if I'm sick. An off-duty doctor, he says.

"Is that so? Well, I'm Cock Robin, but still on the job. Not very sick either. At least not so much I don't know what she's up to."

"Know when I tell you."

"See? She's egging me on."

She also crinkles her face like a potato-chip bag.

Back to the notebook, except she wiggles her ears.

I slam my pencil down. "I can't concentrate with those ears."

Her eyes get funny.

"What have you done to your eyes?"

"So happy we."

"Don't be ridiculous. I hate you."

"Yet flapping together beyond dreams never shaving but real plush life. You ask, I give."

"What, a migraine headache?"

"Everything."

"Everything?"

"For you me."

"Let's get this straight. I see swimming-pools and sports-cars and rainbows in bathing-suits. A dazzling villa set against pastel hillsides. Am I right? I wouldn't take a penny less. We wake up at noon, cocktails at one. Cuban stogies a foot long. Separate sleeping quarters, by the way. I have to insist on that. No ties that bind."

"Hardly any."

"You mean it? Shopping sprees and call-girls and you leave me alone? That has to be understood or I'll get Pablo to blow you up."

"Sound good?"

"Like music."

"For you me."

"Can I have a motorboat?"

"For one favor."

"Name it."

"Godmommy," she says, meaning the godmother, "must we never permit..."

"Okay, I know that song. Goodbye Forever. But where's that leave Vivette and the baby? High and dry, where else? Blacky I want to keep. Race him down the beach mornings and evenings, chucking sticks, chasing crabs."

"Ack!"

"What do you mean ack? He has to piss on time. Me too. I need a free hand to be happy."

"Away! Away!"

I guess I said something wrong. She throws a hammerlock my arm and my head hits the table, then back against the wall. Which inflames the others. Hoots and hollers as more crowd in. They want to see better.

"You don't understand. This woman is a cannibal. She turns people into pork chops."

That only amplifies the idiots.

"The eyes," I tell them. "Please look and die. Aren't they better than a picture show, better than Sade? Impaled babies, I tell you. Disemboweled nations. Agony and heartache beyond your wildest weekends."

Well, a bit of respect. They subside from snorts to snickers, probably because they see she may be a cannibal after all, the way she's working me over. Preliminary tenderization. Half-nelsons, full-nelsons, with tentacles up my shirt. Her ring digs in. I feel it, the diamond, big between my fingers. That's some stone she has, about the size of a shot-glass. I want to rip it loose and break her neck simultaneously.

"My boy! My boy!"

"Let go! Let go!"

I slither to the floor and pop up like a cork, threatening her with a right-cross. I hold up my pants with the other hand.

"I hate you, despise you and everything about you. Why can't you get that through your thick skull? All I want is the money, money, money."

"Never get it," she says. "Be too stupid."

That tickles the screwballs. Whistles and catcalls even as I lash out. I tumble over tables and break a few dishes. Hot after Auntie, but she's surprisingly nimble. I miss by a mile booting her in the pants. Aiming my head for her nose, I bash a mirror by mistake. That's when the waiters intercede. Two of them. Another comes on the run, but I catch him with a saltshaker. The other two are more talkative. Big bruisers like them! They want to negotiate. I'm supposed to see reason.

"You're on her side."

"Now, now..."

They fan out and close in, forcing me against a wall. I grab a bar towel and snap every eye in the joint. An old locker-room trick. The women shriek and the men hide behind each other. Meanwhile, Auntie sets about converting the furniture into an avalanche. For which I take the blame. That's only to be expected. She flaps her wings and we get a flock of UFOs. My fault again. I point at her and everyone looks the other way. They call me some pretty lousy names.

Lined up like a football team. Which takes the fun out of everything. I plead to no avail, even calling upon instances in history to back up my stance on the evils of mob rule. I'd do as well with sign-language. I fade left, right, then charge up the middle and get slugged in the jaw. The ceiling revolves. Right away I'm disoriented. A sea of beet-red faces tossing me around like a medicine ball. Why is anyone's guess. I try to recall if I was supposed to join a lodge tonight. One moron fits a chair on his head and dives for my knees. He must think he's an elk. Soon I'm rolling on the floor with a fist in my face. Nothing makes me madder. Another one grabs my ankles and hoists me in the air. The off-duty doctor, I think. He wants to play wheel-barrel, yank the kinks from my spine. Probably an osteopath. I kick and thrash and claw at the tiles as small change rains down like silver bells. They won't let me retrieve it. Somebody else even spits. Another sad case. A dame this time. I beg her to come to her senses, but of course the reverse happens. More join the party. I'm draped in saliva and peppered with lymph, managing to get off only one good load of my own. Way off target. It's a bad evening for accuracy. I gather a mouthful of ammo and pick out the wildest-looking maniac, only to spray my own image in the mirror. A funhouse mirror, it belongs on Coney Island. Not only the glaze on my clothes, this mirror has me standing funny. I see a hand on my ass and the ape it belongs to must think I'm a suitcase. We plow through tables like the Bomb Squad. He's not very good at it. We knock over everything on our way to the door. Which nobody holds open. I mention this, but you know where that gets me. Two seconds airborne and a three-point landing by the bicycle rack.

"Goddamn Nazis! You're nothing but a bunch of..."

Well, I may as well forget what they're a bunch of. I can't squeeze a word in edgeways between the laughing and flapping and swinging doors.

CHAPTER 16

WELL IN THE WOODS
Where the miracle of light defies
a bottomless world

My cap and notebook come sailing out, completely over my head. I have to hurry before the lady on the corner has a chance to wipe her feet. She asks me the time, but I don't answer the bitch. Unsure to begin with and fed up to the gills with hags in fur coats. Won't mess with the Metro either. I stalk off erect, Passy in front of me, along with my nose, a mountain of fog and a good five-mile hike.

Is it possible, I wonder, she could expect me to believe her, to trust her, after all she's pulled? Wouldn't I have to be an awful dope?

Never mind the wisecracks. I'm only surprised I have sense enough to consider it. Then why go on? She couldn't draw a straight line from a box of arrows. So why hesitate? Is it simply my destiny to be another Hamlet? Or not to be?

I stop for a second because I bumped into a shop window and can't get over the perfection of my reflection. Slanting my cap in the heroic manner, I deduce in a flash the whole situation in a nutshell. She's not getting any younger, after all, and I am something of a prize in the heartthrob department. Even if I say so myself. Even with the jaw moss and body lice.

Incidentally, my little friends don't seem to bother her. Another riddle. Does this mean you can turn a corkscrew into a daisy chain? Does love really conquer all? Tune in next week and you'll find me behind bars with the answer. That's what gets me, I walk the plank while Auntie sips buttered rum on the poop deck.

If it comes to that, of course, I'll deny the whole works and say the godmother was dead on my arrival.

"Barely twitching, Your Honor. She'd been running on fumes for years."

Good point. I'll explain how poor I am but deserving, and how rich she was but delusional, expecting to live forever with termites in her rafters.

"At my expense!"

Another good point. Not like sandflies. Here today, gone tomorrow. No trials by jury for the true children of sorrow. I hate myself for saying so, but I guess everything will be fine as long as I'm not caught killing sandflies.

Murder! Murder! Murder! echoes with my footfalls through the canyon way of buildings. No moon or stars or yellow brick roads. Only cotton wool double dense and a kind of vague implication, shadows hiding shadows, the Eiffel Tower itself scarcely more than a remote possibility.

"Gold!" says my right foot. "Silver!" says the left.

"Ham sandwich," says my stomach as I round a corner and run smack into a garbage can, my heart pounding wildly because I thought for a second it had run into me.

Opportunity only pounds once, I reproach myself. A treasure at your fingertips and you fuck around garbage cans. An immense windfall and you munch used sandwiches.

Everything about me seemed extremely well informed and eager for change. Wealth! Women! The pageant of life! Mine for the taking. If only I might slip past the streetlamps and their yellow-white veils to partake of such wonders as would turn the Duchess of Passy into one hell of a frog, me the prince. Already she's covered in warts, so just paint her green and live happily ever after at Disney Studios. Among redheads, hopheads and a million luscious blondes, glittering along the pavement in wide sparkling pools.

"Diamonds!"

I'll be damned if I don't reach out and grab a clump of dewdrops. I burp and my cap flips off. That stupid rag. I stare at it in disgust. Swaying. Spinning. I'm a leaf in the wind. I hit the wall laughing. A dumb move. My hand throbs like a drum as I crumple to all fours and vomit up suds. No more mansions or limousines or Technicolor yacht parties. Only lumpy froth and the faintest glimmer of hope, about the power of surrender. If I could find it in my heart to remain on all fours and crawl after her anywhere. Cannes, Rio, Atlantic City. Then just as she's happiest, I'll let her have it.

"Crush her like a bug!"

A fresh sense of euphoria. I scan the mist as though my whole life were there, past plus future, lost and alone, yet strong and growing stronger, like a biographical crescendo building since birth into this gigantic mess that is at the same time the perfect end to confusion.

"If only I have the nerve to follow through."

This last thought pisses me off. I have trouble shouting loud enough. I fly down the street and kick hell out of a bus shelter, roaring so ferociously I have to stop to see if there's a lion behind me.

Orange lights blink on behind green silhouettes.

What time do I think it is?

"Police," I tell them. "Official biz-quiz."

Actually this spot-remover is a stroke of luck or I'd make a swell target. Trouble is, Paris has enough perplexities without navigating blindfolded. I should have asked how far to the river. Downhill seems easiest, especially with my ankles flopping around, randomizing every step, which makes for difficulty finding people to walk on the same side of the street with me. One scaredy-cat I have to chase half a block for a cigarette. He gives me the whole pack, bringing tears to my eyes. Charmed by smoke and the milk of human kindness. My heart swells with gratitude as I survey the panorama of shrouded landmarks and peek-a-boo statues, lovely lamps in a row, exactly like a row of zombies.

"Brrrrrrr!"

I'm giving myself the willies. I pick up the pace and tumble down a flight of stone steps to a gravel path. An iron railing helps me up. Rococo filigree. Hinting of the Gaslight Era and the hues of Lautrec. A long steaming leak, then I make a beeline down the promenade, under the tower and across the river to the Palais de Chaillot. Then horsing around the back streets, one blunder on top of another, finally I'm in an awful pickle. No streets, no sidewalks.

"No Paris, for Christ's sake!"

So maybe I'm in London. Except why all these trees? Offhand I'd say I wandered into the Bois de Boulogne, but might just as well be at the bottom of the ocean.

"How could I lose the whole city?"

It's puzzling all right. I remember being on a narrow path that got narrower, winding to the right and left, then I guess it unwound.

"Balls!"

Ceiling zero. I step in a hole and boom! I'm climbing another tree. Which makes for cautiousness about charging forward too energetically. I take it slow, inching my way along, shaking hands with the bushes while peering into the distance about eighteen inches. I forgot to put my pecker away, so I do that now.

Eeeeeeek!

A funny noise. Lovers, I'm thinking, except I'd prefer not asking lots of questions of this enchanting forest. I'm tired and would rather locate a trail and toddle on home. But how can I locate anything when I have to bend in half just to see if my feet are tied on?

Hey, cinders!

This is lucky. Crunch, crunch. I'm on a cinder path and paths always lead somewhere.

Buddabuddabuddabudda!

Another funny noise, this time like a hundred window-shades flying up. I do five or six pirouettes and bounce off a tree. The fog swirls and a naked little girl comes galloping from the thickets followed by what looks like a gorilla. That's enough for me. I take off the opposite way for about a hundred yards of fast action, my lungs squeaking as the path opens out onto a mushy basin, like an enormous bowl of chili, steam pouring out of it and twisting into odd contortions of vaporous monsters. Mostly lizards and snakes, but also Mrs. Wilcox floats by and I can't believe her tits. Her dogs either. They have everything so tugged out of whack her legs resemble harps as she does a somersault and the splits and comes up a complete hodgepodge, a cross between a beehive and a hurricane.

The dogs get with pine cones from me. I bombard them into murkiness and lose my balance. I brace myself against a tree. The wrong thing to do because a snail was there and I have him pulverized to a pulp, his guts oozing clear to my elbow in a kind of quivering sauce. Dead as a doornail, you might think, but on closer examination I see this used-to-be snail actually leads an inside-out existence. Still wreathing with life. Ugly too. He gives me the hiccups. This is followed by the super-heaves. Not just suds. I work my way from honk-honk to blouwee and get a herring to pop out along with about four hundred beer-heads and nearly all of my pride. No holding back. I paw the ground and hug the trees, covering the turf in all manner of wishbones and party hats, a string of redhots, half an inchworm, eight snorts and a thermometer. I sneeze a great pudding for dessert.

"Pheeoow!"

I feel better, but can't find my other shoe. I blow my nose, then blow ten minutes sorting through the wreckage, disappointed not to find my old roller-skates.

When all at once I freeze, unsure what I heard or if I really heard it. The snapping of a twig? I see prairie schooners and Cheshire cats, but nothing very substantial. This is the land of skywriters. When a band of paleface Indians sneaks up with lassoes, I don't even flinch. At the last moment they shift gears and explode very quietly into a slow-motion puffs.

Time to locate my other shoe. There it is, finally! Boy, am I ever glad but wrong. That's a size-10 pot-roast. My shoe is over there under a plate of lamb stew. It slips right on, kind of squishy. It slips right off again.

"Christ Almighty!"

I carry it to the edge of the path and scrape with leaves, figuring I may as well do a good job and clean off the snail guts while I'm at it. What's another few minutes?

"I'll never get any sleep tonight!"

Then how about jogging to make up for lost time?

I go this way, that way and meet myself coming back.

"Goddamn it to hell!"

No more meandering paths. I decide to cast half-measures aside. I'll strike out across country and get home right away, the idea being that if I run fast enough, far enough and straight enough, I'm bound to hit a road or a river or at least a border crossing.

But once again I'm making a mistake. Almost the worst mistake of my life. Little did I realize. This is partly because I really know how to move. I have these million-dollar legs and my ass is wired for speed. The only trouble is a hole I run across. It's round, black and about forty miles deep. Of course I don't know it's there or I'd have skipped to one side or hopped right over it. As it is, I'm not skipping, hopping or stopping to pick flowers. I'm tearing right along, trees being my primary concern. They loom up quick and don't step out of your way. One false move and I can kiss my profile goodbye. Zigging this way and that, I zag like the dickens. It's a steeple chase and obstacle course. I hurdle all the scrub-brush and vault every log. I leap, bound and don't linger on the hillsides. I'm practically telegraphic. Until along comes this bush, this insignificant bramble. It's no higher than a picket fence, so I take it in stride. Up like a deer, then down, down and down, I'm headed straight for China, saved only by my chin and elbows as they hook on some planks that were partly covering this hole.

I don't know my good fortune, not right off the bat. First I have all I can do to stop screaming. My one leg is twisted backwards, the other pointed south in a kind of precision balance. At the same time, I have the most sickening feeling my execution just took place and this entire nightmare may be exactly that, a jumble of frantic brainwaves as I drop through the trick floor. I snap out of it quick. I swing out like a monkey and roll to my belly, kissing the dirt and kind of feeling myself up.

"Thank God! Thank God!"

I sound like my mother-in-law. Not for long. Soon I'm grumbling about my chin hurts and everything is lousy. The crabs, for one thing, woke up crabbier than ever. I ram both hands down my pants and scratch like blazes, when scarcely a minute ago, dangling from my whiskers, I wouldn't have harmed a fly. I'd have anointed him with oil and wiped the blood from his feet.

"Goddamn insects!"

Nothing to do about it but hope the alcohol in my veins would eventually anesthetize them. I might also hope for a rescue party, or lean back and do a complete inventory of frail hopes, something that should keep me busy the better part of the evening, whereas an inventory of the day's accomplishments needed no time whatever.

"Why can't I do anything right?"

My book came to mind, that classic reject that recently returned from the Great Melting Pot. Lemon among lemons, they say. I say they must be crazy jealous. It bothers me though, that book, since it's beginning to look like my only chance. If it's a hit and brings in some dough, can you imagine? I'll probably go out of my mind.

Meanwhile, I'll wait for the fog to lift. There's this hole to contemplate. I don't want to bore anybody with holes, but this one isn't a sag or a dimple or one of those slight indentations. Of course it's not a volcano either, but deep.

That's my central conclusion after peeking over the brim to see what the chances are for my shoe. It disappeared again and this time it's really lost. I drop sticks and stones, but as far as I know they're still dropping. No light, no sound. Plenty of odor though, the incredible kind. One whiff and I discover my stomach was holding out on me. I bark like a seal and send a high-velocity tidbit straight for the center of the earth. It's bound to reach bottom before my shoe. If there is a bottom.

"Not even an echo."

An ancient well is how I finally write this hole off. The remains of a windmill perhaps, except who would be dumb enough to build a windmill in the middle of a forest? Or did all these trees grow up later? I think it over, ticking off possibilities, such as maybe the contractor tapped into the sewer system and went bankrupt. I yodel, spit and drop more sticks and stones. If there is a bottom, it must be made of feathers, black ones, otherwise the stuff I'm tossing would have to be sailing out the other side of the world. Of course this would at least switch the blame for odor from my shoe to Shanghai.

Finally I'm staring so long and so fruitlessly, I wonder if my eyes fell out. I blink up at the sky, and when turn back, I see a speck of light deep down in the hole, rising higher and higher, like a spark up a chimney. A moth, that's my first impression. An electrical one, judging by the sparkle and shine as it flits here and there and everywhere at once, fluttering past my nose to dance among the fog-flowers like a very young sunbeam. Or something akin to glowworms? Another possibility. This would implicate the Chinese again and leaving my shoe out of it. Either way, he's cute as can be and charming to the limit, a regular acrobat and stunt pilot, never satisfied with where he's at. I watch and wonder, full of admiration, a big smile cracking my face until he buzzes my ears and I swat like crazy, sending him back where he came from and nearly doing a half-gainer in the bargain to save my cap. It was never designed for inspecting holes of this depth. I stick it in my back pocket and make myself comfortable, folding my arms under my chin and letting my brain race in and out, deeper and deeper, like a yoyo. Full of ideas. The kind that get nowhere? We'll have to see about that.

No encores from little Sparky. In the end I'm not sure he was a moth exactly. More of a firefly. Or nothing whatever? Glowworm on a sky hook. Not that it mattered. There were thornier issues to chew on. The longer I went at it, the colder I became, especially the foot with no shoe. I didn't leave until dawn. Birds began to chirp and the fog brightened into an immense pearly dome. I sprinted most of the way and disappeared into it.

CHAPTER 17

DOUBLE WHAMMY
Where dire legalese gives inertia a hotfoot

Life settled down a good deal during the weeks that followed until day before yesterday Pablo got arrested and Auntie's lawyer dropped by to warn us to clear out. Great news on both counts, according to Homer. Now everything should come to a head and my days as Number One Cluck will at last draw to a close. With Pablo I agree. We'd been meeting almost daily to compare notes and get drunk, and the sonofabitch had me up to my ears in cold feet. First red wine, then white, and always in such absurd quantities. It's nothing to smoke a pack of cigarettes an hour when you're with that powder keg.

But the real payoff was Auntie's lawyer, the sober Stan Stenko. I say "lawyer" like everybody else around here, when we all know he's little more than a guardian of rubber stamps and go-between for bribes. Better than most lawyers though, when you come right down to it. Less expensive or conceited and equally shifty. The most glaring contrast is juxtaposing him with our Honest Abe Blacky.

He's with me now, Blacky is, both of us damp and stinky because we got soaked during our walk. I'm hunched over the typewriter with a poetical look on my face, while he hangs out by the door, an eye glued to my every move for signs I'll throw a fit. He knows something's wrong. Last night we crept through the darkened apartment and I had a sharp bottle-opener in my hand, ready to puncture their windpipes if the godmother hadn't been spying on us from the sand dunes. I nearly fainted because that's the kind of face she has. Just a splash of moonlight and you're ready for a good scream.

"Cigarette," she says.

"Forget it, sister."

We let her smoke crayons and clothespins, never tobacco. Her regular brand is pretzels. But last night she crawled over and hugged my knees.

"Cigarette!"

What the hell, I should worry for her health? I lit one for her and one for myself, then sat by the windows admiring her latest construction project. Medieval splendor is what she aims for. Castles, canals and lemonade moats. I fixed her a cute flag out of a Gauloises wrapper.

"Eeeek! Eeeek!"

She knows how to clap her hands ten times per second.

"Shut up and smoke."

The Wilcoxes had a party going across the way. Music and champagne corks. Maybe fifty guests. I followed the drift from room to room, the exquisite gestures.

"Fairies make their home in such places, did you know that? It's their universe."

"Where's Daddy?"

"At the end of the pier deep-sea diving."

I caught my breath just then because the Wilcoxes danced by the windows and you don't run across such magic every day, their shadows swirling madly in the courtyard with the leaves. She wore something white and charming, while he had on a black dinner jacket with a red sash slanting across the shirtfront. An award for pure luck perhaps, or a gentleman's shoulder-holster. I wondered what they'd think if I were to waltz in with my graceful nicotine fiend.

"Stop it!"

She was trying to poke the cigarette in her crack, so I slapped her hand, only to have to come across with another to quiet her down.

"Enjoy yourself. It'll put hair on your chest and your chest X-ray."

The baby let out a squawk down the hall, then went back to peeping and cheeping. I could hear Vivette too, sobbing in her sleep. Drip. Drip. Even in her sleep! It's like bunking with a broken toilet, my pillow always sopping wet and slab-sided like a halibut.

Not much from the others. A faint click when I passed Auntie's door, then nothing. Stash was off somewhere, and even Mama, our champion night owl, had turned in shortly after dinner, disappointing me somewhat because I can usually count on her to pass the time and maybe play a game of Parcheesi.

Later, after the Wilcoxes' kicked their guests out, the moon ducked behind the buildings and the courtyard became really black. Godmommy curled up with Blacky under the buffet. I threw some cushions on the floor and stretched out with my thoughts, mostly about lawyer Stenko. As soon as a few clouds roll in that prick has to start crowding all the lifeboats. No more confidential counseling or intimate powwows, he made that clear. We're free agents from now on, all because the nephew has been raising too much hell at headquarters. Stenko thinks we don't fully comprehend the danger.

"Why pay me if you're going to ignore my advice?"

Good question. He repeats it over and over to each of us in turn.

"Well..." says Auntie. "Aack!...On the other hand... Aack!..."

Out with the lipstick and she's dolling up the old bazoo. That's some mouth she has. Trimmed in red, I'm reminded of the evening the Ferris wheel caught fire on the Place de la Concorde.

"Are you listening, young man?"

"Yes, sir."

He seemed doubtful. I'd been napping and still felt groggy and half-dressed when they herded us into the living room around ten that night. I sat on the sofa with Mama and Stash while Auntie and Stenko took armchairs by the fireplace. Vivette perched on the godmother's rocker with the baby on her knees, inching closer my way in case I decided to blow my top. This was possible because Stenko wouldn't lay off us for registering with the cops, afraid we'll crack under the Third Degree, if ever the occasion should arise.

"As it damn-well might!"

Our futures appear dim to his eyes, our days at Passy very iffy, awful and riddled with pitfalls. Of course he's telling us nothing new. We've always known the nephew would be our downfall with his loud mouth and wild accusations, around-the-clock phone calls. But it seems some corner-office bigwig has finally become interested. Steps may be taken. Tomorrow maybe. Then where will we be?

"Why not have him arrested?"

"Who?"

"The nephew. Before we moved in, wasn't he forging her checks all over town? If the police come, we'll tell them."

"Quiet, Michael."

Auntie hates any mention of forged checks. But I think Stenko understands. He gives me a knowing look.

"The law..." he says.

"To hell with the law. He wants to fix it so she has to have her head examined, right?"

"A competency hearing."

"Then pack her off to Shady Acres and swipe everything in sight. It won't take long either. I give him two weeks at the outside, then feed her hot peppers. No more chicken soup the way Mama makes it. He'll have her dining on applejack and firecrackers."

"Michael!"

"Next stop the bone orchard."

"Quiet!"

Okay, but that nephew is a menace. If Stenko weren't so well-dressed, I'd have suggested inviting the bastard over for a bloodbath, then bury him in that well I found.

"We must be realistic," says Stenko, placing his fingertips together and getting everybody interested in certain realistic cracks in the ceiling. "We must organize our thoughts and face the situation with a clear eye."

Good. We're all organizing our thoughts and clearing our eyes, when he abruptly points at the godmother, who happened to be pouring sand from a tea kettle. If the nephew ever manages to have her dragged before a judge looking like that, we're dead ducks. Vivette and me in particular on account of our registration. He shakes his head and paints more dreary pictures of witness boxes and slanderous evidence. Nothing short of mass hypnotism, he feels, could obscure the essence of the case. The core. The kernel. Everything, in fact, rests solely on the godmother herself, on her soundness of mind.

We all looked at her in horror.

Indeed, this wouldn't be the aging but alert dowager the Defense cracks her up to be. The contrast would be hair-raising.

"You must remember, before your arrival this woman was worth a fortune."

"Then how about if Auntie..."

No, Auntie is in the clear and that's that. Vivette and I are the ones to whom the police will direct their inquiry on account of our fucking registration. Every time I hear it mentioned, I have to watch my blood pressure.

"But..."

"No buts. Picture the worst disaster imaginable."

Stenko is the sawed-off, plump type, with quick little eyes and stubby, ring-bespeckled fingers. He had one aimed at me for a long time before switching to the others.

"You," he says to Auntie, "and you and you," to Mama and Stash, "will simply know nothing. If the police claim to have witnesses, people who say they've seen you here, you may agree, certainly. She's an old friend. Naturally you're in the habit of visiting."

"To bring bread," says Mama, which got her the once-over.

"No," says Stash, folding his arms across his chest and swinging his feet onto the coffee table. "Buy guns for peoples. Turn ugly artifacts for guns into."

He deserved even closer scrutiny than his mom. I couldn't help laughing.

Auntie motioned for Stenko to ignore Broomface and the two missionaries and get on with it. We were making her nervous. At the same time, I could see she had Stenko fairly jumpy the way she kept hiking her skirts and crossing her legs, perhaps hoping to interest him in trading fees for services. I winked at the godmother, who was taking everything in with wide eyes and a slack jaw, then busied myself with buttons and snaps. At least I wanted to tie my shoes better, but kept breaking the laces. I'd splice them together only to break them again. Vivette very kindly poured me a cognac.

"Are we boring you, young man?"

"Not at all."

There was an intelligent brain behind Stenko's beady little eyes, although I could see he didn't exactly reciprocate the sentiment. He looked at me like I'd been hatched from a dodo's nest.

"Tell me, what's your name, Michael, why don't you take your wife and child to the United States?"

"That's what I'll do some day."

"What're you waiting for?"

Vivette lurched forward to hear my answer. But my pipes felt rusty and my tongue tasted like a furry sardine. I drank Mama's tea for her, choking somewhat on the lemon seeds, then drank Vivette's and forgot the question.

"Well?"

"Well what?"

He shook his head and launched deeper into his ocean of eye-openers and terrifying predictions. I guess we needed the lowdown once more. One last cold shower to thoroughly dampen our spirits and put an end to all notions of wellbeing. The future is armed and dangerous, that was his theme. Soon this entire apartment could be a-patter with size-12s.

"Understand?"

"Sure we understand. You want no courtrooms whatever."

"Under any circumstance."

"Right. But how about everybody moves to Auntie's place? Just Vivette and I stay here. When the police come, we'll say the old lady's on vacation. We're the maid and handyman and have no idea where she is or when she's due back."

Quite a clever remark, except everybody started jabbering like I hadn't said a damn thing. Stash offered to invite some comrades over to guard the doors, while Mama knew a Latvian priest who would make a great character witness. Auntie, for her part, thought a psychiatrist of our own could spruce up our dossier and confuse matters indefinitely.

"My idea..." I started again.

"Would you like more tea?"

"Or how about..."

"Ha! Ha! Ha!"

He finally shut us up with a stupendous laugh, mopping his brow and kind of whistling. Psychiatrists! Character priests! Boy, would we ever be sorry. There were tears in his eyes and I noticed his hands had begun to tremble.

"Hang on a minute," I told him, putting extra authority in my voice while raising a palm to silence the other windbags. "I have a friend who knows a policeman. Also several meter maids, but that's neither here nor there. The thing is, this friend has access to stationery from the British Embassy. If we could get him to..."

"No."

"What do you mean no? You don't let me finish. What I'm trying to say..."

"No! No! No!"

He slammed his hands on his knees and shook his head so violently anyone would've thought I'd been trying to get him to switch from tea to castor oil.

"A thousand times no!"

To do legal battle is out of the question. It's precisely such fantasies he'd meant to squash with points one, two and articles thirty-six through seventy-five. Weren't we paying attention? The French judicial system may be blind, and he admits his superiors drag their feet all over the place, but once in their clutches our lives would be laid bare and dissected like wormy turds, each fact scrutinized and cross-checked, then passed through one wringer after another until all lies leak out the sides and our defense resembles a confession, after which they'll fasten us to a wall and drape cobwebs on his ears.

"Then how about everybody gets registered? Tomorrow, say, we could meet you during your lunch hour..."

"No!"

"But if all of us..."

"Please don't interrupt."

Shit, he's the one interrupting. And I was only thinking it would be a good idea to spread the blame a little bit.

"Absolutely not."

Run, hide or take up astral projection, but stay far from the halls of justice.

"Steer a wide course."

"We shouldn't panic though, should we?"

Panic? Of course we should panic. One gander at our bathing beauty and they'll have us slapped in the cooler so fast our assholes will wince. We mustn't kid ourselves, the impending inquiry must be shunned like green meat.

"At all costs!"

And I noticed he raised his voice quite a bit, which isn't normal with Stenko. He's usually a very cool customer. It's just that our rosy outlook was getting him down.

"Awake, my friends!"

He made it perfectly clear, for instance, we're not to salute him in the street. He's off the case and henceforth won't know us from atoms. He examined his tea and checked his watch. How time flies! He looked me square in eye.

"No talking."

"No, sir."

Modesty will be our saving grace. We'll imitate totem poles and wooden Indians, void of all knowledge. And if the fuzz do swoop down and catch us here, red-handed, we can act gay as fan-dancers and pass out the snacks. What a pleasant surprise! Then clam up tight. We're straight off the boat, see? Only visiting for the afternoon. Our favorite word is "Duh". He gets me to say it.

"Excellent."

I'm a load off his mind.

"If only you'll remember not to deviate."

Never. This is pure coincidence, the cops running into us here. Wouldn't happen again in a coon's age. Because we're innocent, clean, blameless as babes. Tots in Toyland. The truth is we're hardly ever around and don't really live here. Haha! Whatever gave them that idea? Neighbors? This will be a shock. We're unacquainted with the bullshitters. Let them step forward. We'll shrug our shoulders and cross our eyes, very duh. As for the lady in question, the dignified old mistress, she's simply too far above us. This is a part-time job Vivette and I do for pin money, otherwise we're snubbed, ignored, and rightfully so on account of our peasant ways. We'll confess this freely, then belch. No use hiding our rough edges from the captain. If he wants to know how long she's been crapping in her sun-suit, we haven't the vaguest. The smell? Hmmm. Now that he mentions it. What a clever detective! But it's the first we noticed and isn't it a shame? Her aroma escaped us due to our humble origins. The hills, see? Rural types. Shepherds. We make our own cheese. Everything will be news to us.

"No statements."

Certainly not. Perfect tranquility. No soliloquies, explanatory reports or voluntary gabbiness. We're strangers to these parts who hopped the wrong bus and got turned all around. Foreigners. Innocent tourists. No speaky Frenchy.

"Get the idea?"

Well, it's beginning to sink in. Lawyers hate gassy clients, but he seemed fairly satisfied now, even smiling a bit as he looked first at Vivette, who had her hands folded primly, then at me. He saw two honest mugs staring blankly at each other like statues in the park.

"Splendid."

We might visualize stagnant lakes, but more important than that, a thousand times more, was to never allow things to go so far. No flatfoots if we can help it.

He stood and sucked in his belly. Auntie did the same as they guided each other to the door.

"Better take the old lady out of the country," he tells her, sending a sharp glance my way. "Every chain has its weak link, so I recommend no delay. You say she owns a chalet near Lausanne? Take her there. The sooner the better."

We all got sharp glances when he pulled on his coat.

"If she's not here to receive a summons...well, maybe you'll manage a while longer."

"Can't you stall them at least another couple months?" I put in.

No answer. He took Auntie's hand after she slipped him his envelope. They lowered their voices.

Blahblahblah.

"Farewell, Madame. Adieu, my friends. Bonne chance."

He backed into the corridor without pressing the light button, then zipped down the stairs like a shadow, leaving us bug-eyed and dumbfounded. I hopped to the windows for a peek, and it gave me a chill, him galloping across the courtyard with his collar way up. He looked like the Headless Horseman.

"Well," I said. "What do you make of that?"

Apparently not a thing. Right away they took his advice about not talking. It's been the same for two days. They practice on me. Auntie is at least twice as quick-tempered as usual, while Mama and Stash fly right up the walls with my clumsy intrusions. Nobody can stand my face anymore, which is about the only secret they don't try too hard to keep.

"Why all the whispering?" I've asked Vivette.

"Nothing."

"What do you mean nothing?"

Even Blacky senses trouble. I had to slap him around yesterday and today to keep him in line. Probably it's against him he thinks they're plotting instead of Godmommy. Which is the real reason, of course. Her days are being numbered and what I have to do is more obvious by the minute. No more if-I-could-I-should-I. The time has come to strike while they're still in a daze.

CHAPTER 18

BYE-BYE PABLO
Where partnerships dissolve as one
lives for one's art

I awoke next morning a bundle of nerves. Blacky got his walk, then I called a crisis conference with Homer and Pablo. Three o'clock at the Select.

"Don't be late."

Homer drifted in around four and Pablo a little after seven.

"You stupid sonofabitch, I told you this is important!"

He had a bandage on his head the size of a football helmet, and the story he hands us, he walked into a bistro off the Rue Rennes and everybody jumped him for no reason.

"Absolutely without provocation."

Then he wouldn't sit still. The Select was already filling up with the usual oddballs and he wanted to show them his bandage, especially the red spot in the middle, dirty fingerprints all around.

"Get back here!"

"Let him go," says Homer. "You can see it's not going to work."

"What isn't?"

We had a table near the bar and were hashing over various contingencies and slippery side issues. Of course I told him about Stenko, the urgency of the time element. I also wanted his slant on a list I'd drawn up of damn near every murder weapon imaginable, plus timetables of Auntie's habits, her crazy movements, trying to pinpoint the tender weak spots at which eternity might slip in on her unawares.

"Not bad," he says, thumbing through the ten or twelve notebooks I'd brought along. "You put in a lot of work. I'd say cut chapter five, but the rest looks salvageable."

"What chapter five?"

"How do you see the end?"

"One dead aunt, how else?"

He smiled. "I mean afterwards. I assume you expect to get away with it. How's that going to happen?"

"Well, I have different ideas. My favorite is where Auntie falls out the window of her own *locked* room. Something to keep the inspectors guessing for a long time. The only clues would be an unhung picture and the poorly glued leg of a chair."

"That's your favorite?"

"Except I worry sometimes she can read my mind, like she knows what I'm thinking before I even think it. Her eyes actually darken, turn black like a rattlesnake's, like she sees where I'm going and how to get there first. All my intricate schemes and well-oiled trains of events go sailing out the window, the chair breaks and she lands on the fucking bed instead."

"Maybe you want something less fancy."

"The beauty though, if I use the chair trick, I won't have to stay in cahoots with the mad artist."

"Screw you," says Pablo, who returned just then from his travels, his bandage completely haywire, exposing his runny bump.

We had a thirty-second shouting match during which he insulted my courage and said I'm a lazy couch-potato whose spine got traded for a television antenna.

"Mastermind of the rumpus room," he calls me. "He lays around all day with his dick in the cheese dip."

Homer intervened with a round of cognac, Pablo's favorite, encouraging us to be nice and put our heads together, come up with a workable plan.

Fine, except Pablo wouldn't stop elaborating our strategies and flying off the handle. No surprise. I'd learned long ago to soft-pedal the visions of a golden victory over the powers of darkness for fear he'd swallow his tongue. At least he had to quit blabbing to every stoolpigeon in Montparnasse or there'd be hell to pay with the cross-examiners. The rate he was going I saw a blazing finish with searchlights and a hail of hot lead, up in the maid's room maybe, swimming in glory and teargas.

"Would you shut up!"

Not that he was uncooperative. He even introduced some reasonable suggestions. It wasn't long though, the hooch took over entirely and he had us back at the OK Corral shooting it out with the Dalton Boys.

Another shouting match led to more cognac and more shouting until I lost my temper and gave him a shove. His chair tipped over and he ran backwards on his heels into another table. The people there objected, but of course Pablo never apologizes. He spit in a lady's hair and pulled out a knife I'd bought him almost two feet long. That's when things got complicated. Four waiters dashed over and wrestled him to the floor.

"Do you feel like a bite to eat?" says Homer, stuffing my notebooks into a plastic bag.

"What about Pablo?"

"Forget about Pablo."

He was to repeat that several times during the remainder of the evening, so often in fact I got the impression he's a little cold-blooded. On the other hand, he treated me with unusual warmth.

"You know, Mike, I feel responsible for you."

A nice thing to say.

While Pablo tangled with the waiters, Homer and I trotted across the boulevard to the large café-brasserie La Coupôle. The dining area was too crowded and noisy, so Homer suggested we have a beer on the terrace but eat somewhere else.

"Italian opera," he says, nodding across the boulevard at the Select.

We could hear muffled screams and could see Pablo racing back and forth inside, his bandage streaming behind him like a comet. And after a minute, he burst through the swinging doors with two waiters on his tail.

"Mike!" he shouted. "Homer!"

The waiters wore white coats, appropriately enough, and one waved a bar bill.

Homer chuckled. "He seems unlikely to leave a tip."

"I better go get him."

He grabbed my arm. "Just watch the show."

After galloping toward the church, Pablo stopped and doubled back, dodging the waiters and a handful of patrons who'd taken the opportunity to blow without paying. He fell down a couple times, scrambled over a parked car, then made a break for the Metro but collided with a line of movie-goers by the corner cinema. An argument ensued during which Pablo turned his pockets inside-out and passed his watch around. A few fists flew. Then a woman stepped forward to referee. Pablo knocked her for a loop. He sent the waiters crashing into the newsstand. When the woman stood, she got it again. A double loop. Now everybody was pissed off. Hitting a woman! They were all against this but Pablo. He's no good at public relations. He kicked the newsboy in the balls.

Meanwhile, Homer paid little attention. Even after the police arrived, he preferred yakking about the publishing trade and how wonderful it would be if I got a book in print.

"Think of the prestige," he says, laying a hand on my notebooks. "I want to keep these, see if I can whip them into shape."

"Yeah? And who's going to whip you into shape?"

Just then Pablo bounced by the corner of my eye with a desperate look on his face and a six-foot cop on his ass. When he spotted us, he let out a yowl, rolling his eyes and craning his neck while the cop kept moving, frog-walking him to the corner and into the arms of a squad of colleagues by the Café Dôme. They had a paddy wagon waiting, but Pablo would have none of it. When they opened the door, he kicked it shut.

"I'm an artist!" he shouted, which tickled the fuzz.

They tripped him up, laid him out and came down like a ton of bricks, showing creative urges of their own, their clubs rising and falling in rhythmic disarray.

"Critical acclaim," says Homer.

"You think it's funny?"

Pablo's face appeared now and then, all aglow, crushed between two huge rear ends, until one cop leapt from the pack and did a kind of unicycle backpedal into the street. He held an ear with one hand and fumbled for his gun with the other.

"Just wait!" he shrieked.

His pals had to restrain him. They sat on his chest and removed his holster.

Pablo broke free in the confusion, but got snagged by the fish stand and hauled back in a blur of arms and legs. They filed in the wagon and the driver started the engine. Pablo came to the bars as the wagon pulled away, making super-expressive faces like a silent-film star.

"Mike! Homer!"

Homer nodded and raised his glass in a kind of farewell salute, which gave me a queasy feeling.

CHAPTER 19

NEW DEAL WITH HOMER
Where compromise is struck with an infuriating catch

"Well," says Homer, setting his glass down and smacking his lips. "That's that."

I eyed him sourly. "Funny joke for you, isn't it? What am I supposed to do now?"

"Celebrate."

"Celebrate!"

"You wrote a book."

"Fuck books!"

"It's time to move on."

"Where to, the North Pole?"

"How about Spain?"

"Spain?"

"Anywhere really, there're lots of places."

"Places where I can live on a dollar and a half?"

"You'll get by, don't worry. Guys like you never starve."

"How about Vivette?"

"You leave her, of course. Leave Passy, the kid, everything. You're young, you have to learn to live."

"Shit, nobody has to learn that."

Another round of beer to calm my nerves, then he hiked us up the Rue Delambre to a small restaurant behind Montparnasse. Steak, fries and a carafe of red wine. The air was soft and unseasonably warm, so we took a table outside under little lanterns in the trees.

"The first breath of spring," he says, opening his arms to the night sky as though he owned property in this neighborhood. "The wind, Mike, do you feel it?"

"Yeah, looks like rain."

"That's a south wind. Know what I smell in that wind?"

"Girl Scouts?"

He made a face to show I'm a bit too vulgar for him. "Come on, we better check back at the Select. I think I owe them some money."

"Damnit, Homer, how long do you think I could survive on your bullshit? With the godmother now I have my first chance for a real haul. You wouldn't pass it up either, would you?"

"I sure would."

"You wouldn't."

"Yes I would."

We retraced our steps down the Rue Delambre, him peering into shop windows and trash baskets while I nipped after him like a frantic puppy.

"It's easy for you, you have money."

"You're young, that's worth all the money in the world. What you need now, what might actually help, is to have your whole world turned upside-down."

"What's wrong with inside-out?"

"It's time to concentrate on your writing."

"Fuck writing!"

"This book is finished. Or almost. In need of severe editing, of course, that goes without saying, and a chapter or two to round things off. That'll be easy enough. Finding a publisher might prove more difficult."

"Fuck publishers!"

"I'm afraid we'll have to look for one whose readers don't mind their literature a bit low and loopy."

"Fuck readers!"

He bought a racing form and tossed it away, then just loafed from one side of the street to the other, hitching up his pants and diving into more trash baskets.

"Look," he says, holding up a toy kangaroo.

"I don't want it."

"You can give it to your kid."

"Let's get inside. It's starting to rain."

A fat drop hit me on the head and a dozen more flashed between us like silver dollars. The nearest café was only a few steps away, but Homer wanted to sit outside and discuss the soul-expanding aspects of world travel.

"Hell no, we'll get soaked out here!"

"The Mediterranean, Mike. Little blue fishing boats and African sunsets."

"Tell me about it inside."

"First we'll work the Metro."

"Oh, no. I have too much on my mind to help you bother women."

"We won't have to wait long. I figure that one exit coughs up an easy lay every ten seconds."

"I'm going home."

"To murder the aunt?"

"What choice do I have?"

"You mentioned robbing her shack."

"What of it?"

"Not a bad idea."

"Really?"

"I've been thinking..."

Suddenly it didn't matter what he was thinking. Thunder and lightning nearly made me jump into his arms as the wind picked up and the rain cut loose, sending a barrage of twigs and branches shooting up and down the boulevard like bows and arrows. The newsstand exploded and the trees touched their toes, jackknifing and swimming like squids.

We took off for the Café Dôme, shoulder to shoulder, until a sharp pain struck the back of my head and my ass lost altitude. I awoke in the gutter, wondering why he would want to cold-cock me. I needed a change, he said. My whole world should be turned upside-down. I sprang to my feet, ready for combat, but found I'm the victim of trash baskets. Homer was waving from the Dôme, laughing and pointing at whole flocks of tumbleweed blowing in from the Fifth Arrondissement.

"Get in here," he says. "A quick cognac, then we'll try for the Select."

Okay, a mad dash through the tempest and another spectacular entrance. I spun at the door after clipping my shoulder on a large rubbertree plant, while Homer slid on his ass, cackling like a mad scientist.

"My friends!" cried the proprietor, welcoming us with open arms, imploring us to help save his gold mine.

No problem. While he examined insurance policies, Homer issued messages to the fleet and got us pitched in with the waiters to tether the awnings. We juggled chairs and tables and tossed rags in puddles, flexing our muscles and winking at the ladies, until everything was shipshape.

The kitchen staff cheered as the proprietor licked our cheeks and showed us the best booth in the house. Absolutely free drinks.

Homer proposed a toast. "To jet planes, speeding trains and killers like Mike who have no brains."

"I know you think everything I do is crazy."

"That's the first step toward mental health. The second would be to ask the waiter to leave the bottle."

"If you hadn't got Pablo arrested..."

"Forget Pablo."

"They're liable to kill him, you know. Last time they really worked him over."

"We'll drink to his health and full recovery." He raised his glass. "The Three Musketeers."

That cheered me up. "See, that's how I'd like it to be. The Three Musketeers."

I was ready for another toast, but Homer had already begun to exchange friendly gestures with nearby cutie pies.

I touched his arm. "You said it's a good idea."

"What is?"

"Robbing the aunt's shack. I'm sure she hid lots of stuff out there."

"Go get it."

"We both do."

"You're better off on your own."

"How better?"

"More amusing."

"Damnit, Homer, why can't you be serious? Something's in the wind, and not little blue fishing boats. Ever since Stenko's visit, they act squirrelly as bedbugs."

"You're mixing your metaphors."

"Fuck metaphors! Lend me a hand and I promise you'll clear at least ten thousand dollars right away."

"You haven't got *ten* dollars."

"I mean right away afterwards."

He laughed. "Life," he says, "is definitely a freak. Sometimes a squirrelly bedbug, sometimes more like that bottomless pit of yours."

"Listen, man, we don't have to kill anybody. I agree with you on that. A crazy idea. But we could burglarize her shack, couldn't we? I mean, there's nothing crazy about that, is there?"

He patted my hand. "The way I see it, you need a clean break, start a new life. Head for Spain or wherever and write new stories...Where're you going?"

"To Spain."

"Finish your drink."

"No, I thought you were my friend, but I see you're not. Our relationship has no meaning."

"You sound like a woman."

"And you're a hot air balloon!"

"Give my regards to Blacky."

"Why can't you be serious? Auntie doesn't trust banks, you know. Especially French ones. And I guarantee for a fact she's been riding the train out there every day or two with her bags loaded. Or Stash drives her. But she doesn't trust him either! You see what that means, don't you?"

"Enlighten me."

"She's salting it away."

"Maybe."

"No maybes. Sure as shit. Give me a hand and I'll prove it."

"Call me when you get back."

"Come on, man, there must be thousands, even hundreds of thousands."

"Millions."

"Why not? You saw what was in the safe-deposit box you helped her empty. We'll bring shovels. At night, of course. Tear up the whole fucking place if necessary. What do you say? Just one night's work."

He shook his head. "She has everything in a safe place by now, probably not even in France. You said yourself she's been phoning Swiss law firms ever since you moved in."

"That's just to throw me off the track."

"Well, I'd say she did a good job."

"I should just give up then, is that what you're saying? I should just let her take everything?"

"She already took it."

"I'll get it back. Otherwise it's too humidifying. I mean dubiliating. Humilitating..."

That set him off laughing again.

I stood and rubbed a snowstorm from my beard. "Look, I'm losing my looks. My hands are filthy, my nails black. My clothes, Homer, they'd embarrass a dead man. Quit laughing! I'll die some day, probably before the godmother. Is that what you want, youth slipping through my fingers while Auntie waddles off with Fort Knox? What're you laughing for? Shit, I'm getting out of here."

"Hang on."

"Hang on hell."

"Finish your drink."

"If I miss the last Metro, I'm going to kill myself."

"Maybe you have a point."

"What point?"

"Maybe she's hiding something out there."

"Sure she is."

"I guess it wouldn't hurt to take a look."

"Now you're talking!"

"Sit down."

I do exactly as he says.

He leans over. "We're doing this for money, right?"

"Of course."

"No more talk of murder."

"Well, it would be better if she was out of the way."

"But we're forgetting that, right?"

"Right."

"Tell the waiter to bring the bottle."

"But it's a deal, isn't it?"

"You talked me into it."

"Then we should discuss details, like when do we do it? I made her shack sound pretty flimsy, but actually it may have been built by a locksmith. We'll need tools. Do you think we should rent a truck?"

"That's up to you."

"We could run out there tonight, except I imagine you're pretty tired."

"I'm not running anywhere."

"Tomorrow then. There's not lots of time."

"That'll be your problem. Mine is how to pick up the pieces."

"What pieces?"

"I already know where I'm going to put you."

"What're you talking about?"

"Whatever you find or don't find is up to you. I'll take care of the rest."

"What rest? There is no rest."

"You'll need help peddling whatever you find, then you'll want to disappear. I can't see you facing the aunt afterwards."

"But you have to help with the whole thing, busting in and all."

"No thanks."

"That's the deal, isn't it? Going it alone isn't the same."

"It'll take some courage."

"It's not a question of courage."

"Brains then."

"Stop that shit!"

"Go get the waiter."

"You think it's not going to work?"

"I hope it does. I hope you walk away with a sack full of diamonds. If nothing else, it should at least finish you with that family."

"But Homer..."

I tried talking him into a real partnership, fifty-fifty, but he closed his ears.

"Give me a call in the morning."

"No, you won't hear from me until I have something to report."

"Okay, report to me in the morning."

CHAPTER 20

VIVETTE HAS A SECRET
Where Mike quells marital treason without knowing any better

I had to hurry because I'd promised Vivette I'd be home early. That wasn't possible, but I thought it would look better if I arrived out of breath. As it turned out, my breathing was of no interest to anybody. Lots of screaming and shouting and stomping around the living room, which was fortunate in a way because I could skip the apologies and assume the moral high ground.

"What's going on here?"

Dirty looks, that's what. They scattered like cockroaches while Vivette landed on my shoulder like a tidal wave.

"What's wrong?"

She wouldn't say.

I stroked her hair and advised deep breaths. No use crying over spilt milk. She should just rest against me and let her worries melt away.

"Fuggisyou!"

I let that pass. Vivette is never easy to comprehend, and this time was made worse by gurgles and gasps and a raspiness in her voice that made her sound like a ventriloquist.

"Try not to talk."

"Go fuggisyouself!"

"Now, now, it's bound to look better in the morning."

Fresh air was the thing. Blacky needed a walk, so I herded the two of them out the door and around the corner to the Bois.

"It's always darkest before the dawn."

"Fuggisyou! Fuggisyou! Fuggisyou!"

"Yes, but the thing you're missing is the big picture. Actually everything is fine. Homer says we need a change and I know how to make that happen. He's agreed to help."

"Fuggishim!"

"Right."

I couldn't elaborate, of course. I'm going to kill your aunt, how would that sound? Even though my intentions had been refined to the point I'm only going to rob the old bitch.

"On the subject of travel..."

"America!" she insisted, and wouldn't let me drift to other interesting continents.

My own fault, I suppose, for all the bum steers I'd given her about the fantasia of life in America and the size of my parents' estate. My reluctance to return struck her as eccentric. She said I must be nuts. I told her it's not a question of nuts or berries but the mysterious nature of literary genius.

"It takes adversity to create first-rate art."

"Adversity I give you!"

"And I'll give you a poke in the jaw!"

We argued back and forth while crunching along the bridle path, under the trees, the leaves dripping down our necks, although the storm had moved off and only rumbled in the distance, maybe fifty miles away, casting out great sheets of rippling light over the city.

"Pretty, isn't it?"

"Don't care."

"Sure you do."

Another tour of America might get her under control, so I bounced from Maine to the Pecos, then up and down the Mississippi and all through the Prairie District, dropping hints only about my true itinerary. America wasn't the absolute focal point. It would take too long to explain to a foreigner. She'd just have to trust me.

"Shit! Shit! Shit!"

I braced her against a tree, but she clubbed me in the ear. She's not my wife, she says, not anymore, not until I behave like a proper husband and introduce her to the folks, buy a penthouse and a washing-machine, a block-long car.

"Jesus, Vivette, didn't I just tell you I know how to fix everything? What more do you want? Your aunt's behind this, isn't she? She has something up her sleeve. What were you guys hollering about?"

"You soon see."

"See what?...Shit, don't cry!"

We circled the racetrack and Polo Club and came out on a grassy patch overlooking the river. Far off, the storm still rumbled on, pulsating in the clouds and all along the horizon like an artillery barrage.

"Listen, Vivette, you don't hate me, do you?"

She looked up with startled eyes, her mouth opening and closing like a fish.

"The reason I ask is something Abraham Lincoln said. A house divided cannot stand. What he meant is people like us should work together more instead of pulling north and south all the time. Remember how it used to be? Two against the world. I'd like it to be that way again. How about you?"

"Bahwoop!" she said, and dug her nose in my chest.

A good sign.

"We're still friends, aren't we?"

"Bahwoop! Bahwoop!"

I slipped an arm around her waist and headed us for home, yapping a mile a minute in order to nail down the mood, while she went on weeping, but softly now, not angry like before.

"Everything'll work out, you'll see."

A cold breeze had moved in, partly clearing the sky. The moon appeared intermittently. And as we neared the boulevard, we could hear the sticky sound of wet tires, and could see Blacky on the far side knocking over garbage cans.

"Funny fellow, isn't he?"

No answer, but the weeping eased off to more of a background wheeze, like a saxophone accompaniment, as I continued to explore various ways of saying nothing new. I understood when she didn't pay strict attention. By the time we reached the courtyard, I'm pretty sure she was sound asleep.

CHAPTER 21

TURN OF THE WORM
Where Mike stalls Auntie and goes for broke

This has to work! this has to work! rattled in my head like the clickety-clack of the rails. Outside, the grand boulevards had faded away, replaced by factory walls and bleak canals, a few Stalinesque housing projects, followed by no-hunting zones, an ocean of blowing weeds, winter stubble and one moonlit gravel pit. Auntie's station was coming up. I clenched my teeth and shivered from head to toe. She'd come a long way, I couldn't help marveling. From the Bolshoi to a hobo jungle, then right back into the chips again.

Stumbling off the platform, I made straight for my comfy café, but found it in ruins. Apparently they'd had a fire. Most of the roof was gone and the charred façade had been plastered over with commercial fliers and civic announcements.

Partake of the Great Pig Roast.

"Kiss my ass!"

I stared at a circus poster for a minute, wondering what my next move should be. A clown with green hair stared back at me. Not only did it seem a bit early for her neighbors to have turned in, a convivial hour with my rustic pals would've been just the thing to bolster my spirits. I'd forgotten how lonely the country could be. When the moon slid behind the clouds, the night took over entirely, seeping through my clothes and deep into my belly, threatening to turn firm resolve into scary notions about the thorns and thistles and maybe the fence posts are hobgoblins. The trees reached out like murderers and one actually tried to cut my throat.

"Nobody said it would be easy."

Actually I did say it would be easy, but that's before Homer punked out. I worried now I was making a mistake. Stenko might be wrong, after all. The nephew could settle out of court and let us go on milking the godmother indefinitely. Free room and board! It hadn't been so unbearable. Auntie might even make good on her thousand and one promises to treat me decent.

"What a joke!"

Yet I couldn't be sure. The very fact she's nuts might mean she's serious. It was hard to decide.

The evening before, she waylaid me in the kitchen while I was rustling up a snack. I hadn't switched on the light and still felt keyed up from my walkie-talkie with Vivette, so I nearly dove out the window the way she floated in from the shadows.

"For new clothes," she says, shoving a wad of banknotes in my face. "Must look proper for journey."

"What journey?"

I did a two-step into the sink, trying to recall if I'd gone too far with Vivette. Had she squealed on me? That didn't seem possible. I'd left her in our room scarcely a minute ago, and hadn't disclosed much to begin with.

How about bigmouth Homer?

"Did Homer phone while I was out?"

She pressed my nose like a doorbell. "Tink you I forget when just to need me most?"

I wasn't going to answer that. I lunged for the door, but got snagged from behind. She has these midnight urges of her own. I humored her as best I could.

"Time be come," she says.

"Time for what?"

"Hmmmmmmmmm..."

"Godmommy, you mean? You're taking her out of town?"

Good guess. Our eyes met in the dark and I knew where I stood.

I cleared my throat. "You'll have to give me a day or two to settle loose ends. The middle of the week, let's say, I could let you know definitely."

"Yet time be..."

I didn't give her a chance to hit her stride.

"I'll think it over," I yelped, and practically flew to my room to toss and turn with Vivette.

That's it, I told myself. No more fooling around. The following night wouldn't be a moment too soon. I slammed my fist in the pillow. In twenty-four hours everything would be settled.

Such decisiveness made me sleepy.

The shack retained the same gruesome appearance as the last time I'd seen it. A veil of snow covered the ground and an icy wind had turned the trees into xylophones, but I saw no smoke from the chimney or slivers of light from the windows.

"So far, so good."

I marched up and down the road, reconnoitering the fence and the sturdiness of the shutters. No organ sonatas or flashing cleavers, yet who's to say she wasn't waiting inside?

To spring a trap?

"Ridiculous."

I continued around until a newspaper blew past and flapped against the bars. Of course I jumped at the chance to hide behind a tree. Better safe than sorry.

At the same time, I knew I'd never be able to see through the walls. If anyone was in there, I'd just have to go and find out. Simple. I tiptoed to the gate and scurried right back for no reason at all. She certainly had me spooked. I wouldn't have been surprised to see a witch fly by.

I lit a cigarette and chewed my mustache, switching my worries to the house next door. No gargoyles at the windows. Only one dim lamp behind burlap drapery. But as I crept across for a closer look, a timber wolf leapt out the way Blacky likes to do it.

"Rooooof!"

His bark set off a chain reaction among the other monsters of the neighborhood. I scampered back to my tree and lit another cigarette, deciding to give myself only five more minutes. Meanwhile, I'd concentrate on Auntie's fence and the best way to get over it. I poked my head in my sack of tools. No grappling hooks. Even so, the fence wouldn't be that difficult. The question is, what would I find on the other side?

Disappointment, according to Homer.

"Over the fence and into the s-soup."

My teeth chattered like a brace of crickets as a high-voltage chill shot up and down my spine. I was losing heart.

"T-t-this isn't going to w-work."

CHAPTER 22

FITS AND STARTS
Where strangling Mama threatens domestic bliss

Earlier in the day I felt different. It began around noon with
a long hot bath. I shampooed my hair and scrubbed every
nook and cranny seventeen times. A fresh start is what I had
in mind. The previous evening's encounter with Auntie had
made it clear that the time for hesitation had passed. With an
ounce of gumption, this entire nightmare could soon be
written off as a mere blue period in my biography. Homer
would pawn Auntie's nest eggs, after which I'd spend the
rest of my life patting myself on the back. What a wonderful
thought! I nearly ate the soap.

Climbing out of the tub, I toweled myself down and
doused the crabs with a whole bottle of Witch Hazel. That's
something they hate. One tried burrowing in a crevice, but I
pried him loose and held him up to the light before cutting
him in half.

"Die, motherfucker!"

A new man is how I felt. I trimmed my beard and shadow-boxed with Auntie's soap-rope, then brushed my teeth until the gums bled white. Aristocratic flamboyance is what beamed back at me from the mirror.

"Finally! Finally! Finally!"

Luck, I felt, had swung my way. I sniggered and snorted, then kind of shrieked. Vivette tapped on the door.

"Out in a minute," I told her. "What's for breakfast?"

Donning Mama's bathrobe, I hugged myself with deep affection while waltzing to the kitchen. How simple life was, how beautifully sweet and simple when you know what to do and aren't just mulling things over like a stupid cow chewing some stupid, indigestible cud.

After an omelet and coffee, I cruised the apartment for useful items to bring on my expedition. A battering ram, for instance. Stash caught me borrowing a set of underwear and launched into one of his windy lectures on the Rights of Man. I sat politely at first, letting my mind wander, until it wandered too far. Suddenly I realized I'd have to kill him. No way around it. I'd annihilate the bastard, nail his tongue to his forehead and pour lye down his throat.

"Fry you in electricity!"

He noticed my harsh tone and called for Mama. She came on the run, followed by Auntie, Vivette, the young one, the old one, Blacky and Puss-Puss. A rare get-together.

"Whaz wrong wittim?" asked Mama, tilting her head at me like an intelligent poodle.

"Lectricity," says Stash.

"Ah!" says Mama, as though that explained everything.

Vivette checked the wall outlet to see if I'd been connected to the power supply, which gave me an idea. Why not pretend I'm mentally unbalanced?

"Yip-yip!" I yelled, and vibrated all over like a fishing pole.

Stash pinned me to the floor, but I goosed him where it hurts and scooted off on my knees like a Russian dancer. No one could catch me. The baby yowled and the godmother called me "Anton!" I guess I reminded her of somebody.

Make-believe, of course. I'm a gifted actor and was able to change colors for the hell of it. They tried boxing me in by the dining room windows, but I slipped away easily and could've made it to the living room if Blacky didn't bite me in the ass, thus giving Mama a chance for a full body-slam.

"Be gone! Be gone!" she says, pressing her prayer-book to my forehead and damn near gouging an eye out doing crosses. When she switched to high-speed Latin, I did the same, my tongue flapping so unbelievably fast whole paragraphs emanated at a single burst. Mama couldn't keep up. She sneezed like a horse, threw a death-grip on my ribcage and got us rolling around like that, from the parlor to the hall and back into the parlor, the two of us snapping and snarling like angry chipmunks. When she clutched my windpipe, I clutched hers.

"Ack! Ack!" she said, because I have a strong grip from typing.

My ambition was to see at least one of them turn blue. But Stash booted me in the breadbasket. I maneuvered us under the table and he kept them coming. Finally I had to weaken. Just a moment too soon. They bent her over a chair and brought her back to life with a few measly love-taps.

The next ten seconds would be difficult to describe because not much happened. Mama's dentures had swiveled off kilter and her brassier somehow made it to the top of her head, but she caught her breath okay.

"He...He...He..." she said, swallowing a couple times and pointing. "He tried kill me."

We all knew that already.

"Everything went black," I explained. "Then I heard bells. Must be something I ate."

They couldn't be sure, of course. Mike a murderer? The very idea had them adjusting their eyebrows. Especially the docile way I laid at attention, flat on my back and tame as a corpse. Dangerous? They couldn't quite swallow it. Actually I'm more to be pitied. They pulled at their ears and stroked their chins, exchanging sly grins. The necktie party was off, I could see that.

Even so, I whooped and wailed just to be on the safe side. No time for subtleties. I slammed my head on the floor and rolled my eyes nearly out of their sockets. Vivette zipped to the rescue with a large cognac, even though I protested I didn't even want a small one. Stash hoisted me onto the daybed and Mama stroked my brow, humming a tune similar to *Beautiful Dreamer*. I kissed both her hands and begged forgiveness.

"Oh, Mama! Mama!"

"Michaelishkoo! Michaelishkoo!"

Witchcraft was the diagnosis, brought on by hot baths and arctic drafts.

"Writing his book too much," said Vivette.

His book, huh? My nitwit rating shot sky-high. Once again I was too cute for words and too dumb to take seriously. They brought pillows and blankets and loaned me Stash's furry slippers.

"Skin awful pasty."

True, about eight quarts of blood had rushed to my biceps.

They made me sit up and stick out my tongue. Chicken broth was the answer. Not too heavy, not too light. With plenty of scalding tea.

Vivette massaged the back of my neck while Stash treated us to a fugue on the piano, which got me shivering again. Sleep would fix that.

Auntie eyed me intently. "Better fast."

"Yes, I'm feeling much better."

Vivette fussed throughout the afternoon. More broth, more curative tea. Rest was the main thing. No wine. She wagged a finger in my face. It gave her a charge to boss me around. Later, she brought cookies and milk, which I shared with Blacky, then dozed off for a while, waking up and dozing off until the room darkened and grew smelly with the dinner cabbage. Vivette rattled in with a big steaming platter. Blacky made short work of it.

"Wish me luck," I told him.

"Careful," he seemed to say.

I trailed Vivette to the kitchen to say goodbye.

Our last goodbye!

"I can't sleep all day and all night too. I think I'll take in a movie."

Stash was at the table, shoveling in a mountain of grub.

"Gurgle," he said.

His last gurgle!

I chuckled to myself while strolling up the hall for my raincoat and cap. I took a last look around. Mama was on the sofa with the baby at her feet, the godmother hard at work in the sand, a one-woman skeleton crew. Auntie sat by the fire with a newspaper in her lap and a liter of ice cream.

"See you guys later. I'm going to the movies."

"What movies?" asked Mama.

"It's in English," I blurted, afraid she might get it in her head to tag along.

She hopped over to feel my brow. "Piping hot."

"No, I'm fine."

She loaned me her babushka because my neck was wide open.

"No drinking," said Auntie.

"No, ma'am."

She aimed her spoon at me. "You sure?"

"Yes, ma'am."

I descended the stairs in long graceful bounds, then crossed the courtyard to a spot under the archway where I could see anyone spying from the third floor. I flipped up my collar and crept along the wall to the garbage room. That's where I'd hidden my war-surplus spade, the collapsible model. The first thing that went wrong, I slid it in my shopping bag and the bottom tore out. Time to reconsider. It was mighty chilly, for one thing. A cold front had moved in. I should've worn a sweater. On the other hand, am I a man or a mouse? I found a large potato sack for my tools and slung it over my shoulder. Now I looked like a rat-catcher.

At the Gare du Nord, I found my train okay, but loaded with drunken sodbusters. My potato sack helped me blend in. I kept it tightly closed so no one would notice the bottle of calvados I'd bought at the station. Already they were passing their own jug. Somebody bounced a French fry off my ear, but I ignored it.

"You a foreigner?" asked the scarecrow across from me.

"No, I was born right here in Chicago."

He offered me a pinch of snuff.

CHAPTER 23

TREASURES OF THE AUNT'S SHACK
Where Mike breaks in and breaks out

About twenty of us piled out at Auntie's station. I waited for them to move off, then crossed to my comfy café. I already mentioned that great sadness. I spit out the snuff and climbed the embankment to the far side of the tracks, then tramped through the marsh, around the city dump, all the way to Auntie's private dump, hiding behind several trees before settling in at my favorite, glaring out at Auntie's twelve-foot fence, which turned out to be almost ridiculously easy. No need to glare or get worked up. The bars were tipped with sharp spikes, but I merely pushed my sack through, shimmied up like a monkey and dove over like a jackass.

"Damn!"

I heard something rip and wished I'd brought a flashlight. My feet felt wet. I struck a match and saw one of my coattails waving from the spikes and my feet were ankle-deep in an ice-flecked mud puddle. This deserved a drink. Uncorking the calvados, I took a long pull just as the moon slid from the clouds like a flying saucer, casting an eerie glow over tin cans, oil drums and other interesting paraphernalia, some of it dating back to the First World War. Scrambling up a slag heap, I tumbled down the other side after snagging my ankles in a ball of wire. Now my cap was missing. I sorted through rusty springs, shell-casings, L-shaped shoes, empty paint buckets, broken piggy banks...you name it. I picked up a rat pelt by mistake before locating my cap beside a 1914 eggbeater. Slapping it in place, I stepped through a disemboweled panel-truck on my way to the door. Before reaching it, I hit another trip-line and landed on my kisser. Now my hands were really dirty.

"I should have worn gloves."

Not because of fingerprints. I laughed that off. Even when she finds out, how could she ever go to the cops? I certainly had her over a barrel. My plan was perfect, as long as I got inside. But that appeared more difficult than previously predicted. And how about out here? The prize I was looking for might be small, a jewel box perhaps. But I could take my pick from a thousand hiding places, in the house or under any of these crap salads.

On second thought, if I managed to scale the fence, that meant the local delinquents could do likewise, meaning Auntie would've figured this out herself and stashed everything inside. I was using psychology. Skip the yard and concentrate on the shack.

Fine, except the door wouldn't open. I hadn't expect it to, of course, yet even when I laid into it with all my might it wouldn't budge.

I took a seat and sipped at my apple brandy. There happened to be a chair handy. Looking closer, I saw it wasn't a chair exactly but a toilet bowl with a plywood cover. Right away it tipped over and sent my head crashing into the door, which still wouldn't open.

My mood sagged.

The shutters too were built to last. I checked my sack. Four pliers, nine screwdrivers and a salami sandwich. No dynamite. I should've planned ahead better. This was plain stupid. What I needed was a crowbar or an axe, and an acetylene torch wouldn't have been overdoing it.

On the other hand, while eating the sandwich I wondered if this might be a blessing in disguise. The shack being so well sealed, once inside I could pour on as much light as I wanted without fear of any leaking out to alarm her neighbors.

This triggered another thought. Actually a memory. The summer we lived there following our marriage, Vivette had mentioned a hole Auntie cut in the roof to keep an eye on her enemies. I remembered seeing a ladder in the kitchen. Did it lead to a watchtower? This was my chance.

Steel bands on the rain-pipe made excellent toe-holds, so up I went, sacrificing a few buttons on the way, but eventually reaching the roof and slithering along the shingles until I found the hole okay, totally boarded up and nailed down, tight as a drum. To make matters worse, somebody had slopped tar all over it. Scraping with my spade proved worse than useless. It sprang the wrong way and skittered down the shingles, bang! against the gutter and boom! off the panel-truck.

"Shitballs!"

I skittered down myself, cringing in the shadows in case her neighbors weren't stone deaf. Their dog whined and let out a couple nervous yelps. I waited him out.

"Nice boy."

And as my pulse normalized, I got to thinking about makeshift tools. Certainly her yard offered many possibilities. Snooping here and there, I ran across a six-foot length of pipe that was more or less ideal. I took it to the roof and pried, wrenched and tugged for over an hour, eventually removing all the planks except the last one, which lay directly across the middle. The toughest plank of all! Attempting a shortcut got me stuck on one side and I couldn't fit through the other. More buttons lost and a good deal of my poise.

"That fucking plank has to go!"

I grabbed hold with a roar and tore my pants.

"Sonofabitch!"

Another drink, another smoke, then I busied myself with the planks I'd already loosened, stacking them neatly by the chimney so as to find them easily when the job was finished. That way I could fit everything back in place and nobody would be the wiser. Not that I expected to see my in-laws again. Just Vivette. I'd left a note for her to check the mail-drop at the American Express the first of each month.

Don't worry, everything is fine.

"Stupid, nothing is fine!"

I stretched out on the shingles to recharge my batteries, locking my hands behind my head while ruminating about time and space and joyous childhood events, especially Christmas and Santa Claus. I leapt up and examined the chimney. Too narrow.

"Why is nothing ever easy?"

Reaching under the plank, I felt the bent ends of the nails. More like railroad spikes. The plank itself appeared to have been soaked in concrete. My pliers and screwdrivers were pathetic. The pipe too couldn't be angled properly for leverage. Only one thing to do, I'd break it in half. Stepping to the center, I hopped up and down a little, testing for flexibility. It seemed to have some, about a quarter of an inch. An encouraging sign. With the pipe held across my chest, I bounced higher, figuring if the plank broke while I was doing that I'd only fall a couple feet before the pipe caught the sides.

Boing! Boing!

I started too enthusiastically and nearly sailed into the yard, my heart smacking the roof of my mouth as I hugged the chimney and watched the pipe wheel off in a slow arc to the far side of the house. Stepping back in position, I went at it more cautiously, boinging little by little until I got the hang of it. Which eventually worked. Lots of play in that plank. So I increased my efforts and came down harder, rebounding higher, more and more altitude, until I could've clicked my heels if I'd wanted. Except my foot must've slipped. Or the wind blew me off course. I'm not sure. I shot up like a rocket, flapping my wings at the zenith, and came down like a bronco-buster, one leg on either side of the plank, my ass in the middle, absorbing the full impact.

Rolling to the shingles, I rocked back and forth, my hands cupped to my groin, Mama's babushka clamped between my teeth, ready to call it a day, go home, slash my wrists.

Yet the plank had cracked. I heard it. I'd cracked it with my nuts. Blue flames shot from my nostrils as I scrambled to my feet and gave the plank a good kick. Then two minutes to cool off. I wiped the tears from my eyes, smoked half a cigarette, rinsed my mouth with calvados, then adjusted my pants and did eight or ten knee-bends, shaking the kinks from my joints and generally priming myself mentally for an all-out tug of war. First I wrapped Mama's babushka around the middle of the plank, tying loops at each end for handles.

I closed my eyes, took seven or eight deep breaths and gave it all I had, heaving and hoeing and straining to the limit, until my arms went numb and my ears hummed with blood.

A snapping sound was the first indication of success. This was followed by creaking and crunching and a low grinding noise that grew louder and louder. I dug my heels deeper and pulled harder with my arms, swinging my ass to and fro through a crescendo of snaps, pops and finally an ear-shattering crash that sent splinters flying up and my eyeballs leaping out like cuckoo birds.

"Arrrrrrrrrrr!"

A second later, I knew I'd made it. The plank remained where it had always been, but I was downstairs now, wrestling with stovepipes. Instead of pulling the plank loose, I'd pushed myself through, feet first, straight through the roof.

"What's she going to say when she sees that?"

Twin skylights. One had a plank over it, the other wore my raincoat.

"Damn! Damn! Damn!"

Hacking and hawking, I stumbled in circles through clouds of soot, spitting out long black licorice whips. My sneezing was out of this world.

"Shit! Shit! Shit!"

Not only was I filthy beyond belief, I'd given my head such a rap against the Ben Franklin stove I could still hear the repercussions. If I hadn't been locked in, I think I'd have left then and there. I was sorry now I'd ever come.

It took a minute to see the bright side. As the soot settled somewhat, moonbeams slanted in to reveal many familiar objects, some belonging to the godmother. Also a box of candles on the organ. I decided to shoot the works. Twenty in three rooms disclosed more familiar objects, but no gold laying around. I sat on the bed to gather my thoughts. My throat felt dry, but when I went to the kitchen I found the tap on the blink. No watermelon in the icebox. Halfway up the ladder, it disintegrated before I could reach my calvados on the roof. Not only did I smack the stove again, I had to swallow a second avalanche of coal dust before washing down the first.

"Fuck! Fuck! Fuck!"

The stove caught my eye. A fine hiding place, I thought. Crawling over pipes, I patted its belly. But when I opened the little door, I my tongue cracked like a bullwhip as a black plume rushed out and sent me racing into the living room blind as a bat. I hit the far wall and went out like a light. When I came to, I felt strangely refreshed. I guess I needed a few winks. What did it matter if I got dirtied up and banged around a little as long as I found what I was looking for?

True, and so far I hadn't searched very diligently. I did that now, trotting from room to room with a candle in each hand. No pearls, no rubies, no Stars of India. I sat on the bed to gather more thoughts. I glanced around. Nothing very exciting about the godmother's stuff. Mostly cooking utensils. Where could the rest of it be? The paintings, the silverware, the endless end-tables?

"Going, going, gone."

That was the answer. Auntie had sold it off. Saving me the trouble? I laughed, but not ecstatically. Right away I was scared. Even Auntie's personal crap appeared in shorter supply than I remembered. Fewer boxes, and those that remained contained less in the way of overflow. I split one open. No doubloons, no Kruger Rands. Only an armload of rags and one of those miniature vodkas I'd seen so many of at my engagement party.

How about in the mattress? It was sure lumpy enough. I flipped it to the floor and noticed a telltale rip underneath. My spirits soared. It doesn't take much. Ramming both hands inside, I pulled out a horse's tail and another miniature vodka.

"Why would she want to hide this?"

It was puzzling all right. I drank it anyway, then headed for the icon cabinet where I knew I'd find more. But the cabinet was gone. Not her bicycle. She'd removed it from the ceiling in case I felt like swimming in spokes. As I hit the floor, the top of my head blew off. Frenzy took hold. Bouncing to the ceiling, I ricocheted off the walls and charged everywhere at once, smashing this, that and whatever I could lay my hands on, sloshing through the debris like shuffling leaves in the park. No ermine capes, no mink dusters. Only rags by the ton and more and more bottles. Plenty of those. Not only here and there, but inside her five-gallon cookie jar and everywhere else I looked.

It didn't make sense. If I had a mess of diamonds, I'd have tucked them in the wall behind the icebox where I noticed some amateur patchwork. What I found was a family of mummified mice and another two-ounce eye-opener. It rolled out at my feet. Three-Star Supreme.

I dumped the icebox on its side and became more wild-eyed and stormy as the evening wore on, pitching empties at the stove and plowing through everything with a vengeance.

"Is she pulling my leg?"

I reeled back and got beaned by a hatbox. Inside was a smaller box, labeled *Cartier*. I closed my eyes and said a few magical words, becoming somewhat religious. Don't open till Christmas? My hands shook as I lifted the lid. I shut it fast. I punched the wall.

"No! No! No!"

But it was true, just another of her hundred-proof pranks. "Impossible!"

Why? If I second-guess her, why can't she second-guess me? Or is that third-guessing? And while we run around forth-guessing each other, maybe it's really me I'm fifth-guessing.

This called for scratch paper.

My jaw jutted forward as I knuckled down in greater earnest, examining every square inch of the whole damn place, well into the small hours, hunting for secret compartments and hollow books, tapping the walls like a demented woodpecker.

The icebox contained a camembert cheese.

"Yum! Yum!"

Poking through the coal pile, I uncovered a cigarette case. Silver? Platinum? It was dented and badly scratched, not too valuable. I could barely read the inscription.

ALL MY LOVE ALL MY LIFE.

I stamped it flat and slipped it in my pocket along with the camembert and about half a pound of dust cookies. The cheese was runny but eatable, indicating Auntie had been visiting recently. I ran across a train ticket too, dated about a week ago. I wasn't wrong, in other words, just too damn late.

"My timing stinks!"

I kicked the organ in the teeth and knocked the stove into a cocked hat. No longer worried about forensics niceties, I ripped a post off the bed and lashed out at random, pounding gashes in the sashes and jagged lightning down the walls. The whole shack sort of leaned on its elbow. I didn't care. After all I'd been through, to come up with dog biscuits and one moldy old cheese was just too much. I drained gins and whiskies and used the empties for batting practice. What did moderation matter? I'd go down swinging.

Clinging to the void, Pablo would say.

Tis better to've loved and lost than just lost and lost.

"Fool! Fool!"

I kept at it long after reason had past and the shack was in shambles, refusing to call it quits before the sun had a chance to make it over the brim and get the neighbors rinsing their tonsils.

Pattooie! Pattooie!

I bashed a hole through the kitchen wall and wandered into the backyard, rooting up waffle-irons over here, crankshafts over there. Halfheartedly, you could say. I just didn't have the old zip. Halfwittedly too, since Mama probably knew a thing or two about hallucinating temperatures.

One uplifting thing, the seasons had changed.

Springtime, no less!

Always extremely welcome.

Radiant heat. Blinding light.

As the sun rose higher and hotter, sweat streamed down my face in shiny rivulets of coal dust.

Next door, an old woman threw a window open and yawned at the new day.

I ducked down and giggled, wondering if I could catch her between the eyes with a canister of mustard gas. She disappeared after a minute.

"Who wants a pancake?"

I nibbled a corner off the camembert and washed it down with Old Number 7. No longer angry. Surprisingly sober too. I suppose I'd worked off lots of piss and discord while demolishing the shack. I wondered if Vivette found my note or if it mattered.

Suddenly somebody screamed and it turned out to be me.

CHAPTER 24

COLD FRONTS, WARM FRONTS
Where reason smiles, bows and
marvels at perfect holes

The dog hit the deck and a burly man barged out with his suspenders flying.

Enough mistakes for one day.

I beat it the back way, over the fence and down the road, across the fields to the city dump, clawing my way to the top of the mountain where I could see Paris in the distance, floating way out over the sparkling tin and broken glass, a kind of island in the waves.

I stayed there an hour or so, frolicking in the sun and wallowing in slime. Why is anyone's guess. Unsatisfied with Auntie's private garbage, I suppose taking a crack at what the public had to offer seemed logical enough.

Seagulls circled overhead. Crows strutted nearby. I aimed shrapnel at them and at the beautiful clouds, great fleets of them passing and re-passing, all billowy and white.

In the end, I tumbled down kind of snow-blind and nuts. We may as well face it, my thought patters had lost lots of symmetry. I stuffed glass in my pockets and rubbed muck in my face, as though I'd struck it rich after all. Pay dirt! Actually I found a pretty good sweater. I brushed coleslaw off the design and spiffed up the colors, then loaded a baby carriage high with household appliances and spare animal parts, mostly chicken feathers and rabbits' feet. Balancing a television on top, I pushed off down the road and into a ditch. The dampness hardly matter. Mud, crud or drainage systems, it was all the same to me.

Fair, equitable or cricket is more the dilemma weighing me down. To find a job, of course. Some means of support. That goes without saying. A purpose in life. In the States, where else? Or with the Wilcoxes, why not? Become their dog and serve them faithfully. I actually dreamt once of licking Her Ladyship's legs.

The *Silver Streak* thundered by followed by the *Golden Arrow*, shaking the ground as two-legged lumps scurried to the station, some of them amused, others startled by my smile. Only one paused to go peepee, causing my smile to lock at full-throttle. I kept it there while pacing the platform and all the way to town, kind of frozen on the upswing. Which went against me with the lunch-pail brigade. The camembert too. Ripe cheese arouses people's suspicions.

"Do unto others as you would," I told them.

It helped land me a seat.

"Virtue is its only reward."

I plucked groceries from my beard and smeared coal dust everywhere, shielding my eyes from the blinding glare and not singing very loud, preferring to concentrate on the center of things. In this crowd that was the conductor. I spotted him about the same time he spotted me.

"Tickets, please."

Apple Blossom Time is what I sang.

Reaching in my pocket, I came up with my ticket okay. Neither of us had expected that. Also a handful of orange-peelings and the insides of an alarm-clock. He wanted to know the date, I showed him the date. No need to ask twice. I even worked it in the puncher for him.

"Allow me."

Polite as could be. I steadied his grip and helped squeeze the handles, nodding approval at the perfect hole.

"Well done," I nodded. "And medium rare."

No one was going to catch me on civility issues. I offered him a rabbit's foot on his way back.

"You're probably an expert on holes like this rabbit was."

He didn't know what to say to that, so I said it for him.

"Thanks for the memories."

At the Gare du Nord I touched my cap and pushed my way to the exit with more courtesy than is called for. Everybody was impressed. I bowed and let the ladies off first.

CHAPTER 25

SPRING FEVER
Where Auntie blocks Mike and has
Godmommy take a walk

Not far from the Gare du Nord is a poor man's amusement park where I once beat the Wheel of Fortune out of a bottle of white wine and two packs of chewing-gum. The surrounding cafés are respectable enough, but hardly the style to enforce rigid dress-codes. Or so I thought. A full circuit got me the same raised eyebrows and refusals of service all around. One waiter said I wore enough vegetables and soup-can labels to give him a taste for minestrone. Funny guy. I didn't mind. I found a shady bench facing a sunny fountain that shot spray in the air full of tiny rainbows.

A gorgeous day.

Leaning back, I closed my eyes and tried to picture myself back in the States. Knocking on doors. Drumming up business. Vivette's fondest wish. My father's too. He says thousands of wetbacks pour over the border every day and here I am going the opposite way. It drives him crazy.

A heavy finger tapped my shoulder.

"Move along."

I loafed downhill to the Champs-Elysées, then west to Passy, sticking discreetly to the shadows like the Memory of Winter among so many colorful clothes and jolly faces.

"Bonjour! Bonjour!"

Big puffy clouds and long ribbons of blue.

Across from the apartment, I fed a line to the barman about being kidnapped by robbers and dumped in the Canal Saint Martin.

"Sure they weren't fishermen? You look like bait."

Another funny guy. He let me clean up in the men's room, but had me shy about my story. I rehearsed it two or three hundred times before summoning the courage to cross the boulevard and climb the stairs. Auntie answered the door.

"Hi! You'll never guess what happened."

She shoved Blacky into the corridor and slapped his leash in my hand.

"I could use a rest," I objected.

"Rest later," she said.

"At least let me change clothes."

She flung the godmother's shawl in my face.

"What's this for?"

She flung the godmother out and slammed the door. I rang the bell, but she let it ring. I thought I'd lean on it all day, but Blacky made like he might crap in the corridor, so I caught the godmother by the elbows and inched her down the stairs until the last three or four we took all at once and skidded into the courtyard like a dance team. The sunshine made her scream.

The concierge poked his head out and asked where we're going. A stupid question because he knows I always walk Blacky around the corner to the Bois.

He chuckled and made a sign to his wife.

"He means the luggage," she said.

"What luggage?"

She smiled and indicated a gash on my forehead. "Does it hurt?"

I had no information about gashes or luggage. I snatched a handful of the godmother's sweater and steered her for the corner. Blacky was already there, prancing from pillar to post with piss on the brain. In the woods I could turn them loose, let them knock themselves out. Godmommy flopped in the dirt while Blacky whirled off like a tornado, snapping at flies and terrorizing pigeons.

What's this about luggage, I wondered. Are they pulling another fast one?

"Daddy! Daddy!" chirped the godmother, splashing dust in the air like a wounded sparrow.

"You think you're at the beach? And how about me, am I a lifeguard?"

She gave me a look like I'm a silly boy, her eyes twinkling, the cataracts gleaming. Seeing? Unseeing? An ant ran across her chin.

"Blacky! Where is that dog?"

He returned peripherally, squirting twenty trees per minute, then swooped in on the godmother and passed his nose under her dress. I gave him a whack, which he took to be playful. He threw his arms around my waist and jazzed my leg, which got him another whack. Both of them were slobbering. The godmother wobbled to her feet only to catch her toes on something and hit the dirt like a sack of oats. Of course Blacky was right there with his nose. When she tried to stand, he gave her a boost. I kicked him in the slats and chased him with a stick. The squirrels threw nuts at us.

"Time to go home."

They wouldn't hear of it. The godmother put on one of her frowns of a thousand wrinkles while Blacky charged into the bushes and returned with a toad in his mouth. I made him spit it out.

On a balcony across the way, a woman sat up in her deckchair and flashed her sunglasses at us.

Fuck it, I thought, and stepped behind a tree for a piss. It came out like tomato soup. Blacky slunk over for a sniff.

"I must've strained myself."

We moseyed downhill to my bottomless well. The planks were back in place and a new sign proclaimed how dangerous it would be to fall in. Blacky tugged at my cuffs as I skipped across for a thrill. Godmommy staggered over and started peeling the sign.

"Lost and Found Department," I told her.

Cold air seeped between the planks, and when I lifted one, a sudden gust smacked me in the face along with the kind of smell that brings back memories.

That's when it dawned on me.

"Why am I so stupid?"

Take a walk! Here's the leash! Where's the luggage?

CHAPTER 26

HOLDING THE BAG
Where craven getaways spark
righteous indignation

"Is it true?" I asked Vivette. "There's no use lying. The concierge told me everything."

"Close door," said Auntie.

"Ha! Did you hear that, Vivette? Close door, she says. Should I close my mouth too? How about my eyes? Maybe I'll blow out my brains."

"Please, Mikie."

"Oh, please my golden balls."

Stash was in the living room wrestling with roadmaps. I ran in there for a peek over his shoulder and he chucked me under the chin.

"Why doesn't anyone tell me anything?"

Mama spotted the godmother and threw her hands in the air. "What you done to her?"

"She fell down."

"Mine God! How we can leave her so?"

I wagged a finger at Vivette. "Who's leaving where?"

"Mama, Stash, Auntie..."

"They're leaving?"

"Yes."

"What about us?"

"We stay."

"Stay?"

"Yes."

"With the old lady?"

"For little while."

"Are you crazy?"

"No."

"What do you mean no? Don't you see what's happening?"

"Yes."

"Look at me, Vivette. I'm trying to control myself."

"Thank you."

"You're welcome. Now listen. Have they coughed up any dough?"

"Auntie send some."

"Send some?"

"Yes."

"In a pig's eye!"

Auntie slapped an envelope across my face on her way by. I opened it and showed Vivette. "See, two thousand francs."

"Yes."

"She just sent it."

"She send more maybe."

"More maybe bullshit! Don't you grasp the situation? We're the fallguys, the patsies. I knew, of course. I knew all along it would come to this. Look at me, Vivette. We're done for. You understand that, don't you? Why can't you look at me? You're in on it, is that it? Sure, you've been keeping it under your hat."

"We go too."

"Go to where, the Big House?"

"America."

"America! And live in Beverly Hills, I suppose. Oh, I see it all. You're an easy mark, my darling, you stuttering imbecile. What have they been feeding you?"

"Mr. Stenko..."

"Ah, Stenko, by all means, let's ask Stenko something I don't know. What a dumbbell I've been!"

Auntie shoved a note at me.

"What's this? Did you see this, Vivette? Instructions, no less. There's your benefactress for you. Chief Crazywhore! We're supposed to follow her instructions inside-out and to the ends of the earth. To America! To the guillotine! Ha! What a joke. It's a funny one, don't you think? A goddamn crying shame! Should I tell her what we think of her instructions? Choreography for the Exercise Yard. I'm not wrong, am I? Should I help them pack? Christ Almighty, hold me back! Don't let me lose my head. Murderers! You won't get away with it. Vivette and me are blowing the whistle. Hear me, assholes? We're spilling the beans. Signed confessions. You want to, Vivette? They'll go easy on us, the cops. I know how they think. They'll suspend our sentences. Because we're young and dumb. Especially you. I can prove it. But that's good, see? We're small potatoes. They'll want the big cheese. Moneybags. Your beloved aunt. Stop blinking, for Christ's sake! Tell her for me, please. I don't trust myself. Go on, put a bug in her ear. Did you hear what Vivette said? Me and her are emptying the bucket, ratting you out. It'll be thumbs down when we get through."

No one seemed interested. Mama paraded back and forth like a hero of the Shipping Department, while Stash juggled suitcases and picnic baskets. Auntie stood by the hall mirror with last-minute beauty secrets.

I ran up to her. "I know a taxidermist."

"Careful what you say it."

"Careful, my ass! We're turning state's evidence. That's what they call it, Vivette. Quit the damn blinking! Tell her what we decided. Self-preservation. It's only natural. We'll save our own skins. You agree, no? I don't exaggerate too much, do I? Am I delusional? Go ahead and say it. He's wacko. Imagining things. Another Joan of Arc. I have visions, voices in my head. I make it all up. Are those suitcases or what are they? Describe what you see. Our reward. That's the thanks we get. Miss Euthanasia over there. Her roots in Boot Hill. Okay, maybe you're right. We'll just stand around blinking. Who cares? My conscience is clear. No regrets. Holy Christ, I'm shouting because I want them to hear! You're a sweet kid, Vivette, but you're thick as they come. Do I have to draw pictures? Palm trees and five-star hotels. Not for us. Hell no! Don't make me laugh. We're the saps, the super-dupes. Isn't that obvious, plain as day? Okay, join them if you want. Take the kid with. I'd prefer it that way. Just me, Blacky and Raggedy Ann. Perfect! You can't improve on it. Drop me a line when you get a chance. Here, Stash, old buddy, let me give you a hand with that crap. You dizzy sonofabitch! I'll see to it you're nabbed at the border. That's right. You won't get far. Take your hands off me. I mean business."

I hauled off with both fists and woke up under the piano, Blacky licking my face. I pushed him aside and flew to the windows.

"Stop those Russians!"

CHAPTER 27

CASHING IN

Where Homer provides travel money and a crash course in salesmanship

Too late. Stash's internal combustion contraption had already swung into traffic. Mama heard me yelling and pressed her crucifix to the rear window.

I turned to Vivette. "We're getting out of here."

"Where?"

"Shut up and hand me the phone."

I rang up Homer and begged him. Anything! If only he'd come to our rescue.

"Slow down," he says. "Start from the beginning."

"I came home. I couldn't find anything. Nothing! Stash beat me up."

"They left?"

"Didn't I just tell you? Gone. Took off. They're not here anymore."

"Let me call you back."

"What's that noise? Is somebody with you? Damnit, Homer, why can't you be a pal for once? I'm sick and tired, running a fever or something. A few minutes ago I was pissing wood."

"Wood?"

"Blood. I was in the woods pissing blood."

"Where did he hit you?"

"Who?"

"Stash. You said he beat you up."

"Slapped me around a little. I didn't say he crippled me. For Christ's sake, none of that matters! Money. Airline tickets. We have to get a move on."

"You said you're pissing blood."

"Probably from when I fell through the roof."

"What roof?"

"Would you forget all that shit. We have to hurry. To the States. That's our best bet, don't you think? Auntie left two thousand francs and I have eight hundred or so. If you could let me have another two thousand, say, that'd put us over the top and maybe leave a little extra to start up on. See what I mean? I figure you owe me at least two thousand for the dining-room stuff...Homer? Are you there? Two one-way tickets. The kid can ride on Vivette's lap. We'll dump Godmommy at a hospital somewhere. I don't know about Blacky. I guess he'll make out. Do you need a dog? He's looking at me right now. Vivette too. She's jumping for joy. How about it?"

"The aunt left two thousand francs?"

"And a list of instructions. Go to America, she says. Her first good advice. I'd like to take Blacky, but I guess that's out of the question. Another two thousand should do the trick. Three thousand would be better. What do you say?"

"What time is it?"

"How should I know?"

"Can you meet me on the corner in an hour?"

"Half an hour."

"Make it an hour. And don't come to the house."

"Shit, I know what that means. This is serious, man. My whole life depends on it. What's that noise?...Homer? What's going on there? Who the hell is that?"

"See you on the corner."

"Don't let me down, old friend. It's the last favor I'll ever ask."

"One hour."

"Wait."

I wanted to ask which café, but he hung up.

"That does it," I told Vivette. "Get packed. And wipe that stupid smirk off your face."

"We lunch first."

"I'm not eating with crazy people."

No time for a bath. I changed clothes, splashed around at the sink and headed for the Metro. Homer's corner is actually six corners. Three cafés, two shoe stores and a church. I saw him at none of the cafés, so I sat on the steps of the church until a wedding party burst out and scared the life out of me. I'm not sure why. I jumped a mile in the air and galloped down the street like the whole world was after me. I rested under a tree, trembling so bad I could hardly light a cigarette.

Maybe my last day in Paris, over three years of solid failure.

I cruised the cafés again and finally took a table at the one with the best view. I ordered a beer and right away spilled it.

"Sorry," I told the waiter. "I guess slobs like me ought to use glasses with two handles."

He must've misunderstood, because he brought two more beers. I emptied them the same way. They simply floated to the ceiling like balloons, then crashed to the floor like beer again. Homer appeared just as the waiter was rounding the bend with an evil look on his face. I slapped twenty francs on the table and raced out the door, past Homer, clear to the corner and across the boulevard.

"Hey!" he yelled. "The car is over here."

I ran back. "What car?"

He had a Volkswagen parked by the church with a grandfather clock strapped to the roof. In the back seat was an Ethiopian girl named Dominique whom I knew slightly from Montparnasse. She normally hung out with her ugly sister Honorée, but was on her own today and appeared to be asleep.

"Shouldn't she be in school?"

"She's old enough."

"Do you have the money, Homer? Vivette's packing."

"A thousand francs, you say?"

"Two thousand. Three would be better."

"I'll have to go to the bank."

We crossed the river at Invalide and wound through side streets for ten or fifteen minutes.

"Where is this bank?"

"You'll get your money, don't worry."

"I notice you're even double-crossing the river."

He frowned. "How are you going to live in the States?"

"On interest-bearing notes."

"Seriously."

"I'll get a job like everybody."

"You won't be happy."

"Yeah, not like now."

"How about sending Vivette and the kid and you stay here? Your parents won't mind."

"With Interpol on my ass?"

"You're hardly an arch criminal. Anyway, Paris is big. Just steer clear of Passy and you'll be fine."

"Should I pitch a tent at the Select?"

"That's where Dominique can help. She and Honorée have a studio by Pasteur." He smiled at the rearview mirror. "You're going to help old Mike, aren't you, sweetie?"

Dominique opened her eyes and yawned, which I suppose was as good as an answer.

"So I divorce Vivette and marry Dominique?"

"You move in with her and Honorée and write up a storm."

"Look, Homer, if you don't want to pay me, just say so."

He swerved around a bus onto the Champs-Elysées.

"When would you leave?"

"As soon as possible."

"You'll be sorry."

"So what? I've been sorry all my life."

He pulled to the curb by the bank and climbed out. "There's a bottle of wine under the seat."

"How long do you think you'll be?"

"Where do you think you're going?"

"I thought I'd grab a beer. I don't feel like wine."

"Get back in the car and keep her company."

I'd forgot about Dominique. "Sorry," I told her. "This must be boring for you. Other people's troubles and all. How's your sister?...She's fine, I imagine. Would you like a cigarette?...I don't blame you. Nice day, isn't it? Excellent weather is what I mean. False spring, the French call it, so I guess we can expect a cold snap by the end of the week. I always say...Well, never mind what I always say. I talk too much. Not like you. Thoughtful. Discerning. I admire that in people. Self-control. Are you looking at that cloud over there? How about this one over here? Like a swan."

"You come live with us?"

"What?"

"Homer says you come live with us."

"No, honey, I'm married. It's nice of you to offer and everything, but you shouldn't listen to gasbags like Homer. One crazy idea after another. Cultivate boys your own age, that's my advice. Finish school first."

Homer slid in and dropped a sheaf of banknotes in my lap. "Five thousand."

"Gee, thanks! I'll never forget this."

"We both know you're lying." He started the engine and jerked a thumb at the back seat. "Has she been bending your ear?"

"A quiet girl."

"The perfect roommate. You ought to think it over."

"How about an airline office? I think there's one by Etoile."

"What you plan doing with the godmother's stuff?"

"What stuff?"

"They didn't sell the beds, did they?"

"No."

"Well, there you are."

"What do you mean?"

"Is the piano still there?"

"Yes."

"You could probably get two thousand dollars for it."

"Dollars?"

"Sure."

"Really?"

"Now that you have free run of the place, why not take advantage? A quick sale could net you ten or twelve thousand."

"Dollars?"

"Sure."

He had me chewing my lips and massaging my thighs. "To tell the truth, I was toying with the same idea, but thought there wasn't enough time."

"Two or three days. It'd be worth it, don't you think?"

"I guess so."

"I'll give you a hand."

"Would you?"

"Sure."

We stopped for a beer and to discuss details. Actually I had five or six and became fairly euphoric.

"It can't miss!"

Homer suggested a light snack, but I told him Vivette could handle that, so we drove to Passy and spent the rest of the afternoon taking inventory. The chicks tidied up the place while Homer hung his thumbs in his belt and tramped from room to room, rattling off a barrage of rapid-fire Blarney stones concerning value enhancements, margin differentials and discounts for bulk. I stayed one step behind, banging into him now and then, trying to jot down all he said about asking prices, selling prices and whether anything was flawless, semi-flawless or chipped. The godmother wanted to play hostess and kept getting under our feet, so we put her in a three-legged race with the hall coat rack.

"Better keep her out of the way on the day of the sale."

He sent Dominique out for labels and got Vivette shoving the vacuum around. A discreet auction is what he envisioned. Two days to pass the word throughout the heirloom district, then off to the States with my pockets bulging. He talked so fast, I had trouble catching half of it, my head ringing like a cash-register with crazy markups, write-downs and all kinds of hidden features. The bathtub, for instance, was cast in 1888 and big enough for a sea lion.

"You think it's worth anything?"

"Six hundred easy."

I'd never have guessed it. The stove too was a luxury model, as were the refrigerator and toaster, while many lamps and chairs would fetch at least a hundred francs apiece, not to mention the rugs and wax apples, the curtains, the mirrors, maybe the whole damn fireplace.

"They no longer make them like that."

Anything not sold at our rock-bottom minimum would go to Homer at ten cents on the dollar.

"You don't want a real cut?"

He smiled sweetly. Seeing me rake it in would be reward enough. All he asked was that I give serious consideration to moving in with Dominique and Honorée while my wife and child sail off for the unknown like Lewis and Clark.

Homer never gives up on an idea.

He tested all joints and seals, fingered materials, and even felt Vivette up a little. That made me see red, but they laughed me out of it. I'm such a prude! Vivette blushed like a tomato and Dominique pinched my ass.

"What's this?" says Homer.

"A toilet, what's it look like?"

"Antique."

He flushed it six times.

"Who's going to buy a toilet?"

"You'd be surprised."

Even Blacky's rug had a special pattern to it.

I waved a hand at the walls. "How about these paintings?"

He shook his head sadly. "Forty francs for the frames."

We stood in somber silence, scanning the many clean patches where the best masterpieces had vanished.

He slapped me on the back. "Cheer up...Does this clock work?"

"No."

"Sure it does."

"I'll be damned!"

All it needed was coaxing. He spun the dials and got it to chime.

"Gee, Homer, you think I could get a hundred for it?"

"Five hundred. I'll give you twenty right now."

I was proud of our merchandise. So was Vivette. She started repeating everything he said like a parrot. Even Dominique livened up with a happy hoot and clapped her hands when I presented her with a seal-skin coat I found behind Auntie's wardrobe. I squeezed one of her tits when Vivette wasn't looking.

In the end, he had us all on Cloud Nine. Me the worst, I'll admit that.

CHAPTER 28

AUCTIONS AND AIRPORTS
Where America gets an influx and Godmommy a nursemaid

Vivette and I watched Homer and Dominique cross the courtyard as the sun went down. They looked up and waved, and that's the last we saw of them, otherwise things may have turned out different. As it is, we couldn't get over the mighty leap in our fortunes. Joining hands, we waltzed around the living room like a couple Viennese barn-dancers.

"You're going to love the States."

She thought so too.

Too keyed up to sleep, we stayed up all night waxing floors, typing fliers and strategizing about prices, always hiking our estimate of what we'd take in, until finally fixing our sights on seventy-five thousand dollars as dawn shimmered across the rooftops in a golden haze...although Homer had said eighteen thousand was more or less the upper limit unless the godmother could be passed off as the long-lost Czarina.

Two days went by. One o'clock Saturday afternoon is the hour we'd set to receive buyers. Wealthy connoisseurs is what we had in mind, whereas the kleptomaniacs who showed up must've been straight off the flea markets. I couldn't blame Homer for that, except he promised to be on hand and wasn't. I phoned all morning, but he never answered or showed up. I don't think I'll ever forgive him for that.

Now the apartment is empty and I've worked up a whole new set of aphorisms on the subject of suicide.

The time for courage is when all else fails.

Vivette and the baby left over a month ago. It's just me, Blacky and the old lady. The cat ran off the day of the sale, or he got himself bagged. Godmommy searches high and low, but she'll never find him.

"Jacques!" she calls.

It's the same name she calls me.

To set an elegant tone, I wore the silk suit Auntie bought me for my wedding. Robin's egg blue. I chopped my hair to the nub and even dabbed powder at the temples to create the illusion I'm older than my years and a man of distinction. A lot of good it did.

I may never speak to Homer again. If he'd shown his face those first hours afterwards, I think I'd have killed him. Everything changed hands but money. We were unloading like hotcakes and I got to thinking I'm a natural-born auctioneer. I could sell anything! But it was all carry and no cash. A real letdown, especially for Vivette. I think it affected her brain. Once the vultures had left and the full impact of our disaster struck home, I thought a philosophical outlook would be best. I could see she was upset. I shrugged my shoulders and gave her a little pat.

"Well," I said, "at least they didn't get the stove. Do you feel like a cup of coffee?"

She threw both her shoes at me, then stormed out of the apartment and didn't return for several hours, barefooted and inconsolable, a screwy smile on her face. Understandable, of course. Dashed hopes and all. I let her simmer for a while before introducing friendly small-talk and trying the coffee gag again. It got me nowhere. Without a word, she tipped the cup upside down and went to bed.

Understandable, like I said. The day of the sale she woke me bright and early and really knocked herself out. Final preparations. The place already looked great. Billowing curtains, glistening floors, an overpowering smell of wax. Still, Vivette isn't one to settle for spic-n-span half-measures. She tied her hair in a bandana and chased down all those pesky details that make all the difference - dusting light bulbs, polishing doorknobs, then she fixed little sandwiches. I rigged up a kind of podium by the fireplace.

"Hear ye! Hear ye!"

The buyers arrived in twos and threes and set a nice steady pace. No shortage of high bids. They simply backed up their vans and whisked everything out the door like magic, even fighting each other for the privilege. I never suspected antique dealers could be so unscrupulous. Vivette collapsed on the staircase trying to save this and that, mostly bathroom and kitchen stuff. If she hadn't put her foot down and her life on the line, I think they'd have swiped the clothes off our backs.

No question of calling the cops, of course. Everybody seemed to know that. One toothless hoodlum pushed me in the snoot and said I should make more sandwiches.

Now the floors creak and there's an echo-chamber effect from the lack of furnishings. Only a few francs are left. I count them at night and panhandle during the day. No shoplifting. We get by the good old honest way. Cleaning. Cooking. Shoe repair. Funny how new routines set in really fast.

Godmommy ties me down a good deal with laundry and stuff. General hygiene issues. I also worry she'll wander into the street. She's not exactly muscle-bound, but can just about turn the knob on the front door if she uses both hands.

Blacky reminds me about meals. Stale bread and slippery meat. I mix everything together in a big iron pot.

There's a hammer by the door in case the nephew instigates a police invasion. I intend braining the leader and the others can fill me full of holes. I'd actually welcome bullets. Especially at night. I sit by the windows, smoking, dreaming, envious of distant worlds. I never answer the door. When the phone rings, I pretend we're a Chinese restaurant.

"I can hear you breathing," says Homer. "Is everything all right?"

"Try chow mien, very good today."

We had a disgraceful scene at the airport, Vivette and the baby completely off their rockers. Me too. Bloodcurdling shrieks and big bubbles out our noses. The boarding area was the worst.

Vivette had no idea what I was thinking. And to tell the truth, neither did I until we were already in the taxi and rolling down the river road. We'd put Godmommy to bed and cut Blacky loose on the corner. He chased us down the block like Rin-Tin-Tin.

The idea was to phone the cops about Godmommy just before takeoff.

"No turning back," I told Vivette.

Oddly enough, that's when I decided to turn back myself. I said nothing in the cab, but just stared out the window at the lights on the water. The Eiffel Tower drifted by. Not until we were loping down the concourse with the other globe-trotters did I poke Vivette in the ribs and step out of line. I was the only one carrying fourteen shopping bags. I dropped them at her feet and handed her our bankroll and tickets. We were near the boarding area. Our eyes met and filled with tears. People pushed ahead.

"Be happy," I told her.

"No!"

"Yes!"

A traveler's-aid lady pitched in with a box of Kleenex. I had them scattered far and wide as Vivette turned on her heels and marched off, ramrod straight, the baby's tiny hand in the air. I wound up dancing with a security guard.

"Splitting up with the missus?"

Blacky was in the courtyard when I got back. I petted him so hard he gave me a nip. Apprehensive about the godmother, but when I opened the door, I could hear her snoring. I threw the windows open for the smell and hunted up dry blankets. We have a good supply from the maids' rooms. Also three mattresses from up there and a few salable items. A mahjong set, for example, and two art deco statuettes. Lissome nymphs. Eighty-five francs for those, with a pair of cavalry boots thrown in. Nothing at all for a painting of her son because the frame was warped and the painting itself too dark and creepy. Muddy colors. So dark, you have to move in close to see it's him as a young soldier standing under a stormy sky with four medals on his chest, his hand resting on his own tombstone.

Looking back on it, Vivette's objections didn't amount to much. One symphonic moment, then adios and goodbye. I went to the airport bar until they kicked me out, then paid a floor-sweeper to buy me a bottle. I drank it in the men's room and roamed the waiting areas, half expecting to see familiar coconuts bobbing in the crowd. One big one, one little one. I checked the departure board and inquired about upcoming flights, but the ticket agent acted nervous and signaled to a gorilla in a bulletproof vest. I hotfooted it for the exit. I couldn't pay anyway. Vivette took both tickets so the baby would have a seat.

"The poor baby!"

I erupted on the bus and again when I saw Blacky. I fixed him a special dinner, then did a turn with him in the woods. Later, we sorted through the godmother's personal keepsakes. About ten boxes of them. Cracked photographs and things like that. Thick packets of letters. Postcards from the Dark Ages. The kind of crap even our antique-stealers didn't want.

The concierge shoves our mail under the door, but never says anything. It's like we're in cahoots. Even his wife, the neighborhood magpie, keeps to herself and only yelled at us once about Blacky watering her geraniums.

For grocery shopping, I patronize the open-air market across the boulevard, usually waiting for the price-drop at closing time. Knobby potatoes and limp leeks, whatever's on sale. Free bones for Blacky. He's the only one with an appetite.

The godmother drinks buckets of tea. I stick to the hearty red. She likes honey in it, but I told her honey costs money.

"Money?" Her eyebrows fly up. "I can get you lots."

Twenty naps per day, but she rarely conks out for good before midnight. I roll her into the blankets and fasten a towel underneath. That's when Blacky and I take our longest walks. Prowling the bridle paths, we check out the neighborhood garbage on our way back. He's crazy for leftovers and once found an entire roast chicken. When we get back, I usually tackle the irrigation problem before turning in myself. Or I just let her marinate.

Her keepsakes needed organizing into different piles. A Cyrillic Bible, for instance, goes in my special pile for salable items along with a 1949 railroad pass good for first-class travel between two impossible places. Curiosity pieces, not worth more than a franc or two.

The letters are mostly from her mother. Nobody knows how old she got to be. I've gone through the ones in French. Good spelling. Excellent penmanship. Zero value, of course, although I ran across an interesting death mask and a 1942 document certifying that she was not of the Jewish race. Something for the Holocaust Museum? An envelope taped to the mask contained a crushed rose with a lock of colorless hair tied to the stem.

The rest is dime-store doodads and miscellaneous eyesores. Estonian postage stamps and Holy Land travel brochures. A foot-long cigarette holder. Also a copy of *War and Peace* with a place-marker that turned out to be a snapshot of Tolstoy and Gorky. Pals of the pen. Tolstoy is dressed peasant fashion and Gorky's boots are on the wrong feet, that's what's most striking. All of which raises questions as to the soundness of the literary mind and if maybe I have a chance.

Junk, that's the long and short of it. Broken pens. Punctured parasols. An ivory hairbrush set. Opera glasses. Square kopecks.

The death mask might've been worth something if I hadn't felt a false eyelash stuck to the plaster and thought it was a spider. I tossed the whole works at the ceiling and it came down in a million pieces.

The letters are boring for the most part. Mother-daughter stuff. I read them at night. Only an occasional hint about foreign bank accounts and a real estate deal in San Francisco. Mostly family gossip and fashion tips. Xs at the bottom. The standard advice about balanced diets and Paris is wicked.

"What a load of bullshit!"

School reports. Library lists. Maybe fifty birthday cards. Frayed reminders. An invitation to the ball.

Blacky doesn't get the point. He nudges my arm and sniffs like crazy at the door.

The opera glasses come in handy for spying on the Wilcoxes, whom we haven't caught kissing. Eight o'clock is when they eat dinner. Quite a lesson in manners.

Blacky doesn't get the point of this either. He whines like a violin and knocks my cap off the knob. When I reach for his leash, he spins like a top.

Prostitutes take over the woods from sundown until around four in the morning. That's when the Vice Squad closes in. The girls skip from foot to foot, then scatter in all directions like a hundred Cinderellas. Seventy francs is what they charge. I happen to know from casual inquiry. Even twenty is enough. Which hardly seems fair when you consider the robberies and slashings and how last November one of them turned up facedown in the duck pond.

Blacky stays far ahead and never wants to go home. I pitch stones at his asshole while perusing the gutters. A couple nights ago I found a patent-leather purse containing a hundred francs and a can of tuna.

Vivette writes twice a week on average. The baby is shooting up, I should hurry and join them. Apparently the craze for America hasn't worn off. She landed an "awksome" job dancing somewhere. She doesn't elaborate. "Girls! Girls! Girls!" I suspect.

She also enrolled at a junior college. Drama classes.

Anyone who saw her confrontation with our bargain hunters would give high marks for stagecraft. She managed to stem the tide, but came out of it no better than me. Two fat lips.

My father scratched a few lines. "What the fuck you doing?"

When I returned from the airport, I phoned Homer to say I never wanted to see his face the rest of my life, although I could certainly use a friend more than ever.

"How about coming down for a beer?"

Sometimes it's hard to resist.

Auntie phoned with amendments to her instructions. I imitated a police siren and slammed the receiver in her ear. She promised to send money, but I haven't seen any.

Anyway, it's like I said, we manage well enough, surprisingly so. Shitty prospects and ominous forebodings hardly count for much.

Blacky and I usually bed down by the front windows. There's often a breeze and a slice of moonlight. The godmother has a double mattress. I put it on the floor the other side of the sand pile. Plenty of blankets and pillows, everything salvaged from the maids' rooms.

The electricity will be cut. The phone too. I'm not sure how that works, but judging by threatening letters, Auntie stopped paying a long time ago.

No cops, that's the main thing. No pests to speak of, aside from the nephew. A minor pest. He drops by now and then, always in a stew. Today around lunchtime. He tapped politely at first, then blew his top, raving about torts and malfeasance and all kinds of shit. I thought I'd jump out and push him down the stairs, except this is supposed to be a respectable building.

The Metro station is where I beg for money. Five francs per hour on average. I'm not pushy about it, but just stand to the side with my hand out, perfectly still with the vending machines.

Blacky won't mess with the godmother since she took to whacking him with her shovel. Full-force in the nose. Or she sneaks up when he's asleep and jabs him in the balls.

Not so much lately. She mainly only sleeps, dicks around in the sand.

We let her dress however she pleases, sometimes in multiple outfits. When her arms tangle, the frustration makes her wild and the gravy really flies. Laundry, that's my big headache. I strung a clothesline by the fireplace or nothing would ever dry.

Both of us caught cold the first week and she came out of it with a nasty cough and the complexion of a rubber. I'm okay, a bit run down.

I boil tea nonstop.

We found a doll she likes. "Bijou," she calls him.

The way she sleeps is what worries me. Everything slows to a halt and she actually stiffens. That puts me in a panic, yet she never fails to come around.

"Quack! Quack!" she goes.

I rub her arms and legs to get her started, then fold her over the tub and pull phlegm out like taffy. Gooey gobs of it. She sweats and gags, but if I don't keep pulling she really would sleep.

I'm not the picture of health myself. It's a low fever we have, which can be the worst kind according to the lady at the pharmacy.

People pass in the street.

The click-click of high-heel shoes.

"Où est ma voiture?"

I'm thinking things couldn't have turned out worse if I'd planned it.

Vivette says I should put the bite on her father for travel money. Good idea, except he never answers his phone.

Probably Pablo is a better bet, assuming he's out of the clink. Whenever I call, I get an out-of-service recording, so I'll have to go over there. Not for money, but he could let me stay with him when the time comes. Which might be any minute. I'm afraid I'll walk in some morning and find I can't wake her. I figure that's how it'll be.

CHAPTER 29

BLIND AND BATTY
Where Pablo reminisces and
Godmommy holds her breath

No luck reaching Papa, so I gave Pablo a try. Now I'm sorry I did. He looked like his own grandfather.

Coming up the passageway and into his garden, I could hear singing, a reedy tenor, and looking up, saw him on the roof, splashing paint at a weather-vane. He appeared about six inches shorter and his hair was perfectly white.

"Hey!" I called. "You look like your own grandfather."

He glanced left and right, then straight up at the sky. "Who's that? Who's there?"

"Me, I'm down here."

"Me who, the Avon Lady?"

"Mike. I'm down here."

He dropped his brush and tottered to the edge of the roof, squinting over my head at the yard next door. "Go away, please."

"When did they let you out?"

"Who did?"

"The cops. Looks like they really knocked the tar out of you."

"Where's your partner?"

"Is something wrong with your eyes?"

"No, thank you. I have to finish this by nightfall, then there's the shutters. Up to my ears in shutters. Hold the ladder, as long as you're handy. Don't let it wiggle. Okay, I'm coming down. Steady as she goes. Don't trip me up, young man. I'm not myself these days. Lost my bearings somewhere."

"I'm over here."

"Some kind of piss-poor peep show."

"Can't you see me?"

He cocked his head. "Is that a cigarette or a bomb?"

"A cigarette, you want one?"

"You get plenty of smoke out of it, don't you? What brand? Volcanoes, I bet. Are you old enough to buy them on your own? I didn't start until Fifth Grade. Not in the classroom. Miss Sullivan wouldn't allow it. Read newspapers to us. Moon Mullins, the Katz and Jammer Kids. Never taught us anything. If you chew gum, you're supposed to stick it on the end of your nose, that's what I learned."

"What happened to your eyes?"

"They couldn't make me stick tobacco on my nose, so I chewed the stuff. A lesson in life, try to remember it. Maybe you could light this for me. Your name's White, you say? Bob White?"

"Mike."

"What do they call you?"

"Mike."

"I guess I remind you of somebody. That beard rings a bell. You're not the roughneck who used to steal my plums, are you? Of course not. That cap, it throws me off. Anyway, you're not him any more than me. See for yourself. He hangs out at the Youth Center, they call it. A government billiard hall. You're made from the same mold though. Nip and Tuck. He bought himself a motorcycle. Never owned a beard. Wait a second, I almost got it. Harold. Your name's Harold. What the hell you want, Harold? Can't you see I'm up a stump? Pressed for time. A strict diet of pills. These are the best. Have one. They'll help you play the bongos."

"Stop clowning, Pablo."

"You're spoiling my day with that cap."

"If you see my cap, you must see my face."

"Now, now, Mr. White, hands off. You some kind of homo sapiens? Who'd forget a cap with a beard? Selling something, are you? Brushes or vacuum cleaners? Try next door. Encyclopediacs, they fall for anything. Insurance. Lightning rods. Tell them you're working your way through college. You could unload that cap on them. Out you go. That's a good boy. No Tupperware today. I'm an artist with no vision. Scar tissue. The work of John Law. Those knuckle-dusters at the Sixth Precinct. They tied me to the bars and stole my watch. No trick escaped them. Cry uncle, that's what they want. I should wither under the strain. Never! I spit at their badges and peed down their legs. That's shortly before Dreamland. Probably I bumped my head. Blue stars. No idea what time it is. My knees buckled and my hearing buzzed. For a while there I thought I was in New Jersey. Awoke in my present fog. The long arm of blindness. No perspective. Can you imagine? A painter with no perspective! I warned them. Go easy, I says. Pretend I'm wearing glasses. Poor listeners. We sit down to piss, my wife and I. Never married the woman, but she'll bring home the bacon. Faithful. Devoted. She sticks like glue. Take my hand, she says. I will be your eyes. Can you beat that? I'm supposed to paint the roof with her eyes. An hour ago I landed in the bushes. Could've broke my neck. Not that I'm complaining. That would be the best for everybody concerned and unconcerned."

"Don't say that, Pablo."

"Say what?"

"Your eyes will get better."

"You think so? Have another pill. I've changed my mind about you, Harold. You want a drink?"

"No, thanks."

"Me too. How about them cigarettes?"

"You can keep the pack."

"Want to buy me a carton?"

"Tomorrow."

"Don't forget the matches."

I caught the first bus for Passy and found the godmother worse than ever. Every day it's worse, her skin pastier, the saliva stickier. I shoved ten fingers down her throat until she fought back. That's how I knew she'd be okay.

"Quack! Quack!"

I stripped off her nightdress and drew a hot bath. The hotter the better, it loosens her up. Then lifting her out, I slipped and we hit the floor pretty hard. It set off an explosion in her lungs like a string of firecrackers. Right away she caught the shivers. I hurried and dried her off and wrapped her up like a caterpillar.

Her bed needed a complete overhaul.

Later, I took a bath myself.

A storm blew in during the night. A real typhoon. When I got up to close the windows, I saw her eyes were open.

"Water," she says.

She managed to sip a little.

"Bijou."

That meant hunting for her doll.

We chatted for a while, mostly about how nice Bijou is. Really stupid stuff, even stupider than Pablo. Her throat kept going dry, so I wet a rag for her to suck on and mashed up an apricot with a spoonful of honey.

"Time to sleep."

"No sleep."

Her mattress was damp on the window side, so I shifted it around and shoved it against the wall, stuffing pillows down her back so she'd sleep more or less perpendicular and not drain the wrong way. She wouldn't stop jabbering. Bijou this, Bijou that.

Finally I heated a cup of wine. That always knocks her out.

CHAPTER 30

PAPA COMES THROUGH
Where Lady Luck intervenes to send
Mike on a toot

"You're in charge," I told Blacky, and stepping back, gave the godmother a final inspection. "Whatever you do, don't lay flat. Remember what happened last time."

I'd finally reached Papa and invited him for tea, but he said he couldn't make it. I'd have to go to his place.

"I need help," I warned.

"We all need help, my son."

A noble thought.

He lives near to the top of Montmartre hill, where the big white church, Sacré-Coeur, rises high over the neighborhood like a great magnified moon. X-rated movie houses and transvestite hookers dominate the lower half, making for a sleazy atmosphere that I think Freud would have loved.

I asked directions at a Moroccan snack shop and was told to continue on up until the lampposts peter out in an unlit square. Papa's building is to the left, a low-budget affair of peeling paint and crumbling plaster.

My last ten francs had gone on beer that afternoon trying to work up the courage to ask a doctor at the Neuilly Hospital to examine my medical miracle. The reception lady wanted Social Security numbers and things like that, so I backed off and wandered outside, studying the comings and goings until I noticed a professional type sauntering in from the parking lot. I cut him off at the entrance.

"My grandmother..." I started.

"Yes?"

"She's very old, coughs all the time. Do you think you could take a look at her?"

"Certainly. Have you made an appointment?"

"Couldn't you just drop by when you get a chance, maybe on your way home?"

"You'll have to make an appointment."

I buttonholed a nurse for the same advice and bummed a franc off her. I used it to call Papa.

"Fifth floor," he says. "Red door at the end. I'm here all night."

Navigating his staircase is tricky because the banisters are detachable and the light-timer only activates at three-second intervals. Halfway up, I met a drunk tumbling down from the floor above. He hugged a bottle to his chest while sliding headfirst and upside-down, finally bumping to a stop when his head hit the landing, his legs pointed up the stairs.

"Disgraceful," he says, blinking up at me. "I'm so embarrassed!"

I helped him to his feet and asked if he knew which door was Papa's. He nodded, burped, then back-pedaled to the next flight of stairs, which he took the same way.

I leaned over the railing. "Are you all right?"

"Glitter-Glitter!" he says.

The lights went off, but with the help of matches, I found Papa's door okay. Red, sprinkled with silver glitter. I gave it a gentle rap.

"Enter. It ain't locked."

A modest studio, one room and a kitchenette, but decorated so lavishly I thought for a moment I'd stepped into a greeting card factory. Two overstuffed chairs and a matching sofa dominated the center of the room. Each was covered in psychedelic pillows, multicolored teddy bears and at least one frosted cupid. Between the sofa and chairs was a coffee table made of painted seashells.

"Oh!" said Papa, seeming surprised to see me.

He took my cap and grinned slyly while locking the door, then scooted to a full-length mirror to smooth the contours of the housecoat he wore that appeared to have been sewn together out of flock of parakeets.

"Sure it's okay, I'm not disturbing you?"

"Sit, honey."

"Thanks."

I chose the sofa. Lavender velvet. The wallpaper was raspberry red, the carpet electric blue.

"Want coffee, honey?"

"Thank you."

He zipped into the kitchenette and swung out with a tray-on-wheels.

"Who sends you?"

"Nobody. I'm alone now except for Vivette's godmother. You know, the one in Passy."

"Others leave?"

"Yes. Six, eight weeks ago. Vivette's in America."

"California?"

"Probably. I was supposed to join her, but something came up."

"I see."

"Actually, that's why I'm here. The godmother isn't at all well and I can't really cope anymore. She needs to be institutionalized."

"You can't stay here."

"No, no, I had no intention..."

"Want sandwich?"

"Thank you."

He slapped ham and cheese into half a baguette and dropped a pickle in the middle. "Nice flat I got, ain't it?"

"Yes, very nice."

"Curtains is new."

"Yes, very new."

"Trouble is him."

"Him?"

"My friend."

For a moment I thought we were discussing the plaster Adonis on a stand by the windows, but Papa abruptly leapt to his feet and dashed past the Adonis to poke at the curtains.

"You expecting somebody?"

"Any minutes."

"Well..." I put the sandwich down and checked my watch, even though I wasn't wearing any. "I better be going. Thanks for the sandwich."

"Thought you need money."

"I do."

"I give you some."

"Really? That would be wonderful. Of course I can't pay you back right away, but when I get to the States..."

"How much you need, honey?"

"Whatever you can spare. For the godmother, you understand. I found a top-notch doctor, but he wants cash in advance, to paint her palate or whatever." I examined my wrist again. "Actually I should hurry. She's not safe on her own."

"Five thousand okay?"

"Fine! Great!"

I cleared a place on the coffee table for him to count it out.

"Must leave then."

"Sure. Right away. Like I said..."

"Be terrible jealous."

"Who, your friend?"

"Mr. Trouble, I call him. See hands?"

I joined him at the windows. "Is he at the café?"

"Umbrella. Strong, strong hands."

Half a dozen men stood at the bar across the street, but only one carried an umbrella, open, as though the roof leaked. I couldn't see his strong hands, but judged his shoulders to be about two yards wide and his height around nine-foot-six.

"Great-grandfather killed Rasputin."

"His great-grandfather?"

"Strangled him."

"Do you have the money?"

"No."

I did a quick jig. "You said five thousand francs."

"He got it."

"Him?"

"Always lots of money."

"Would he give it to me?"

"No give, we take."

"Take?" I eyed him up and down. "How do you mean?"

"Like that," he says, snapping his fingers and cackling in such a way I realized I must be awful stupid to think I could deal with this lunatic.

"Thanks anyway," I said, and headed for the door.

"Wait."

I didn't. I continued across the room until he caught me from behind and rushed me smack into a pile of clothes hanging from the door. I tried to break free, but Papa has pretty strong hands himself.

"Stay," he says, smothering me in overcoats. "I get you the money."

"You can mail it to me."

He pressed a finger to my lips. "Shshshsh."

Somebody was coming. Heavy shoes clumped up the stairs and across the landing, stopping outside. The knob rattled.

"Feets," Papa hissed. "Hide feets."

"The dishes," I hissed back at him, getting into the swing of things. "Get rid of the dishes."

Boom! Boom! Boom!

Papa buzzed here and there, fluffing pillows and clearing away debris, while I flattened my back against the door and buried myself deeper in overcoats, wondering what my chances would be of landing on a hay wagon if I dove out the window.

Boom! Boom! Boom!

"Who's it?" chirped Papa, tossing me my cap.

"Me!"

"One minutes, please."

"Open door!"

"Is open, no?"

"No!"

Papa paused by the mirror to tidy his appearance, then trotted to the door and jammed the key in backwards, fiddling with the latch and winking at me, as if to say we're having lots of fun with Mr. Trouble.

"Lock don't work right, darling. When you going to fix it?"

"Open blasted door!"

Boom! Boom! Boom!

Click!

"Entrée!"

Wooosh!

I rose to my toes and swung with the hinges. The door slammed shut and I tiptoed back with the clothes, blushing now because they were kissing. Time to beat it, I thought, except Papa indicated with his eyebrows I should hang on. I didn't want to, but he got them wiggling really fast, meaning I should get ready to catch a wallet between my teeth. I never saw it coming. It bounced off my face and I snagged it before it hit the floor. A nice fat one! I could've kissed Papa myself, except three is a crowd. He implied this himself with more eyebrow language.

I'm pretty tactful with hinges. In two seconds I was out the door and tearing down the stairs at a hundred miles an hour. On the ground floor, I removed the cash and slid the wallet in Papa's mailbox. Eleven hundred smackers! Not what he'd promised, but worthy of celebration nonetheless. I lit out for Montparnasse, figuring an hour or two on the town couldn't be held against me after all the misery of the past weeks.

An aperitif at the Select, steak and mushrooms at the Dôme, washed down with premium wine and a couple top-shelf cognacs, then a beer across the street, four or five at the Cosmos, another two or three at the Rotonde and the Rond

Point, a bowl of chili at the Rosebud, topped off with more beer, more wine and a jug of absinthe, I think, although I'm not sure where.

I awoke in the Cemetery of Montparnasse, soaked to the skin, a gentle rain falling.

"Sonofabitch!"

Rising to my knees, I noticed a smudge of light in the eastern sky.

"Holy Christ!"

A plastic bag hung from the headstone in front of me. Inside were cough drops, razorblades, aspirin tablets, dry mustard, a tube of toothpaste, one smoked sausage and two cartons of Gauloises. Apparently I'd found time to go shopping. Fumbling in my pockets, I came up with only forty-one francs.

"Goddamnit to hell!"

No telling what I'd find at Passy. I tried to recall if I'd fed Blacky before I left. I pictured him standing over the godmother like a mountain lion.

"The poor old lady!"

CHAPTER 31

DEATH OF AN OLD DOLL
Where the godmother finds her way in the absence of moonlight

Blacky met me at the door. No blood on his mouth.

"Is everything okay?"

He sniffed out the sausage and downed it in three gulps.

No sign of the godmother. I cocked an ear and listened. No snoring, no sound at all. I did a quick turn up the hall, glancing into bedrooms, the bathroom, the kitchen, the parlor, then trotted through the dining room and living room, weaving around yellow-brown puddles, past the sand pile, and found her on her mattress, more or less how I'd left her, except completely hidden under blankets, one cramped hand sticking out like in a horror movie.

Rigor mortis, I thought, but hadn't the nerve to make sure. I only stood and watched, a lump rising in my throat.

Blacky kept sniffing my pockets.

"Go away."

Finally I inched closer, knelt down and threw off the covers. Her mouth and eyes were open, the eyes pegged to the ceiling, the mouth frozen in a kind of silent scream. Death, I thought, that's what it looks like. But when I brushed the hair from her brow, I felt a cool film of sweat and saw no dilation to the eyes. Pinpoint sharp. And I thought I heard something, a crackling sound in her throat like a Geiger-counter. Not very loud. I put an ear to her mouth and heard it again.

"You're going to be all right."

She erupted before we reached the bathroom. Bubbly white ribbons from her nose and mouth. I laid her on the floor and got the water going, then stripped her naked and bounced her on my shoulders to keep things moving. She couldn't scream through all the goo, but as the room filled with steam, she stiffened in my arms and rolled her eyes like crazy when she saw what was coming. I boiled her like a lobster, dunking her over and over until the water clouded up. I drained the tub and did it again, pounding her back just short of breaking her bones. She fell asleep that way, limp as a rag, but breathing much better. Short and shallow, but much better than before.

The floors needed a good scrub-down. That took an hour or so. I aired the rooms and felt her pulse a couple times, then walked Blacky to the woods and did two loads of laundry before relaxing in the kitchen with a glass of wine. Not much appetite, but I thought I should eat something. A can of peas for Blacky and I sliced a potato for myself, simmering it in mayonnaise. Blacky lapped up the peelings.

We did the walk routine twice more in the afternoon and again after dark. A steady rain had set in. Whenever I checked on the godmother she seemed fine. Resting comfortably.

Around midnight, I stretched out for a snooze. Blacky clunked down and gave me a look, his chin on his paws.

"Go fuck yourself," I told him.

He woke me an hour or so later, yelping and carrying on because I think he trapped a mouse under the stove. When I lit a candle, I saw the godmother had crawled from her mattress to the sand pile. I let her stay there.

"No moon," she said, craning her neck to see out the windows.

"Because it's raining."

"No raining."

I fetched blankets and pillows and bundled her up to the ears, wondering if I should drop a pillow on her face. That's all it would take. If I could rest my hand and concentrate on something else for a minute, everything would be settled.

"Bijou."

I found him in the dark by stepping on his head. I'd have to try fixing him in the morning.

The candle seemed to frighten her.

"No moon."

"I told you it's raining."

"No raining."

"Are you calling me a liar?"

She smiled and arched her back, then said my name, "Michael," which gave me a jolt, her getting it right for a change.

"You're feeling better, I think."

Her nostrils flared and her chest heaved up and down, crackling away. A little popcorn machine. I stretched out beside her and listened for a while, a faint whistle in her nose, her eyes darting here and there over the walls and ceiling with the dancing candlelight. Then her lids drooped and I guess mine did too.

The next thing I knew, someone was pounding on the front door. The candle was out and my mouth full of sand.

CHAPTER 32

TAKE IT OR LEAVE IT
Where rain sets the tone for a few empty words

The neighbors were in a white-hot fury because the deluge in our bathroom had seeped through their rafters. I raced in there to empty the tub and tighten the taps before trotting down the hall to put their minds at rest. My ankles were stiff and my head in a spin, so I lurched like Frankenstein and had trouble formalizing my French.

"Cool it!" I shouted through the door. "Whomever may excuse these what-you-call-it's is justified in the extreme. I mean, there you have it. Everything goes well. Hopefully the circumvention will complete itself upon acceptance of my compliments, if pleased you would deem it to be so gracious, holding forth as I do to the distinction of your jollity."

They gave up after a minute.

Blacky slunk in with his ears slicked back and his tail between his legs.

"What's with you? How come you didn't bark at them?"

He trailed me to the kitchen to boil water for breakfast. I poured it over a teabag with six lumps of sugar, then grabbed a handful of crackers on my way to the living room. I'd paid no attention to the godmother in my rush to wake up, but had my suspicions now the way Blacky squeaked and walked on his elbows the closer we got to the sand pile. I stopped halfway across the room. Her eyes and mouth were open like the previous horror show, except the eyes were milky white now, like crystal balls, and alongside her pillow nestled a gob of blood, rusty brown, about the size of a golf ball.

I placed the tea and crackers on the floor and stepped closer. Her face and arms were bluish and blotchy. I stooped down and lifted one arm. Just a formality. I let it drop. Blacky stayed by the door, half in, half out.

"Now we have a stiff on our hands."

He seemed to know that already.

I lit a cigarette and went to the windows to watch the rain beat down. The same lousy weather almost every damn day. The wind whipped it against the glass and rattled the frame, sending a fine spray through the joints that smelled of wet wood. The concierge was in the courtyard scrubbing trash cans. Saving on water today. He held a bucket in one hand and a long-neck brush in the other, hopping from can to can like the captain of a sinking ship. Out front, a taxi stopped and a young woman scampered off with mincing little steps. Not much traffic on the boulevard. The cafés were open, but not the market. Two schoolboys galloped through the empty stalls with backpacks held over their heads.

The concierge wore a yellow slicker with matching hat and boots.

Having fun, I thought.

Then my nose filled up. My cold seemed to be getting worse. I couldn't decide if I wanted to sneeze or cough, so I kind of did both and felt my eyes brim over. Water streamed from the roof and off the tin overhang of our balcony, then down to the courtyard. Other streams fell from all sides, smacking the cobblestones like clapping hands. The sky was gray, of course, but lighter toward the east where the sun shone through in a silvery patch that reflected off the slate shingles above the Wilcoxes' place and off the roofs farther away, those that cut in from every angle, overlapping and rolling like the sea.

I motioned for Blacky to help himself to the tea and crackers. He crawled on his belly and ate very noisily but fast.

I boiled oatmeal for him and fixed coffee for myself, then fetched a bucket and rags to clean the mess. A couple times I thought she might be clowning and would liven up, but the hours passed and she grew rigid. I covered her with the least repulsive of our blankets and took Blacky to the woods for an hour or so. When we got back, I brought keepsakes to her from the dining room. The sand-bucket and shovel I placed by her head and arranged photos and letters all around. I smoothed the sand and swept it toward the center. Her doll was easy enough to repair with tape. I propped it beside her and stepped back for an appraisal. Pretty hideous. Her tongue protruded and turned black as an eggplant. The washing made her skin glossy. I scraped the crust from her mouth and nostrils and weighed her lids down with twenty-centime pieces. Later, I lit candles and tried to press her legs together, but they'd grown springs in them now. I'd been screwing around too long. In the end she looked like the letter X.

"Rest in peace," I said, unable to work up very personal remarks. I hardly knew her, after all, and certainly not before she'd lost her wits.

"She died as she lived, happy in the past."

That sounded better, but stupid nonetheless. Probably her family and friends would've had heartwarming stories to tell from when she was young. The promise of it all. I couldn't really picture it. Her father might've jumped off a bridge. That's what the police were going to ask me to do. I should've called a doctor. They'll point that out. I should've taken her to the hospital or at least been nicer. Earlier, I'm talking about. I blame that on Auntie. We could've robbed her blind and still...I don't know. Once everything is clear, it seems to lose all meaning.

CHAPTER 33

AN ANGEL FOR THE SELECT
Where Mike strikes out from what he wants to what he gets

I drank two glasses of wine and that's it. What I really needed was a Bolivian passport. I paced the apartment the rest of the afternoon and evening and all through the night, trying to dope out an intelligent strategy. Blacky could be shipped to the States if my parents didn't mind. Or even if they did. Except I'd have to put in an appearance at the embassy and fill out their questionnaires and inoculation forms, livestock certificates.

"You're a Black with no papers."

Around three in the morning, I decided to put off calling my parents until first checking with Homer. I packed my personal belongings, selecting what to save and toss, then whipped together a big breakfast of leftovers for Blacky. I didn't see Homer until mid-afternoon. The sky had cleared and the weather turned really beautiful. Still, it took half an hour of hammering on his door to get a rise out of him. The battle-ax across the way inquired if I'm his son.

"Parole officer," I told her because I'm such a quick wit.

We were chewing the rag, when Homer poked his head out. "The corner," he says. "I'll meet you in five minutes."

Not a chance. I breezed straight past him and ran smack into a Japanese girl coming the other way. She dropped an armload of clothes, gathered them up and bustled off without introducing herself.

"Hand me those socks," says Homer.

I managed to hold his attention for a full ten seconds before he ordered me to pipe down so he could arrange my future by remote control.

One phone call, that's all it took.

Later, he helped me lug my stuff to where I live now. With the Ethiopian sisters, in case you haven't guessed. Dominique and Honorée. They tossed it in the street because their place was too cramped to begin with. Four garbage cans got filled to the brim with notebooks, manuscripts and practically everything else I valued.

The idea was to leave nothing behind. No evidence. They pitched the whole works when I wasn't looking, damn-near all trace of my existence.

"Have you eaten?" says Homer.

We chatted as though nothing had happened. I buttered toast while he explained how lucky I am to know a hero like him who can sell people on my attributes. The world turns. He settled my entire destiny in five minutes.

So here I am. Actually I'm at a café by the corner of his dead-end street. I have him bottled up there. Mainly I only visit to bug him for roomier living quarters. One room and a closet, that's all the girls and I have.

"Even three bats would collide!"

He pretends to listen and pays for the beer. Not much different from the old days. Better in many ways. Enough dough, for one thing, and my roommates need an accomplice only at night. Mornings and afternoons I'm totally my own man, free to loaf through the public gardens to my heart's content. The Luxembourg in particular. There's a military band on Sundays, and I enjoy watching tennis matches and pony rides, toy boats on the pond. Mostly it never rains the past two months. I haunt the gravel paths like a sentimental millionaire, stumbling backwards half the time, trying never to forget what I see. I jot it all down in black and white. The people, the places, the essence of the rooftops. Cloud formations. Already the trees are dusty, their leaves brown and crisp at the edges. Ecstatic shrieks from the play areas stab at the heart like music. There's no question this is a town for sensitive souls.

Pausing by the cement railings, I try to out-staring the statues. Can't be done. Many Queens of France have been at it forever, as have two past presidents and various beasts of the jungle. Stony-still beasts. They hide in the bushes with a poet in bronze, a past-poet, unperturbed by the lion who never blinks.

Pigeons glide from one to the other and high over the fountain to where Apollo and Aphrodite pose on their pedestals twenty feet in the air, thirty yards apart, gazing at each other from opposite ends of eternity.

Such devotion puts me in the mood. Not that I make a pest of myself. Generally I mind my own business and steer for the narrow end where the park takes the shape of a frying-pan handle. There's another fountain to contemplate. Green horses and sea turtles. Which brings me pretty close to the Select. I look out over the flower beds, but not eternally. Usually I cross to the boulevard or sneak around from behind and leave through the side gate with pollen on my nose. A couple days ago a dragonfly bit me. It's hard to fit everything in one book.

June was gorgeous, now it's August. Lazy days, fragrant nights. What more can I say? The race track opened, but I haven't the knack for gambling. I still drink, of course. No change on that score. The girls nag me to slow down or switch to ether. I'm growing a liver like a Strasbourg goose. Mainly this is due to the rich grub we feed each other. Homer won't touch my deviled duck gizzards. When he visits, he almost always brings sandwiches.

"A closet case," he calls me because that's where the girls make me sleep, on top of their dirty laundry.

Disappointed about the crabs, that's what started it. Honorée told me to scram the first night, but Homer talked her out of it. The thing is, I have my good points.

We were supposed to bunk together, the girls and me, that was the original plan. Three in one bed.

"Gosh, Homer!"

"Don't worry about it."

He gave himself a sponge-bath before tucking us in. I think he screwed them both while I was out fetching beer.

"Why can't I stay with you?"

"You're staying with them."

We picked Dominique up at a student café in the Latin Quarter and went directly to their place. Sixth floor. Honorée was waiting with a stern look on her face and her arms akimbo.

"Humph!" she says, reminding me of somebody.

She made me sit with my mouth open while outlining my duties. Homer cut her short so I could describe in my own words why I'm the best man for the job. I preferred facing Dominique because she doesn't bite your head off.

Honorée kept spinning me around, trying to pin me down on salary expectations and how I felt about living in a sardine can. Did I intend sharing expenses? Well, I could hardly sign on for big expenses without an inkling of what my salary would be. And it seemed poor etiquette to gripe about the lack of deck space in front of my hostesses. So I stuck to more universal topics and eventually drifted pretty far afield onto claustrophobic generalities and theories of racism.

Homer cut me short too. He finished all my sentences, took charge of the wine and shot off his mouth for a solid hour. Which eventually sealed the deal. Honorée wound up ninety percent sold and Dominique probably a hundred percent. Me, more or less half a percent. He pulled Dominique on his lap and coaxed Honorée to sit on mine until our chair tipped over.

We ate country bread with blue cheese and dry sausage while Homer filled them in on my adventures in Passy, not exaggerating too much, except to make Auntie and them sound like jet-set royalty who specialize in high-society swindles. I told the more realistic parts myself, like Godmommy throwing up in my face. They laughed fit to burst and soon I was the life of the party, all set to move in. We were obviously headed for a sex orgy. Honorée brushed all misgivings aside and said I'm exactly the livewire type she was looking for. The details of employment could be ironed out as circumstances evolved. She blew in my ears and Dominique hopped over and started devouring me with her romantic eyes. That's when Homer said I should run out for beer.

"There's still plenty of wine."

He peeled off a hundred francs and said not to hurry. "Try to pick up some pig's knuckles."

"Pig's knuckles!"

"And stuffed olives." He fluttered his lashes at the girls. "Do you feel like a pizza?"

After his grand buildup, they'd begun to zero in on me more than him and I think he got jealous. When I returned, the room smelled musty and Homer had to beat it.

"Why the rush?"

All at once we were shaking hands and I remembered about the crabs. He wouldn't let me walk him to the corner.

"Could you loan me your soap?" I whispered.

He laughed and skipped down the stairs with one of my manuscripts under his arm.

Right away the girls stripped to their panties and urged me to do likewise. Homer had told them I'm an athlete of some sort and they couldn't wait to get a load of my physique. Honorée yanked my shirt over my head and Dominique humped my leg while unlacing my shoes. I think he also lied about the size of my cock.

I dashed to the communal toilet out in the hall to give myself a wash, and when I got back, the only light came from the radio dial and the girls were dancing. I ran back for more lather, but couldn't keep that up all night. It was time to hit the sack. We stretched out in a row, me against the wall and Honorée the Horrible in the middle. Dominique had the far edge and kept tumbling off. We all caught the giggles. I jumped up for a smoke, but they pulled me back. Finally there was no way around it. Everything grew quiet. Too quiet! The moment of truth had arrived, my itching powder with legs.

"Shit of God!" said Honorée.

It's been bitch-bitch-bitch ever since. My fault, according to Homer. I don't apply my ointment properly or flatter their vanity the way he does. I should smooch and slobber and hang out my tongue when they bend over.

"What irresistible bosoms!" he whines.

Sickening and unnecessary. Taming unruly clients is the only reason for keeping me, and I do it cheap. Every morning I hold out my hand and don't kid myself about the golden hearts of whores. Twenty francs is all I ask. Homer bullied them into a raise, but I refused to go along with him.

"Twenty is plenty."

Honorée knits her brows and sniffs for rats.

"Come off it," says Homer. "You have to demand fifty at least. She thinks you're up to something."

Already she grilled him at length about my career objectives and IQ.

"He's just a super-sweet fellow with literary pretentions."

Dominique was impressed. Actually she's pretty sweet herself and doesn't get a square shake around here either. Honorée controls the purse-strings and is tight as drum. Not as bad as Auntie, of course. That goes without saying. Prompt payment every morning, plus weekend bonuses to ensure I'm on my toes when they trot in with one of their midnight snacks. Time to hit the ball! There's a chair by the closet where the suckers drape their pants.

Need I say more? I'm still vacuuming wallets for other people. The only difference these days, I chase no more windmills. Every morning I pocket my twenty francs and strike out for the boulevards with a song in my heart, even if I'm settling for less than five percent.

"See you beauties tonight."

They don't understand. I save my bellyaches for Homer. Not about money. It's the size of the closet that gets me. And the smell! These babes aren't hygiene fanatics. No deodorants or American sprays. Our bidet leaks and the jokers they pick up are always full of booze. The girls too. I hear them jabbering and banging around before they're halfway up the stairs. Time to rise from their unmentionables and prepare to pounce, a baseball bat handy in case one of these Romeos isn't too blind to count. We could be in for an ugly scene. The meekest protest and I fly from the closet like a bat out of hell. Several close shaves have taught me to aim for the bleachers. I addle pate their consciousness and drive home their thoughts.

Afterwards, we give them a ride in Honorée's Volkswagen. She enjoys bouncing them on the roll. I may as well mention that. Or we dump them by the convent with their dicks in their hands. Usually I take the feet and any snazzy clothes that fit, while Honorée takes the arms and all the cash. Six flights down. Dominique keeps lookout on the street, palming whatever she can when Honorée's back is turned. Mostly jewelry. She gave me an Omega watch the other day and bought a new band out of her own savings. She says it gives her pleasure to see me looking nice.

I only screwed her three or four times. Honorée caught us the fourth or fifth time and raised such hell Dominique confessed everything, including a couple other games we'd been playing on the side. Not for big stakes. I'm mainly interested in snappy threads while Dominique always plows her share right back into the common good.

Honorée has trouble believing such horse shit, so she slapped us around until the whole bag was empty. Then we all had a good cry. No hard feelings. She took us out for drinks and we ended the evening at a wild party where Dominique stole a sheep-skin coat and Honorée walked off with two designer handbags. I got a bottle of scotch myself.

Dominique is the pretty one. She's shy and retiring and not a conversationalist at all, yet she's the one our thrill-seekers prefer following upstairs. Her muscular behind is what intrigues them. Not a bad puss either. Jet-black eyes with little fires in them.

Occasionally I take a turn through Passy. Actually I'm there fairly often. On the lookout for Slavic faces, I draw a blank every time. No one recognizes me either in my stylish new duds. I got rid of my cap and off went the beard. Homer says I could pass for a Belgian porn star the way my wardrobe has expanded. Casual elegance is what I aim for.

Yesterday I wore a bow tie and a straw hat with a feather in it. I took a table across from the godmother's place where they feature imported beers. The atmosphere is reserved. Stuffy, in fact. I don't mind. I perused the morning papers while clipping my nails. We have lots of clippers. Then around noon I ordered a hotdog and literally fell off my chair when Mrs. Wilcox loped by in a very short skirt, nearly stepping on my sunglasses before crossing to our building with that same miracle of motion, calling up many sad memories of my days with the godmother and the others. Vivette and kid especially. I still think about them. Blacky too. All the things that went wrong.

Vivette's letters became so weird toward the end I stopped reading them. Elocution lessons and things like that. Diet regimes. Yoga classes. She also wants to be called "Rhonda", a stage name.

Before leaving Passy I wrote her a ten-page plea to forget she ever met me. I added a few lines about the kid's education. No way to check on replies since the concierge would be holding them and might want to make a citizen's arrest. Already the name changed on our mailbox. I climbed the back steps and found a new lock on the maid's room.

Not that there'd be anything left but the view. I'd packed everything useful and dumped the rest in my bottomless well. At least twenty trips in the pouring rain. Blacky tagged along until I don't know what happened to him. I turned and he wasn't there. I called, but he never showed up. I'd just dropped the godmother's doll and a carton of Gauloises by mistake, which put me in a foul temper. I tossed whatever I could lay my hands on. Leaves. Bushes. In the end I couldn't see straight. I tried to recall if I'd thrown a dog down there. Did I strangle him? I remember having him by the throat at one point. He bit me, then I think I beat him up. I shouted and wound through the trees until his name became a whisper. Around ten, the rain petered out and the sun broke through very hot and bright. People began to appear. I adjusted the planks over the hole and wrote KEEP OUT with a chalky stone.

The apartment felt very empty. I carried my stuff to the maid's room to be picked up later, then said goodbye to the corpse and headed for Montparnasse by way of the woods. Still no Blacky. I tramped up and down the bridle path, but never saw him again.

The Select gave me a big lift. Blazing sunshine outside, cool shadows inside. I had the bar to myself and all the mirrors. Only a few coffee-sippers on the terrace. I ordered a beer and watched the traffic flash by on the boulevard, raising my feet for the scrubwoman and again when an angel swished in smelling of burnt skin and sea breezes. I swiveled to watch. Fine white hairs on her arms and legs. The bartender winked. I hoisted my glass and glanced at the clock, catching the pendulum in mid-flight, the sweat rolling down my back like the beer down my throat, everything going down like summertime itself. I hated to leave. I kept expecting more angels to drag in. Or good old Blacky. We could run a tab and pass the hours. Let the dead bury the dead. It's only a short way to Homer's.

-END-

ABOUT THE AUTHOR

Robert Kettering divides his time between the U.S.A. and France (Colorado Springs and Courbevoie, to be more precise). In the United States, his time fragments among various shopping malls, television stations and a humor website called *dearprofessorknowledge.com*, whereas in France, life is simpler, usually apportioned more or less equally between the café on the corner and the one down the street. Over the years, he has hobnobbed with many famous literary figures, and enjoys dropping names and telling stories about these illustrious characters. Samuel Beckett, for example, was a drinking buddy of his for several months without Mr. Kettering being aware of Sam's full name, professional achievements or mutual eminence. He did most of the talking and all of the bragging. *Ticket on a Crippled Crab* is something else. He hopes you will enjoy reading it.

www.ingramcontent.com/pod-product-compliance
Lightning Source LLC
Chambersburg PA
CBHW020353120726
47904CB00002B/545